NOTHING VENTURED
Nothing Gained

MISTRESS OF NONE : BOOK TWO

PHOEBE DARQUELING

Black Rose Writing | Texas

ISBN: 978-1-68433-558-9
PUBLISHED BY BLACK ROSE WRITING
www.blackrosewriting.com

Printed in the United States of America
Suggested Retail Price (SRP) $19.95

Nothing Ventured, Nothing Gained is printed in Chaparral Pro

*As a planet-friendly publisher, Black Rose Writing does its best to eliminate
unnecessary waste to reduce paper usage and energy costs, while never compromising
the reading experience. As a result, the final word count vs. page count may not meet
common expectations.

This book is dedicated to my husband, who has always encouraged me to venture despite the uncertainty of gains.

NOTHING VENTURED
Nothing Gained

MISTRESS OF NONE : BOOK TWO

New Orleans, LA
October 15, 1871

Mary gazed out over the riverfront from her perch several stories above. If she had been alive, the tiny people below would have seen her and been concerned about her sanity, but as she had been dead for a few months now, no one was the wiser.

After returning from the debacle in Chicago, the ghost was charged with surveillance duties as if she were some kind of spectral guard dog. The groveling she'd been forced to do at the feet of her master had saved her from a far worse fate, but that didn't mean she was happy about her new role in the organization. And much like a guard dog, she had only a short leash to work with.

"It's a nice morning," Abernathy said as he rubbed a misty knuckle against his nose. It was a habitual gesture from a time when he could still do things like feel a sensation such as itch; a gesture that Mary deeply hoped he would lose as he became accustomed to his un-death.

"We may be stuck together," Mary snarled, "but that doesn't mean we need to talk. That goes double for talking about the *weather*."

The younger ghost put his hands before him in a placating gesture. "Suit yourself. Just being pleasant."

Mary dragged her eyes over the scene below, combing the forms for the one she sought. The port was far too large to be able to watch all at once, even from her great height. Later in the day, they would need to move on and actually walk among the living, but this early in the morning there were few of them out and about. It was a silly, inefficient chore, made all the worse for Abernathy trailing her every step of the way. She wasn't sure which was worse, being a guard dog or being a babysitter. When Mary had brought up the idea of splitting up in order to cover more ground, the master had dismissed the notion out of hand.

Mary winced as the other ghost spoke again. "Actually, no. You can't just shut me out. He said—"

"I heard what he said," she snapped, then turned to Abernathy with a sigh. "I have to show you the ropes."

"Exactly."

She would have liked to punch him right in his smug, freckled face, but resisted the urge. Instead, she settled into a seated position on the edge of the rooftop, feet dangling. "Fine. What do you want to know?"

"We're down here to watch over the shipments," he said, touching his nose again. "But what is coming in?"

"Supplies. For the endeavor."

"Well yes, I'd gathered that much. But can you be more specific?"

Mary glowered. Much to her chagrin, she could not actually say more about what was in the crates. The League did not disclose the details to any but their inner circle. She had been on her way to joining it, and then that deplorable medium Annabelle—scratch that, Vi—had ruined everything.

She flapped her hand at him like the gadfly he was and returned her gaze to the riverfront. "You don't need to know that. Ask me something else."

"Did you want to be a ghost, or were you raised like I was?" Abernathy sat down beside her, far closer than Mary would have liked.

"I came back of my own accord, and the Master was waiting for me." She could not keep the pride out of her voice. "He recruited me on the spot. Said I had potential."

Abernathy rubbed his hands against his thighs as he pondered. "Forgive me if this is too...indelicate...of a question. I have not figured out the etiquette of all this yet. But...well, how did you die?"

Mary peered at him out of her peripheral vision. "Hanged. For murder." A wicked smile spread across her face as he gulped and squirmed farther away at her admission. "What, you never killed before?"

"I took care of my fair share of Blue Bellies," he replied, miming holding up a rifle and firing at imaginary Union soldiers along the horizon. "But off the battlefield? Nope. I was a cobbler before the fighting broke out. Not much reason to kill in that line of work. What were you? Before, I mean."

That wiped the smile off of her face. Her exploits and trial had been well covered in the newspapers at the time, so she saw no need to share those details with anyone. Murdering her clientele could gain her respect among the ever-growing number of risen soldiers. The fact that she'd been a lady of the night up until that point, however, could only diminish her in their eyes. If she ever hoped to be a general in the League's army, that was a risk she wasn't willing to take.

"That's my business. Next question."

Abernathy scratched his nose once again and sniffed. "And this woman we're looking for. What's that about? Is it true what they are saying?"

Mary froze except for the fog of her spirit flesh churning. "Which part?" she asked with a voice equal parts cautious and caustic.

"Did she really burn down Chicago?"

"Yes." The tension released and she snickered. "Well, in a way. Though I had my part to play as well."

"Wow. So, the League wants to recruit her? After delivering a blow to the enemy like that?"

"Certainly not," she scoffed. If Mary could still make saliva, she would have spat off the building at the thought. "It isn't as though she did it on purpose. It was just a happy accident for the League. A distraction that benefits us, nothing more."

Abernathy chewed on the inside of his cheek. "So, why are we looking for her?"

"Two reasons." Mary held up a finger. "First, she has access to funds. Money that rightfully belongs to the League. We won't be able to access it unless she signs it over, or we can prove her death to the authorities." She held up another finger, cruelty curling the edges of her mouth. "And second, we're going to feed her to the Master's marvelous machine."

CHAPTER 1

St. Louis, MO
October 15, 1871

Viola Thorne could take a punch.

In any fight, the goal would always be to avoid said blow, but she took a certain pride in knowing she could go a few rounds rather than simply folding up like a fan at the first jab. This unladylike quality, like so many of her unladylike qualities, came from an alchemy of skills she'd first learned from her father, mixed with a goodly dash of her own innate stubbornness, and left to simmer in the crucible of experience.

All the same, when the angry Valkyrie of a dockworker took her first swing, Vi ducked. No sense in getting her face rearranged, even if the arrangement of her face was the source of their argument.

"Get her, Agnes!" crowed a man from the sidelines. His heels pounded against the wooden crate where he perched, his call echoing off the rafters of the warehouse.

Vi sidestepped the other woman, a fat knot of fabric bouncing against her knees where she'd tied up her skirt. More often than not, flashing her stockings also would have meant giving everyone an eyeful of her knife holster, but for better or for worse, she'd elected to leave it at the pension that day. At least a dozen men had followed them from the bar, many still clutching their glasses. The owner probably would have minded more if he weren't similarly equipped and standing alongside his patrons in the ring of onlookers.

"You don't have to do this," Vi said, keeping her slur to a minimum. The room was refusing to stand as still as she'd like, but it wasn't anything she couldn't handle. "This is all just a misunderstanding."

"Tell that to my brother," Agnes bellowed. "If he says you're the one, then you're the one!" She spun, her frizzled, orange hair coming loose from her bun. She stood a whole head taller than the relapsed grifter, and the tawny rebellion at her apex made her loom even larger.

The audience took turns cheering and jeering as the giant rushed at Vi again, but no one was enjoying himself quite as much as Peter. The ghost walked from man to man, mingling his misty, gently glowing form with the vapors coming off the drinks and cigars. Vi caught a glimpse of his infuriating, contented smile as she ducked a wild haymaker.

Before Agnes had even started to move, Vi had felt a slight push against her, like a breeze coming off her opponent's other fist before she moved it. The eddies in the aether broadcast the movement, and even after passing the morning away in a dark corner of a tavern, Vi could anticipate the strike.

Bonnie's voice rising above the din, on the other hand, she had not foreseen. "Are you in here, Vi? I tried the tavern, but the barkeep said everyone was out here for some reason. I've got news!" She all but sang the last word. Then she caught sight of her friend's situation. "What do you think you're doing?" The little brunette's sharp admonishment turned a few heads, but they simply saluted her with their glasses and jeered.

"As I was trying to explain to my new friend," Vi replied as she and the other woman circled each other. "There has been a mistake."

Peter scolded, "The only mistake in this situation was yours. If you had walked into any other bar in this godforsaken river town, you wouldn't be in this predicament. It is your fault for getting recognized. I told you leaving the boarding house was a mistake, but did you listen? Of course not. You never do." No one but Vi could hear the ghost nagging, but she scowled at him anyway.

Agnes caught the sour expression, and assuming it was directed at her, pumped another liter of blood straight into her cheeks. With a roar, she ran at Vi, who deftly stepped aside and wrapped an arm around the other woman's neck. When the copper-headed bear stood to her full height, Vi's feet dangled several inches above the cement. "Please, can we talk about this?" She added a pleading whine to sell the line.

"Stop mucking about," Peter said. "Just finish her already. We both know you can. You haven't even tried to hit her!"

"Quit the act and fight me already!" her opponent growled, echoing Peter's sentiment. "I know your reputation as a muggins and a brawler, Rose Hockley. Or should I say, 'Madame Rosina'?"

Peter's comprehending sigh was cut off by Bonnie's scoff. "This is ludicrous! She's no Rose Hockley. What are you on about?" The tiny woman shouldered her way through the ring of sweaty men with surprising ease.

"I see," the ghost said. "She's one of Rosie's patsies. Good old Madame Rosina. We had a good run with that con."

Agnes stopped her angry thrashing at Bonnie's words, and Vi loosened her grip. She slid away from the frizzled giant, happy for the out her companion was providing. Bonnie wasn't great at lying, but when it came to the truth, there was no better way to sell it than her earnest brown eyes and pixie features. Agnes was more than likely completely correct—Vi had gone by the moniker of Rose Hockley for a time and probably had known her brother. But as long as Bonnie didn't know that, she might be able to convince the dock worker of the lie.

Vi raised her hands in mock surrender and backed away, whimpering. "See? Listen to my friend, here. I'm not who you think I am! And I don't want to fight you." She flicked her gaze to Peter, hoping he would read what she wanted from him in her expression. He'd proven in Chicago that even if no one could see him, he could still be of help. At least, if he felt so inclined.

"You calling Tommy a liar?" Agnes's chest heaved, one part anger, one part exertion. Vi would've preferred to get out of this without giving away her ability in the ring and confirming Agnes's suspicions, but it was good to know the giant was tiring if she needed to start throwing punches.

"Ladies, please." Bonnie stepped between them in a swirl of skirts and placed a hand on each. The ring of gawkers groaned their displeasure at the interruption in the show. The 19-year-old's voice shook a little when she realized both how Agnes loomed over her, and how little Agnes appeared to enjoy being called a 'lady.' "What is it you think she did exactly?"

Agnes spat at the ground beside her. "This snake told my gullible little brother, Tommy, that she could help him talk to my big brother, John."

Vi had not been able to place Agnes before now, but given her various and sundry dealings along the river, she also had not doubted that the other woman's anger was justified. Now that she mentioned Tommy, Vi had to keep from snorting. She was making it sound like her brother was some innocent child rather than the lout with the wandering hands Vi had dealt with.

Bonnie blinked in confusion. "I don't understand. How would this Rose person help with that? Was there bad blood between your brothers?"

"Hell no. John's dead!" Agnes sneered and took a step forward, pushing Bonnie's back straight into Vi. She caught the smaller woman's arm and managed to keep her from stumbling all the way to the packed earth of the floor, both because she did not want to see her friend fall, and it had the added benefit of keeping an obstacle between Vi and the white-knuckled fist at Agnes's side.

The incensed dockworker continued. "He died up in the Alton clink in '63. And *she* charged my baby brother nearly a year's salary for saying she had a message from John. It was a load of malarkey, but Tommy's such a sweet sort that he believed she could actually talk to ghosts. Especially after she plied him with a few drinks!"

The men ranging around them grew restless and shouted such helpful remarks as "Hit her!" and "Get on with it!" at no competitor in particular.

With Bonnie's back pressed into her, Vi could not actually see the dark cloud gathering on her companion's normally sunny assemblage, but she could imagine it.

"I see," Bonnie said, the two words stinging like hail stones.

Vi's time grifting as a medium after the war was not a secret between the two, but it also was not a subject they had discussed openly. It had all been a game when it started, a nice way to turn a tidy profit. Then the day came when Vi saw her first real ghost. She did not stop offering her services, but it was definitely no longer a game.

As a recent widow, Bonnie took issue with Vi's former line of work, even if she had performed the role in reality for her and her late husband only a few weeks prior. The truth was that not everyone became a ghost, meaning that even though Vi could act as a conduit between them and the living, there was not always someone to contact. As far as she had been concerned in the old days, that little detail was not actually vital to collecting their money.

At the sound of Bonnie's tone, a leaden ball formed in Vi's stomach, making the beer she had guzzled all afternoon slosh uncomfortably. "But that is not me, now is it?" She did her best to hit the 'now' rather than the 'me' just hard enough that her friend would share the understanding without tipping off her aspiring assailant.

Bonnie wrinkled her nose at Vi's breath and hissed, "Have you been drinking? *Again*?"

"Well, just a pint or two."

"Or six..." Peter piped up helpfully from somewhere on the far side of Agnes.

"You are unbelievable," Bonnie seethed, and to Vi's chagrin she realized she was still holding onto the other woman's bare arm. The contact had allowed Bonnie to hear Peter's remark, and now she threw her hands up and stepped out of Agnes's path.

"What? I was thirsty," Vi said. "And you can hardly call what they serve in there beer. More like dirty water. I am dandy, really. You worry too much."

Bonnie turned to Agnes. "You know what? You can have her."

"Bonnie, I—"

"You are absolutely right, *Rose*. You can handle yourself." Her smile was uncharacteristically mischievous as she stepped out to join the sweaty men and their sloshing steins. "No need for me to intervene."

"I knew it!" Agnes cracked her knuckles as she advanced.

Vi could already feel the left hook coming her way and got ready to dodge it. To her great surprise—apparently only matched by her opponent's shock, based on her contorted face—Agnes came flailing through the air and knocked her to the ground. Vi tried to scramble out from under her before the other woman recovered, but there was too much dockworker and not enough leverage. There in the tangle of limbs, Peter rose from his place on his hands and knees, his light fading as he made himself fully insubstantial again.

"Sorry!" he said. "I only meant to trip *her*."

Agnes clawed her way past Vi's kicking feet and took her wrists into one meaty paw. "Oh, I'm going to enjoy this." She snickered as she put one knee on each side of Vi's torso. The medium tried to buck her off, but she'd have had more luck moving a brick wall than dislodging the behemoth. The attempt did nothing more than drive the remaining air out of her lungs.

Even though Vi could feel the blow coming, there was no way to avoid it this time. Her head snapped with the force of the clout, her vision a blur of red and black, followed by a scatter of stars. Vi thought she heard Bonnie gasp, but all sound was soon swallowed up by the howling appreciation of the crowd.

The flesh around her eye socket tightened and grew hot. She felt the next blow coming, so she mashed her eyes closed, immediately regretted it, then steeled herself for the impact.

"Let go of me, or you're next!" Agnes cried, and when Vi opened her eyes again, she saw Bonnie dragging against her assailant's free arm.

The petite woman heaved as hard as she could, but when the arm did not budge she gritted, "Get off her!"

A shrill whistle pierced the air, and for a split second everything was still. A gruff voice called, "All right. Break it up!"

As the men scattered, Vi caught sight of a pair of police officers silhouetted in the warehouse doorway. Agnes struggled to standing, lifting her hands up in the air in a show of innocence. Vi rolled out of the way, but not fast enough to avoid the other woman's kick to her ribs as she fled.

"Serves you right!" Agnes yelled before disappearing through the back door with the others.

The strike itself hadn't been all that hard, but Vi was still recovering from a week-old injury in the same spot, and the blow left her coughing and heaving. She was annoyed at Bonnie for not playing along, though she gladly allowed the younger woman to help her to her feet and shuffle them both out the door. Peter had taken off with the rest. He waited for them in the alley, evidently remembering he was incapable of suffering any consequences of the illicit affair. They'd run plenty in their days of confidence games; old habits died hard, even after death.

The afternoon sun shone painfully bright outside of the warehouse. The dry autumn baked the streets, and they kicked up whorls of dust as they made their way down the alley. Vi reached up and touched her throbbing cheek, sucking at her teeth when her finger prodded just under her right eye.

"Serves you right," Bonnie giggled.

"*I* was trying *not* to fight her, if you recall. And I have you to thank for selling me out."

"I cannot say as I blame you. I would not want to fight her either," she evaded. "Look at what she did, and she only popped you once." They rounded a corner. "And to think, I was going to ask you to teach me some day."

Vi shifted her weight off of the younger woman's shoulder and moved away to meet her gaze with her non-throbbing eye. "I did not want to fight her because I was going to *win*."

"Uh-huh. Sure you were."

"I was!" Vi slumped onto one of the empty wooden crates that lined the waterway. "But we are trying to keep a low profile. I didn't want those goons out spreading stories about the gorgeous, athletic—"

Peter chimed in, "Don't forget 'modest'."

"—and regal woman who managed to take down that monstrosity in a moment or two of fisticuffs."

Disgruntled former clientele were not the only people Vi had to worry about alerting to her reentry into society, nor the most dangerous. Getting to the bottom of Peter's murder proved to come with its own set of potentially lethal challenges, and Vi's sins went back even farther than her sham marriage to the Colonel – not to mention some of those transgressions were committed against people who had the means to find her with only a few hints and whispers. The Agency did not take defection lightly.

"Regal, you say?" Bonnie asked archly. "You are awfully dirty for a queen. And drunk I might add."

Vi snatched up the knot in her skirt and worked to free the fabric. "You think good Queen Vic never has a tipple? Besides, I told you. I am perfectly fine." An ill-timed hiccup did nothing to help her make her case.

Bonnie leaned in closer to examine Vi's eye. "Well, for my part I am sorry. You fought off those thugs who killed Tobias, so I did not think something like this would happen." She reached to brush some hair from Vi's face to get a better look, but Vi rushed to do it first. Vi didn't want the attention anyway. It would be even worse if her friend were to make contact again and saw the strange, shimmering wound Vi had picked up in Chicago. She had managed to keep it hidden thus far, a task made simpler by the fact that the living could not see it unless they made the same skin-to-skin contact that made ghosts visible.

"I *am* good at fighting. Just as she said, Rose Hawkley was quite the brawler in her day." Vi's smugness morphed into contemplation. "She should not have been able to knock me down like that. That has never happened before."

"Then what happened? One second, she was on her feet, and the next she was on the ground. But I did not even see you move."

"Peter tripped her," Vi said with a sniff, pointing at her eye. "And I was collateral damage. How bad is it?"

"It's not good," Bonnie replied, her grin spreading as she straightened. "Especially considering what you'll be doing this evening."

"Oh, and what is that?"

"Our ship has come in."

CHAPTER 2

After sending a telegram to every port town along the river, they'd been biding their time for a week. Now, their request had finally been answered.

They didn't waste a moment getting back to the boarding house. Vi sat before the cracked mirror and examined her eye. A burgundy crescent hugged her eye socket and grew darker with every passing moment. She gingerly ran the tip of her finger along the ridge of bone, but nothing felt broken.

"Read me the telegram while I take care of this," Vi said, catching Bonnie's eye in the reflection.

The young widow perched on the edge of the bed and held the card up to the light. "'Dearest Vi. Stop. Been too long. Stop.' How long has it been, anyway?" she asked, her cadence showing this was her own question and not part of the message from Sam.

"It must be something like ten years since the last time," Vi marveled. "It is hard to believe it has been so long! But the war disrupted a great many things."

Vi opened a small pot of minty salve and dabbed it on the bruise. After a week of using the concoction to calm the angry blisters on her neck from an unsavory encounter with a very angry spirit, it was nearly gone. Luckily, so were the blisters. The slash on her cheek, however, still seeped a phosphorescent blue light. No salve would heal the damage the ghost had wrought to Vi's aura during her attack. She had hoped it would close on its own, but unfortunately it hadn't yet shown any sign of change. It did not cause her any discomfort, except for the fact that it existed at all. At the same time, it seemed fitting that she had been marked somehow by the events in Chicago, considering what a mark she'd made on the city.

"Was he a captain when you met him?"

"As far as I know, he's not a captain now." Vi took great care to smooth the cream with as little pressure as possible. "He was the first mate on his father's ship. Unless the old goat already passed and I don't know about it. We have been out of touch this whole time."

"Nice to know you don't just hide from *me*," Peter said sourly from where he lounged in an armchair in the corner. She directed her reflected grimace at the shimmer in the chair. Unlike Bonnie, his reflection was a strange, pale echo of his normal form, as if the image lost cohesion by dint of refraction. If she'd been at her full strength, his presence would have been impossible to ignore, but she had been feeling drained ever since fleeing the fire.

Bonnie resumed her reading tone. "Passing through tonight. Stop. Must have dinner and discuss. Stop. Happy to help. Stop. Just like old times. Stop."

Peter groaned, "Stop is right."

Vi scoffed at his remark, then clarified for her living companion. "I do not think Peter is happy about this arrangement."

The other woman hovered over Vi's shoulder and peered down at the collection of pigments and grease paint she had laid out before her. "Luckily for us, he does not always get his way."

"More like I never get my way!" he grumped. "We shouldn't be going downriver to start with. Let alone with some...some...scoundrel you used to know."

"Oh please. 'Scoundrel' could just as easily fit you as Sam. Or me, for that matter." Vi leaned in to the mirror to get a better angle as she gently smeared a layer of a greenish paint over the bruise.

Bonnie regarded her skeptically. "That is just making it worse."

"Wait and see," Vi said, moving around her face to examine her handiwork as she blended the edges. "This is not the first time I have had to cover up a bruise. Agnes was right about me being the occasional brawler back in the day."

"Where did you learn to do it? The paints I mean."

"One of my mother's friends from the theater. I don't remember if it was Sam's mother or one of the other actresses." Satisfied she'd thoroughly covered the purpling skin, Vi winked her good eye. "But seeing as how he gave me a mouse worse than this one time, it was probably his mother trying to hide it from mine."

Bonnie's reflection gasped. "That's terrible! He hit you? Maybe Peter's right."

"We were children together," Vi said, waving away her friend's concern with a rabbit fur brush. "He did not really mean it. I believe he cried afterwards, in fact. You know how kids are."

"I was a kid, and I definitely never gave anyone a mouse like that!"

"Why am I not surprised?" Vi chuckled as she unscrewed the lid of a tinted grease paint, imagining an even tinier version of Bonnie. Vi held the paint pot next to her face and checked to see how closely it matched her natural skin tone. After her days out on the ranch, her complexion was darker than what would be considered proper in the strictest sense, but she preferred the sun-kissed glow to the porcelain tone most women strove for. She leaned toward the glass again as she dotted the bruise and the dark circles under her eyes with the make-up. The bruise she could blame on Peter, but the puffy flesh below each eye had developed thanks to her nearly 34 years on the planet, many of which included a bottle in her hand. Still, the time she'd spent in California and the work she'd done on the ranch gave her muscles definition and kept her from becoming plump as well-to-do women often did at her age.

"Is there more to Sam's message? You said something about meeting him for dinner," Vi said, trading the grease paint for a final powder.

Bonnie walked back to the bed and picked up the telegram. "Southern Hotel, seven o'clock. We don't have much time. Good thing I found you when I did."

The powder brush stilled in Vi's hand, and she rotated on the stool. "He may be expecting a quiet dinner with an...old friend."

"Just a friend?" Bonnie asked with a suggestive pump of her eyebrows.

Vi could not contain her grin. "We stepped out together, from time to time. After I left Pru, I was in New York again for a few years, trying my hand at following in my mother's footsteps on the stage. Sam was usually off on runs up and down the Hudson. Sometimes, his ship docked to re-supply, and we would spend time together."

The younger woman giggled. "I cannot believe this is the first I am hearing about this!"

"A lady does not kiss and tell," Vi teased.

"So, what is your excuse?" The ghost called from his place in the corner.

Vi turned back to the mirror to apply her lip stain. "Peter, I think it is time for you to go. I shall be dressing soon, and our passage to New Orleans may just depend on what I wear tonight."

He grumbled as he rose from the chair, then stomped noiselessly across the room and slipped through the closed door. Vi finished her last touches before blowing herself a kiss in the mirror. In all honesty, she'd barely given Sam a thought in the past few years. However, now that she was about to see him again, memories of walking arm in arm around New York came rushing back. That was before her first run-in with a ghost, when she could take a man's arm without fear of discovery.

"I have never seen you like this," Bonnie said as she examined an amethyst gown hanging in the closet. "You've had a case of the *morbs* since Chicago. I was not sure I would ever see you smile again."

The giddy anticipation whooshed out of Vi like helium from a toy balloon and she came back down to earth. She'd done her best to avoid reading the newspaper, but the fire was all anyone seemed to be able to talk about. At the latest count, three hundred souls had been lost, and it was all her fault.

With her head buried in their modest closet, Bonnie completely missed Vi's change in demeanor. "Now," she chirped. "Let us get you ready for that date. I hear our quest for Peter's killers depends on it."

"Sam probably is not even thinking of it that way," Vi said, though the admission didn't keep the heat from rising to her cheeks. "He could be happily married with a pile of kids by now for all I know. I was just trying to gall Peter a little."

"Ah yes, annoying Peter, your favorite pastime." Bonnie shook her head, dislodging a stray lock of her brown hair. "Sometimes, I am not sure how the two of you ever got to be friends."

Given the grifter's general tight-lipped nature, Bonnie more than likely did not expect a response, but Vi mulled over her words. At some point, she owed her companion a full explanation. Every time she tried to say the words, however, her tongue couldn't manage to push them past her teeth and onto her lips. Instead, she stood up behind her friend to help tuck her and smooth hair back into place.

Bonnie thanked her before holding up the gown of deep purple. "Well, even if Sam was not thinking of romance when he issued his invitation, he will no doubt be thinking about it when you come to the table wearing this."

"It is rather lovely. For a ready-made, that is." Vi ran the hem of one sleeve through her fingers. "It is a shame we have to travel in secret. I doubt I shall have another occasion to wear it until we reach New Orleans. Employees should not dress so fine."

Bonnie motioned at her to remove the smudged cotton dress she'd worn during her impromptu pugilism. The other woman tossed it onto the vacated chair, then helped Vi into the skirt. "And you're certain we have to ride in steerage?" Her ensuing pout was no doubt meant to be playful, but Vi could hear the truth of her feelings behind the jest.

"Yes, unfortunately." She sighed theatrically and put the back of one hand against her forehead. "We shall have to be but lowly workers. No first-class accommodations this time."

The other woman shifted to the front to cinch one set of laces. "What about just using fake names on the manifest? You've got plenty of aliases to go around."

Vi raised an eyebrow. "If this morning tells us anything, it is that my old names are anything but safe to use. Besides, no one will even glance at employees, no matter what we call ourselves. It is the safest way to get where we are going unnoticed." Once she'd situated the skirt, Vi slipped on the bodice. The ruffles in front hung to her thighs but came to a gathered stop at the small of her back to allow for the bustle. The built-in stays meant she had no need for a corset, a fact she was thankful for in the unrelenting heat. No doubt the breeze coming off the Mississippi would also go a long way to relieving it. "I also do not wish to simply demand free passage of Sam. We should work for it."

"Oh, all right. But you cannot blame a girl for trying!" Bonnie said. Vi crossed back to the mirror and did a spin to make sure everything lay the way it ought. Her friend made an approving sound and clapped her hands together. "Beautiful!"

"*Merci, Madame,*" Vi replied with a curtsy. "And despite my jab at Peter, you are welcome to go to this dinner if you like."

Vi slid open a drawer in the vanity to retrieve the last pieces of the ensemble and was surprised by what she found. Up until this point, she'd been doing an excellent job of avoiding the book that now lay between her and the finishing touches. It has been safely tucked away in the bottom of a carpet bag, and she certainly had not put it in her own way. As she slipped a pair of gloves and a white lace fan from under the battered brown journal, the memories trapped inside hummed at her outstretched fingers, whispering entreaties to open it.

Instead, she closed the drawer with a thud and a scowl.

Bonnie shook out Vi's abandoned day dress, oblivious to Vi's miniature personal drama. "No, that is quite all right. Sam's note said he is only passing through, so we shall need to be prepared to leave right away. I'll tidy up, you go have a marvelous time."

As Vi wheeled away from the offending drawer, she painted on a convincing, sunny smile with the same amount of skill as when she'd hidden her black eye. "As you wish. I really must be leaving." She slipped on her gloves and pushed opened the door with a cheery, "Don't wait up."

Peter leaned against the opposite wall, his spirit flesh eddying and his gently glowing head bowed in thought. His iridescent cerulean eyes flicked up to her face as she emerged.

"No need to wait up," he replied, pushing himself to standing. "I'm going with you."

CHAPTER 3

The sky to the west was blushing like a church lady in a brothel by the time Vi stepped onto the street. Peter had his hands shoved into his pockets, the tatters of the shirt he'd died in strangely still despite him passing through the occasional pedestrian. A ghost strolled along the opposite sidewalk and he raised a hand in greeting. Vi kept her eyes trained on the flow of the living, careful not to reveal she'd been aware of either spirit's presence until it passed.

Even if there hadn't been a ghost to ignore, she needed to watch her step in the press of bodies strolling along the brick-lined streets. Chicago had been crowded, but with St. Louis at the conjunction of the both Mississippi and Ohio Rivers and several rail lines, it had grown at an unprecedented rate after the war ended. As cumbersome as it was to dodge through the throng, the crowd provided cover for Vi's whispered question to Peter. "Have you been going through my things?"

"Hmm?"

"The journal. I know you moved it."

He snickered. "Oh, that. Yes. Guilty as charged. Sorry, waiting around this town is not exactly exciting, and I have to do something while you sleep. You know, it turns out being dead is quite boring."

Vi stepped onto the solid concrete of the sidewalk. "Don't touch it again," she hissed.

"I thought we were through with this," he said. "Or have you decided I am not 'allowed' to move things again? Because you cannot deny that I have been useful."

She didn't like to see him practicing, but it was better than how his rage could tear him apart if given the chance to think on his predicament too long without distraction. "By all means, move anything you want. *Except* for that."

Peter paused, letting a pedestrian pass through him. When he caught up again, he asked, "You really do not mind if I practice?"

"No," she sighed, flicking open her fan and using it to cover her mouth as she continued. "We shall finish your unfinished business and get you crossed over one way or another. Moving around a few things in the meantime probably will not make a difference. And if it keeps you out of my hair, all the better."

"Excellent!"

"However, you must promise to be careful not to call any attention to yourself. Or me. No more waving at random ghosts you pass." She indicated the other side of the street with the flutter of her fan.

"Now, that just seems rude." He nudged her with his elbow.

His gesture knocked off Vi's rhythm and she bumped into a woman. After a mumbled apology, she dropped her voice again and flapped the fan in an irritated blur of lace before her face to obscure her words. "We have a momentary advantage over your killers. They do not know if and when we are still coming, and I'd like to keep it that way."

The ghost smiled slyly. "Is that all?"

"*And,* I do not wish to be dogged by yet *another* spirit or delayed by a request for aid. We already have a mission. I will not jeopardize it because you are trying to be polite."

He snorted. "Well, one of us should be. The dead don't have that many people to talk to after all."

As they turned left, shafts of the waning sun painted the street in citrus hues. A man with a long pole busied himself lighting the streetlamps ahead, but the windows of a few shops added puddles of light to the tableau. Vi squinted into the glare and found a clock tower that read ten minutes before seven.

"This is no joking matter, Peter," she huffed, picking up her pace.

"Yes, ma'am. No calling attention and no touching the journal," he replied, his tone far too earnest to be fully sincere. "And no joking. Anything else?"

"I'm serious. It is dangerous."

"Which one? Calling attention to us or the journal?"

"Both."

As if to add weight to her point, a newsboy stepped into her path. The Sunday evening headlines he bleated all had to do with Chicago and the question of how the city would recover. Vi gritted her teeth and stepped around him.

Peter gave the kid's hat a flick as he passed, grinning at his surprise when it moved on its own. "Personally, I am simply dying of curiosity about Pru's mystery book. I do not know how you can stand not to read it. Don't you want to know?"

"Know what?"

"What you are really capable of."

Before Vi could form a response, they reached their destination and even the chatty ghost lost his words when they stepped inside. Everywhere one looked, the eye came to rest on a surface either plush or polished. The lobby had wooden floors with an ornately inlaid pattern that seamlessly transitioned to the facade of the front desk. Every side table was adorned with a bouquet of flowers, perfuming the air and covering up the muddy smell of the river outside. Through a pair of double doors, Vi could see the tasteful bar across from an archway that led to the dining room proper. The boarding house they had just left was no palace, but this hotel came very close indeed. Sam must be doing extremely well for himself if he was staying here.

Peter let out a low whistle of appreciation. If anyone else could have heard him, she would have been embarrassed at his uncouth response to such a lovely space. Instead, Vi nodded slowly in agreement. This was much more her style than the boarding house, or even her own saloon back in Sacramento. Unfortunately, this meant this was the sort of place she'd worked over during her grifting days, and the laying low for the past four years had required she avoid them. The time away from civilization made her feel unexpectedly out of place. A slender grandfather clock in the corner showed her she'd arrived a few minutes early. Just enough time for a drink to quiet her nerves.

Peter trailed behind her as she entered the bar. The arrangement of the room gave her a pang of longing for her own place. By now, Jimmy and Caroline had no doubt gotten things cleaned up and back to normal. The sooner they got this sordid business in New Orleans figured out, the sooner she could go back to normal, too.

"Bonnie's going to be cross with you," Peter said. He "tsked" playfully as he trailed her to bar.

Vi winked. "What she does not know does not hurt me."

"Except for the joys of alcohol, of course. That little lack of knowledge seems to hurt you on a regular basis."

"True. We shall have to see to her education." Her voice was swallowed by the din of the other patrons as they passed into the bar. Predominantly pairs and trios of men in fine suits were scattered around the room, but almost all of them had their attention turned to a knot of women. There had to be a half dozen of them, tittering and bubbling together, and most importantly, blocking her way. Vi's desire for liquor doubled.

She chose the path of least resistance and sidled up to the far side of the bar. Like the rest of the men in the room, the bartender had eyes only for the clutch of young ladies in their kaleidoscope of dresses. When a few polite throat clearings failed to get his attention, Vi picked up a stray cork and lobbed it at the barkeep. It hit him in the ear, cuing Peter for applause both enthusiastic and silent in his spirit form.

Vi hid her satisfied smirk behind her gloved hand as the man looked around for the culprit. When he spotted her, he snapped to attention. "My apologies, Madame. Would you care for some wine?"

"Scotch and soda, my good man," Vi said cheerfully, but her smile slipped when a cascade of laughter erupted from the flock of butterflies in the corner. "Make it a double."

Peter leaned against the empty bar beside her. "Care to play a game of 'case the place?'" he said, taking in the assorted people in the bar with a sweep of his arm.

"You're on."

Vi retrieved her drink from the bartender, then mimicked Peter's pose to better survey their surroundings. She took a contemplative pull from her drink and nodded to a grizzled man at an adjacent table. His skin was sun battered, making his age difficult to place, but based on the slight salt mixed in with his pepper black hair, he was likely somewhere in his late forties. He was the only man in the entire bar with his back turned to the gaggle of women, a well-chewed toothpick bobbing on his lips as he gritted his teeth. His shoulders hunched slightly over his nearly empty pint, but his spine didn't seem quite willing to slouch fully. He had no more patience for the flower of youth than Vi, evidently, but training kept his back from bending.

"No doubt," she began, "if his shirtsleeves were rolled up, we would see some kind of tattoo, but not fresh. My guess is the crest for his Navy vessel. I would need to hear him speak to figure out which side he fought for, though."

"You are certain he's not just an old riverman?"

Vi shook her head minutely and shielded her answer with her glass. "You do not get nearly enough sun on the Mississippi to acquire that particular brand of shoe leather for skin. He may be one now, but he has definitely spent some time at sea in the past. There is nothing to stop the glare out there."

"All right. My turn. He is sincerely wishing that toothpick was a cigarette, which he rolls himself." The man raised his glass at the barkeep to indicate he needed a refill, and Vi spied the yellowed pads of his fingers and the slight bulge in his shirt pocket where his pouch of tobacco laid in wait.

"Agreed," she said.

Another upwelling of voices from the other side of the bar drew Vi's attention. The group of women would make a fine target for the next round. She gathered what facts she could, using her peripheral vision. Five women posed, each with a flute of champagne, save for one stately older woman with mahogany hair and a tumbler of something dark. It was possible the hotel offered a suite of services beyond the normal wining and dining, but these women didn't show any sign of desperation for attention one could expect among competing ladies of the night. They obviously enjoyed attention, but their next meal did not depend on it. Besides, they would have fanned out and been giving the other worthy gentlemen more of their glances if they were working. Still, there was something familiar about the way they all carried themselves, a sureness of how they moved that came from either practice or masking self-consciousness, or perhaps both. When she could not quite pinpoint it, Vi moved on to their companions.

Upon closer inspection, there did appear to be a few men in the middle of the fray, no doubt the envy of the rest in the bar. They were not dressed as fine as the women, but that was usually the case. One had a thin excuse for a mustache, the other was not so much clean shaven as unable to produce a beard. The two of them could not have been more than twenty, but this also was not out of the ordinary. After the war, the world had been left in the hands of the women and the men too young or too old to have seen action–which was what made the third man striking.

He stood with his back fully to her, head bent toward the younger men in conversation, but he had the broad frame of a full-grown man rather than the loose ease of the gangly boys around him. His hair was a sort of reddish blond, too long to be fashionable. He kept his weight shifted slightly to one foot, as if one leg caused him some discomfort. A veteran perhaps, or a riverman who had been in an accident. The steamships along America's rivers were notorious for two things, racing each other and not surviving more than a few years due to accidents. Hidden sand bars, flood debris, a bolt screwed too tightly on a finicky boiler—any of these could cause a ship's demise.

"Now I shall choose the target?" Peter asked, shifting to her other side and gesturing at the ladies. His brows rose to a smug arch. "They are dancers."

That would explain the way they moved, but Vi was not ready to give him the satisfaction of agreeing too quickly. "Really? Just like that?" she asked, taking a swallow of her drink.

"Yes, I believe we are looking at a troupe in town to perform a travesty. About King Midas, if I'm not mistaken. And they closed yesterday night, so they are celebrating a night off after spending two weeks doing shows."

"How could you possibly get all of that from a bunch of women standing around in a bar?" she scoffed, forgetting to keep her volume in check. A few people turned their heads, including the blond man. Vi spun away and tossed back the remainder of her drink, a rush of warmth settling in her cheeks that had nothing to do with her scotch.

Peter snickered. "I admit, I did not gather all of that information just from them. There was a poster in the entryway."

"That is cheating," she hissed.

"*That* is being observant," he retorted, shaking an ephemeral finger. "You have been out of the game far too long, my friend."

A deep and cheerful voice cut through their conversation. "Vi? Viola Thorne, is that you?"

The voice, the strawberry blond hair, the slant of his shoulders—"Sam, as I live and breathe!" she cried with far more delight than she felt knowing he'd witnessed her little outburst. Unlike Bonnie, Sam had no idea that Vi could speak to the dead, and she planned to keep it that way.

His grin was wide and earnest, his gray eyes sparkling like the Pacific Ocean on a cloudless day as he took her in. They had an uncertain moment as the decade since they'd last spoken stood between them, but he closed the distance by leaning down and giving her light kiss on the cheek. His neatly cropped beard was even redder than his hair, and its scrape across her cheek sent an unexpected jolt through her spine.

"It is wonderful to see you!" he said. "Forgive me, I did not realize it was already time for dinner. How rude of me."

"Not a problem, I assure you. I would have said something sooner, but I did not recognize you at first with such an—"

"Sammy, darling, who is this?" One of the dancers appeared at his side and rested her cheek on his shoulder as she wrapped a possessive hand around his forearm.

"Entourage," Vi finished, offering the petite woman in the canary frock her hand. "I'm Viola, a pleasure."

"Minerva," the other woman replied, "and the pleasure's all mine." She bared her teeth, but it wasn't exactly a smile.

Peter leaned close to her ear. "If our trip down the river depends on you outshining that flame, I doubt we shall ever cast off. Perhaps I will get my way after all."

Sam offered Vi his free elbow. "Well, now that all of my girls are here, shall we head into the dining room? We have much to discuss."

CHAPTER 4

To Vi's surprise, the scruffy subject of the first round of she and Peter's game also rose. Sam introduced him as Bulloch, which could just as easily have been his first name, his surname, or his species. As it happened, he was Sam's first mate on a ship called *The Piasa*.

Between the two fresh-faced boys and the men, there were plenty of arms to go around and properly escort everyone into the dining room, but the leader of the dancers sauntered out ahead of the rest. Vi admired her blithe confidence and felt her own spine straighten in imitation. She may be able to win a boxing match (usually at least), but this woman all but oozed poise and confidence in a way that no doubt commanded every room she entered.

As Vi passed into the dining room, the woman was nodding to the head waiter. He showed them to a central table and rushed to pull out her chair. "Madame Juno, so lovely to see you again."

"I am afraid this is the last time," she said with a voice deep and sweet as molasses. "We closed last night. The entire company leaves in the morning."

"Ha!" Peter said as he circled the table. "I knew it."

"You shall be missed," the waiter said with a polite bob of his head to the group at large. He helped a few of the other women to their seats before excusing himself to retrieve the wine.

Sam pulled out a chair for Minerva, who flashed another too-toothy smile at Vi. "Age before beauty, isn't it?"

There was a reason Vi rarely kept company with women anymore, Bonnie being a notable and recent exception. And despite her years around the theater, that went double for female performers. She would never admit it to her aunt Prudence, of course, but the practiced snideness of competitive women had knocked the bloom off of the rose even before the war interrupted

Vi's attempt at a stage career. Peter may say things that cut on occasion, but at least he was upfront about how he felt. Minerva kept brandishing her smile as both a shield and a sword.

"Thank you," Vi said cheerfully and took the proffered seat. "I am glad there is no need to explain that I come first." Peter guffawed and she had to fight to keep the smirk from her face.

Based on her pursed lips, Juno did not find the remark nearly as amusing. The mustachioed man broke the moment of awkward silence. "Samuel, who is this lovely creature dining with us this evening?"

"Forgive my poor manners!" he said, taking his own seat. "This is a friend of mine from my New York days, Viola. Our mothers were friends."

"And you live here in Saint Louis?" Juno asked.

"Just passing through," Vi said, hesitating over her gloves. If Peter had not followed her, it would not have been an issue. Etiquette dictated she had to remove them, but it meant risking a brush against someone's bare hand and exposing them to her dubious gift. With the attention on her, Vi had no choice but to bow to custom. She busied herself beneath the table, removing them as she continued. "I'm traveling with a friend. I would have invited her, but I did not realize this was going to be a such a large party."

"And I must beg forgiveness once again," Sam said. "Telegrams are so limiting. But, still a marvel, are they not? I never would have found my way back to you at all if you they did not exist."

The waiter returned with an assistant and several bottles of wine in tow. Peter grinned as he followed them around the table, mingling his spirit flesh with the heady vapors of what proved to be an excellent Bordeaux.

The rest of the introductions were made as they poured. The baby-faced man was Charles, and if the roses on his cheeks were any indication, he had been enjoying the hotel bar far more the others. The fellow with the thin, black mustache was called Jack. They were in charge of managing the stage and the sets for the troupe. They got involved through Jack's sister, Diana, a sweet blonde with a swanlike neck and unfortunately for those in earshot, a voice to match.

As they made their way through the various women, Vi realized they were all using stage names. It was the only way to explain the cadre of Roman goddesses all sitting at one table. In addition to Juno, the queen, Diana, the goddess of the hunt, and Minerva of the crocodile smile, Venus and Ceres rounded out the ensemble. Venus had a tumble of coppery curls, a few of which were left loose to frame her ivory, heart-shaped face. She was one of those rare redheads who had the same color of warm, almost orange eyes as her hair. Ceres was about as far as you could get from her in terms of looks, with coal-black hair and an olive complexion. They both appeared genuinely happy to have some new blood at the dinner table.

If anyone could appreciate a good alias, it was Vi, and she nodded to each in turn.

"And together, they make the world-famous 'Jeze-Belles,'" Sam said by way of conclusion.

Vi restrained herself from saying that she'd never heard of them, as that would probably do more to expose herself as out of touch than to diminish them. Her self-imposed exile meant she had missed out on plenty. And given the way the wait staff fawned over the party, the claim might even be accurate.

Instead, she settled on something both innocuous and true. "It is a pity you have already finished your engagement here. I always enjoy a good show."

"You may get your chance," Sam said brightly. "The Belles have an engagement in New Orleans before their tour ends. And if you are taking passage down south with us, you will be there at the right time. It is a wonderful show, and not just the ladies. There are a few different acts and a lot of music. You will love it."

"I am certainly interested in hitching a ride," Vi said. "And my companion and I are happy to work in exchange for a berth."

"A scullery maid, perhaps?" Minerva asked. "Or you could assist with our laundry, if you have enough experience with fine fabrics, that is."

Vi barely heard the remark, she was so taken with the sparkle in Sam's eyes. It reminded her of simpler times, and she was disappointed when he turned his gaze back to the table as a whole. "I actually gave that some thought already."

"I bet he did," Peter grumped.

"And though I know it is proper to wait until the meal has concluded to talk about business matters, it seems I have been offered the perfect opportunity. Though this matter primarily concerns the Belles."

Juno lifted her glass and a waiter rushed over to refill it. "I am listening."

"What would you say about adding more stops to your tour?"

The women exchanged excited glances as Juno sipped her wine. "What sort of an extension did you have in mind? We already have an engagement in New Orleans, and we are due back in New York to start work on a holiday revue in November."

"You wouldn't have to extend anything, just add some stops along the way."

She shook her head. "We cannot possibly book the theaters in time, let alone load and unload all of the sets."

"That is the beauty of my proposal!" Sam said with a wink. "I recently completed construction of a stage on *The Piasa*. I have a piano on board and all tuned up. All we have to do is tie up for a night at say Memphis or Baton Rouge, let the local paper know we're in town, and the audience will come pouring in."

Ceres interjected, eyes alight with possibilities. "You mean you've got a showboat?"

"Yes indeed. They may have disappeared for a spell, but I hope to rekindle the tradition." Sam looked from face to face in turn. "Think about it! I have the space, you've got the talent. We can all make some money."

Minerva leaned forward, fixing Juno with a heavy gaze. "I thought the point of taking a ship rather than a train was to get some rest."

"If we agree, and I'm not saying we are, mind you," Juno said, though the flash of greed in her eyes said she was leaning in that direction. "I cannot guarantee the full company. I have final say over my Belles, but there are the other acts to consider. We usually have something to keep the audience occupied during the scene changes, the intermission. Many of those we have toured with already have engagements booked after this. I've lost two just here in St. Louis."

"Not a problem," Sam said. "I have some gaming tables set up to keep the patrons entertained even after the curtain falls. And I have an idea or two for other ways to fill the gaps." He stole a sideways glance at Vi.

Venus spoke up. "What do you say, Juno? It would be a shame to waste the momentum we've gained on the tour. And maybe some of the Belles could fill in the other spaces. We've got that new number we could add to Midas."

With a thoughtful swirl of her wine, Juno murmured, "It would give us a chance to practice new material. And popping in and out for surprise performances would make for a good story in the papers."

"Not to mention you may finally be able to pay back wages," Charles slurred into his glass. He either did not realize he'd said it aloud or thought no one would hear him. Based on his alcohol-thick speech and the way he ignored the icy hush that fell over the table, either seemed just as likely. Vi had just assumed the Belles were staying in this hotel as well as eating here, but it appeared the burlesque business was not as lucrative as she had first thought.

"Gambling and a show, it seems like a marvelous idea, Sam," Vi interjected into the awkward silence. "I'm sure it would be a big hit with the river crowd. It's about time someone revives the floating theater tradition. And I could help you out with those gaming tables, if you wish."

A laugh rumbled in Sam's throat. "You do not belong with that rabble. It can get...rough among the river sharps. Besides, do you even know how to gamble?"

The note of condescension rankled, but she kept her tone light and pleasant. "In fact, I do. I am quite good at it. One of many skills I learned since last we met."

"Really?" Venus asked. "I didn't think they even allowed ladies into gambling houses."

"No one 'allows' me to do anything. I do as I please," Vi replied, her voice sharper than she'd intended. She gentled it as she continued, "Besides, out West it is becoming quite common."

"So, that is where you have been all this time," Sam said. "Where? Colorado? California?"

On the other side of the table, Peter crossed his arms. "Careful, Vi. The New Orleans lot aren't the only ones who would like to track you down."

"I have been many places," she said, waving vaguely and looking around the dining hall, desperate for a way to change the subject. She was rescued by the return of the waiter and a broad tray laden with bowls of soup. In truth, the stifling air of the dining room rendered what was probably a very nice dish quite unappetizing. All the same, she tucked in to head off any further questions, barely tasting what she ate.

The conversation drifted to other topics, but Vi could tell from Juno's contemplative air that she was still considering Sam's proposal. The favorite subject was the city of New Orleans, and what they would do with their free hours between shows. It would be the first time visiting there for most of them, and they exchanged recommendations they'd heard before bringing Vi back into the discussion.

"What about you, Viola?" Diana asked. "Is New Orleans one of the 'many places' you've visited?"

"Yes, I have been there before, years ago."

"My, my. You do get around," Minerva said. "And all on your own, poor thing."

The verbal jab was accompanied by a pointed glance at her bare ring finger. Vi felt her nostrils flare but channeled her pique into a saccharine tone before responding. "I was not alone when I was there last. I was leaving for my honeymoon."

Sam's spoonful of soup caught in his throat. "I didn't know you were married," he coughed.

"Recently widowed," Vi said, holding Minerva with an unwavering gaze until the other woman shrank away. Her satisfaction at getting the upper hand faded as her mind flitted from the man she had married for money to her first husband, the one she had married for love. That wound was far older, but never missed an opportunity to bleed.

The melancholy must have shown on her face because Sam reached out to squeeze her hand. "I am so sorry, Vi. I had no idea. When I contacted your aunt, she never said anything. I always just assumed—"

"You contacted Prudence?" she interrupted. "Whatever for?"

"Isn't it obvious?" Peter groaned.

Sam startled at the remark, able to hear Peter now that he held Vi's hand in his. She pulled out of his grasp before he caught sight of the ghost or the blue gash on her face, but his eyes were bouncing between the men at the table and trying to decide which one of them had made the comment. Bulloch had been so sullen and silent, Vi had nearly forgotten he was there on the opposite side of the table. He thumbed his pocket watch as he held the pair in his steady regard.

"I am sure she gave you a warm, Thorne Manor welcome," Vi said in an attempt to distract Sam.

He turned his attention back to Vi with a chagrined smile. "She slammed the door in my face."

"Yes, that sounds like her, all right." She chuckled. "I would apologize on her behalf, except that I know she would not be the least bit sorry."

"Based on that one blessedly brief encounter, I think that is probably true," he said with a wink, then his tone became somber. "Were you married long?"

Vi parted her lips to answer, but Peter's sharp "Ahem" reminded her to be prudent. Even though she had run the con under a false name, the less he knew, the better. Instead, she settled on, "I would prefer not talk to about it at dinner. Another time perhaps." Preferably one with a lot more liquor and a lot fewer prying ears in the vicinity.

"Of course," he said, flustered. "I find myself begging your pardon for a third time this evening. How clumsy of me."

She toyed with replying with something clever about how she should apologize for knocking him off-balance, but it had too much of a ring of truth to be a joke. As much as she thought she'd prepared herself for this reunion, she had not expected the abiding affection in his gaze and the way it drew her in.

Juno's voice saved her from forming a more appropriate response. "Samuel. I have considered your proposal." She paused, no doubt to milk every moment for dramatic effect. You could take the actress off the stage, but the stage never really left the actress. "And we accept."

CHAPTER 5

October 16, 1871

The Piasa was set to depart at noon, but the waterfront stretched along the river for miles and Sam's instructions weren't altogether clear. They'd arranged to have their shared luggage delivered; hopefully, the driver would have an easier time navigating the waterfront than they had.

Vi's heart swelled with reminiscence as they wended their way along the slanting shore, dodging horse-drawn carts and barrels taller than a man as they were transferred to the unbroken line of steamships. Before Peter and Vi had their exploits along the river, a good portion of St. Louis had burned to the ground. Now, sturdy, brick warehouses as far as the eye could see added the sounds of their workers and billows of smoke to the damp air clinging to the riverfront.

Vessels of every size bobbed shoulder to shoulder, each with a set of smokestacks and 'scape pipes bristling from the roof. Taut, black lines ran between them to keep the tall pipes vertical and diverting the hot vapors away from the rest of the ship even in inclement weather. Unlike sea-faring ships, none of these had sails, but most sported a paddle at the back or pair of wheels along the side. White-washed walls with bright red paddles was the dominant style, with names in glinting gold script scrawled across the paddle boxes or pilot houses perched at the top.

A few wide, low barges broke the pattern here and there. They depended on smaller vessels with engines to move them, but their shallow keel and wide decks meant they could carry huge amounts of cargo without being stopped by snags and sand bars on their way up and down the Mississippi. Man, beast, and crane worked together to move cargo on and off the main decks of the ships while passengers of every stripe strolled through the chaos looking for their berths.

"It certainly is lively," Bonnie said.

With her horse-headed cane clutched in one hand, Vi flung her arms wide to encompass the whole riverfront. "Largest port in the country, outside of New York." She snatched her hand back just in time to avoid toppling a straw hat from atop a passerby.

Peter walked a few paces ahead and turned his chin over his shoulder. "A little too lively for my tastes."

"Aw, too crowded for you, Freeman?" Vi said with a smirk. "And you accuse me of getting old, you curmudgeon."

"I'm not the one who has to worry about running into people. I'm sure Agnes wouldn't mind picking up where you left off." He turned fully around and walked backwards through a stray crate, his essence leaving a momentary flicker behind. When Vi emerged on the other side, he continued. "But it is the smell that I could do without. The vapors put off by a nice brandy are a fine consolation prize for my current state, but I could do without the miasma of livestock."

"I doubt Sam will be taking any cows along for the ride. So, if you can stand the running water itself, it should be a pleasant enough trip for you."

Bonnie interjected, "What's that about water?"

"Ghosts don't generally care for it," Vi said. "Based on what Pru told me about energy, I assume it must have something to do with how the water is moving but the ground is not. Or perhaps putting distance between the spirit and the earth? We did not discuss the phenomenon in particular. But there may be...effects on Peter."

He pulled a sour face. "Yes, that clandestine escape from the fire was only a day, and that was far from pleasant. I am not looking forward to weeks."

"What sort of effects?" Bonnie asked. "It will not hurt him, will it?"

"I am sure he shall be right as rain."

He glared at Vi as he stomped on ahead. "Nice to know my dear friend is so concerned for my well-being."

"Whatever the *potential* discomfort, it does not change the fact that this is the fastest and safest way for us to reach our destination," she called after him. To Bonnie she added, "It's not likely that another ghost would choose to travel this way. If any spirit *is* following us, this should help dissuade them."

They continued down the row of ships, occasionally stepping around puddles and the bustle of bodies. The sun was almost at its zenith, and without the shelter of buildings, it beat down mercilessly. Thankfully, Vi had the forethought to purchase wide-brimmed hats on their way to the boat. Bonnie's face was covered in a scatter of tiny diamonds of light where the weave allowed the sunlight through. Her brown eyes grew wide as she pointed to something down the shore, and Vi followed her gaze. "That cannot be right, can it?"

The ship bobbing a few hundred feet into the open water was not quite a steamer and not quite a barge. Though it boasted multiple decks, there were no stacks or paddles in sight. The walls were white, but what they could see of the hull was black with white block letters spelling out the name of the craft. All the railings bore red and gold candy stripes, and for all their garishness, her eyes were drawn to the bright red walls of the second story. The word "Casino" was painted across it in letters that had to be several feet high.

"Yes, I believe that is our ship."

"But it has no paddles!"

"If I am not mistaken, Sam seems to have converted a lumber barge. Very clever, really, because that means there is more space on board for the gaming floor and stage, and it is a much quieter way to travel. There must be a tow around somewhere that will push us...Ah, there!"

She directed Bonnie to a smaller craft on the shore parallel to *The Piasa*. *Apple Blossom* was larger than most tows, but *The Piasa* was also larger and heavier than most barges, so the older ship had been retrofitted for the job of steering the showboat. The knee boards that would serve to hold the ships together and offer easy passage between them en route were currently being used as ramps to load wooden shipping crates. Once they were underway, the two ships would function as a single, long vessel. A flash of movement caught Vi's eye at the top of the *Apple Blossom*, and she spied Sam waving at her through the window of the pilothouse perched atop the roof.

"Why is it called a tow boat if it pushes?" Bonnie asked.

"No clue. Many of the naming conventions are strange." Vi waved at the upper deck. "For instance, the second story is called the boiler deck, when there has never been a boiler house there, even on old models. The boiler and the cargo are all held on the lowest deck. That uppermost part with the pilot house on top? It's called a 'texas' because they joined the union around the same time the convention became popular."

"You know, even though I grew up near Boston Harbor, I never once thought to learn about these things. But you sure know a lot about ships."

Vi chose her next words carefully, settling for something that would not be a lie, but was not the whole truth. She trusted Bonnie, but there were some elements of her past she was not free to discuss even though the war was long past, and especially not on a crowded riverfront. "I have had plenty of occasions to learn, and not just from Sam. My father was in the military, as well as conducting other business abroad. Whenever he came home, I would always beg him to tell me all about it. It was never something quite as glamorous as a tunnel to a hidden world in the middle of the Earth, but to a little girl, it might as well have been."

Bonnie furrowed her brow, which only made her look younger. "A tunnel to the middle of the Earth? How exciting. Where is it?"

Vi sighed and placed a sympathetic hand on her friend's shoulder. "Let's hope *The Piasa* has a library. We really must begin expanding your reading horizons."

"I read," Bonnie protested, but she lost some heat in her voice as she clarified. "Though mostly penny dreadfuls."

"Ah." Vi nodded, then recommenced their walk to the ship. "I see now."

The edge of defensiveness returned to her voice as Bonnie followed. "See what?"

Vi chuckled. "Where you get your iron constitution. Most people would find out who, not to mention *what* I am, and run the other direction. But you have been filling your head with murderers and highwaymen from a tender age."

Her friend grinned. "And monsters, don't forget the monsters. I have always thought vampires were fascinating."

"Piffle. There's no such thing as monsters."

"I wouldn't be so sure about that. After all, until I met you, I wouldn't have said there was a such a thing as ghosts."

They were a few paces from *The Piasa*'s stage plank when a male voice rose over the commotion from the front of the towboat. "I am doing the best I can."

"Well, it simply is not good enough," replied a deep, female voice Vi immediately recognized as Juno. She surveyed the scene and found her and a couple cringing under the weight of her commanding presence. The shiny black coiffure told Vi it was likely Ceres being admonished, but the man had his back to her and she could not distinguish his identity.

"This load is taking twice as long as before. It is simply unacceptable." Juno did not shout so much as her voice swelled. "And you, girl, stop distracting him. You have your own work to do."

"See? I told you there were monsters," Bonnie whispered.

Vi pushed her next words out the side of her mouth and watched out of the corner of her eye. "That's the queen Belle herself."

"Oh my. Not a big, happy family, then."

"They seemed happy enough last night. There's nothing quite like being a part of something like a play or a variety show," Vi said, feeling wistful for her own days on the stage. "But there can also be a lot of pressure from the cast, the crew. Charles made a remark last night that indicated some trouble in paradise. Of a financial nature, though."

"And that man is Charles?"

Vi shifted to get a better look as the man resumed his hauling before shaking her head. "No, that one is Jack. Though it seems Charles should be around here somewhere. This is his job as much as Jack's." Her eyes flicked to the deck and Sam had just reached the plank, a warm smile splitting his neatly cropped beard. "And that is Samuel."

He was wearing a smart black uniform complete with cap, though as a nod to the noontime sun he'd dispensed with his jacket. As he reached the shore, the scene unfolding between Juno and Jack caught his attention and he motioned at Vi to wait where she was. Sam crossed to the confrontation and the woman seemed to remember herself and regain some composure. Peter had already reached the stage plank before them and made a rude gesture at Sam's retreating back.

Bonnie giggled. "I see why you were hoping for private dinner date."

Vi's neck craned to better appreciate the view and she smirked. "You know, I do believe he's gotten even more handsome. But he's sweet on one of the Belles, Minerva."

The ghost stood on the wide plank suspended over the water. It did not bob under his weight as it would with the living, but he looked sick and worried all the same. He made uneasy progress as if he were on a tight rope rather than a sturdy ramp of wood.

"I am not so sure," Bonnie's words trailed off suggestively and she nodded in Sam's direction. "That was a very happy look on his face when he saw you."

"If only the same could be true for everyone," Vi said. "Peter looks rather *unhappy* with me at the moment. I should probably go make sure he is all right."

Her friend's insistent throat-clearing stopped Vi from moving more than a step. Bonnie jerked her head over her shoulder to where Sam was jogging toward them. His stride was uneven, marked by the discomfort Vi had noted in his stance before she had recognized him in the bar, but it did little to slow his pace.

"Ladies, I'm glad you found us," he said as he reached them, a light pant shortening the words. He reached into his waistcoat pocket and checked his watch. "We should be departing shortly, so you should get yourselves settled in. Your things have already been sent up to your room on the hurricane deck."

"I suppose you did not have any state rooms to spare, what with all of the Belles and their considerable number of associates," Vi said.

"To tell you the truth, even though it is a bit of a climb, the upper deck is much cooler than the passenger deck. And it has a better view as well." He hooked his thumbs on his suspenders and rocked back on his heels.

She smiled slyly, whispering, "And is that true, or do you expect we shall simply fall for your charms?"

A wash of pink crept up his neck and into his ears, just as Vi hoped it would. He never was good at accepting a compliment. His complete lack of guile was a welcome change from the men she'd encountered in the intervening years.

He placed his right hand to his heart. "God's honest truth. And I should know, that's where my quarters are as well."

Bonnie's murmur was for Vi's ears only. "A better view indeed."

"Looking forward to it," Vi said. She shifted her gaze to *The Piasa* and was glad to see Peter had reached the deck. He was steadier with a wider platform beneath his feet, but no less perturbed. A shimmer of energy on the second deck drew her eyes upwards and she squinted against the glare from the river. It came and went so fast, she could not say for sure it was the blue of a ghost or the white of the living, but sensing any aura from such a distance was intriguing. Her additional sensitivity quested toward the source before she realized she'd flexed the invisible muscle.

Sam's baritone interrupted her examination and the energy contracted. "Vi, I really am sorry for springing the Belles on you like that. And Minerva especially."

A slight frisson crept across her shoulders, but whether it was the mention of the dancer or the hint of otherworldly energy she'd spied on the ship raising her hackles was unclear. She was careful to keep her voice level. "No apology necessary. From the sound of it, you'd had this plan in the works for quite some time. Have you known the Belles long?"

"I've known Juno the longest, though I've met them all before," he replied. His weather-beaten brow creased. "Vi, I do not want you to get the wrong idea. Minerva has taken a shine to me, but we are not close. I do not even know her real name." A steam whistle shrieked from atop *The Piasa*, and he glared at it for a moment before regaining his composure. "That would be my mate keeping me on schedule. If you'll excuse me?"

Vi found herself only capable of blinking dumbly at the news about Minerva, so Bonnie obliged. "Of course," she said. "You go on ahead. We can find our way."

"Thank you." He gave her a slight bow before turning his attention back to Vi. "I would love a chance to catch up with you some more, in private. I really do have something I wish to discuss with only you. Dinner tonight, perhaps?"

Her voice was breathy with surprise. "I would love to."

He doffed his cap before heading toward the stage plank at a brisk pace. Vi watched him go, then her eyes traveled back to where she'd spotted the glimmer a few moments before. The upper deck now appeared deserted.

"Shall we?" Bonnie asked.

"All aboard."

CHAPTER 6

The main deck of *Apple Blossom* was bustling with activity. A crewman strapped down any luggage that wasn't bound for the state rooms, and people mulled about the benches in the shade. After the blaze of the noonday sun, the plunge into darkness was all the more pronounced.

A scrawny juggler practiced his skill, a silhouette against the shifting flow of the river beyond. In addition to the Belles themselves, their entourage included at least a four-piece band and a handful of other people for the variety acts between scenes. Charles was in the middle of assuring the bassist that his instrument had been taken to the stage already as they passed. Unlike the night before, he had a broad smile on his face and gave the musician a hearty slap on the shoulder as they spoke.

Vi's gaze followed the line of the collection of poles and oars hanging from the ceiling with sturdy leather straps, some at least thirty feet long and others more akin to ten. Even the big steamers often had a few of them around in case the crew needed to shove off from an obstacle during the journey. With no real steering abilities aside from the towboat, they also might need them to push *The Piasa* away from shore and get around snags. The river was so deep in places that even the longest ones would not be able to reach the bottom, but their purpose was more to do with horizontal rather than vertical reach. Several six-foot crates took up floor space on the open deck below them, spread into three corridors to keep the ship balanced.

She ran her hand over the nearest crate, the rough wood snagging on the lace of her gloves. Some of the crates bore faint chalk markings she couldn't make out in the dimness after the glaring sun, but others had words like 'sets' and 'costumes' painted in block letters. Several had posters plastered onto them sporting a brightly smiling woman and information about the main show, "Midas."

"My goodness, is that all for the Belles?" Bonnie asked.

"That appears to be the case. Though Sam has probably got some other cargo as well. There is always someone who needs something to go south from here." Vi peered into the gloom beyond the crates. Despite the other performers, two more rows of wooden benches lay vacant. "Though I am surprised he hasn't taken on more passengers, even just for the day."

"You said the performances are meant to be a surprise, right?" Bonnie said. "Perhaps he is just trying to maintain some secrecy until they are ready for their audience."

The air beneath the overhang was hot and close with the crates blocking the airflow, and Vi wished for the fan that was packed with their things upstairs. She took off her hat and waved it in front of her face to cool herself instead. "I cannot wait to get moving."

"Do you want to go up higher and get some air?"

As nice as that would be, she was more concerned with the other presence she'd sensed than cooling down. "Not just yet," Vi replied. "Peter is around here somewhere, and I need to speak with him."

Bonnie bobbed her head and made her way to the port side staircase. Vi considered whether she should have let the other woman in on her suspicions, but it was too soon to know if what Vi had sensed was worth worrying Bonnie over. If whatever it was proved to be unfriendly, they would definitely need to find some excuse to disembark without it following. One step at a time.

As if on cue, the deck shifted below her feet as *Apple Blossom* cast off from the shore. The tow progressed backwards, the water churning and bubbling in its wake. Getting it to align with the stern of *The Piasa* and connecting the knee would be no simple matter, but she took comfort knowing it was Sam's experienced hand at the wheel.

Vi continued her stroll, taking in the details of what would be her home for the next ten days. As she rounded a corner, she nearly bowled over Bulloch. Agnes must have addled her head more than Vi realized because she had not sensed anyone, and the first mate was hard to miss under any circumstance.

"Pardon me." Vi's hat was the real victim in the collision, and she put her fist into the crown to try to restore its original shape. "I was not watching where I was going."

"A habit you should break," he grunted. It may have been his tone, or perhaps the rank smell rolling off him, but Vi found herself instantly repelled by the man. Though he softened his gruff demeanor as he continued, Vi's shoulders grew tauter. "Wouldn't want you to end up in the drink. The river will swallow you up."

She replaced her hat. "And we would not want a tragedy to befall *The Piasa* on her maiden voyage."

Even through his thick whiskers, she saw his jaw tighten. "We're already courting disaster, if you ask me."

"Oh?"

Juno's disembodied voice shouted at her performers, and he jerked his thumb in her direction. "I'm not sure the captain realizes what he's unleashed."

Vi chuckled. "I am sure things will calm down once we are underway."

"Let's hope so." Bulloch slipped the scuffed watch into his pocket and crossed his burly arms. "I am not used to having so many aboard."

"What, passengers?"

He grimaced. "Women."

It was a myth, a holdover from the early days of sailing. Nowadays, women traveled on ships all the time. Vi smirked. "Don't tell me you are superstitious?"

Apple Blossom's engine quieted, leaving them drifting backwards for a moment as they completed their turn. The engines reversed and they jolted forward. Vi grabbed the railing to steady herself.

"I am many things, miss," Bulloch replied gruffly. "Including busy. If you think you can manage not to fall overboard for the time being, I have to oversee getting us connected, unload the sets over the knee, and avoid having my ears bleed in the process. Some of us have *work* to do." Bulloch gave the barest of taps to his hat brim before stepping away.

Vi scowled at his back as he disappeared around the corner, her shoulders relaxing as the distance between them grew. No doubt, she would encounter the odious man occasionally during the journey, but she definitely would not go out of her way to speak to him again. He must have some redeeming qualities for Sam to have such an ogre as his first mate. Though from where she was standing, she could not see any.

The two ships were connected without incident, and as Bulloch had predicted, the crew immediately began to open and unload the cargo containers. The back of *The Piasa* had a set of wide doors for them to haul over scenery flats and the various and sundry required for a production. Vi slipped across in between loads to search for Peter.

When she finally found the ghost, he was standing at a striped railing at the front of the ship and gazing into the lapping water. She joined him but did not interrupt his contemplation. Though at a distance, the river reflected the robin's egg sky, up close it was a dull brown from the pounds of silt it carried with it all the way from Minnesota. The surface may have looked placid, but there was no telling what lay beneath.

"How are you feeling?" she asked eventually, eying the way he swayed.

"I've been better." The swirling fog that made up his body had not darkened nor thickened with irritation as she'd expected. Instead, he looked faded, insubstantial, like his reflection in a mirror rather than himself. The only part of him that remained unaffected was his eyes, which were the same startlingly bright, unbroken blue of the dead. It was the part of his transformation that always unnerved her the most, and Vi diverted her gaze to the water once more to stem the tide of guilt.

"It is only for a week, ten days at the most," she said. "And we shall be stopping sometimes, so it will not be all day every day."

"That is probably good for you as well."

"Why?"

He reached out and stroked her cheek with the back of his knuckles. The touch was feather-light, but held the coolness of his spirit-flesh. His fingers grew brighter for a moment as he brought them away from her invisible wound. "You're bleeding even more freely now. There must be some connection between whatever is happening to me and whatever that is." He studied his hand for a moment before grinning. "As uncomfortable as it is, this is rather fascinating, though, don't you think? I'm curious to see if it makes a difference to get higher. I wonder, is it the water itself that is the problem, or my distance from the earth?"

Vi snorted. "I'm glad you can find the amusement in this."

"Not amusement. Science," he said, a hint of mischief in his voice. He shook an ephemeral finger at her. "Really, this is something you should be recording for posterity. And I know just the book to use."

She evaded the innuendo but met his gaze as she leaned one hip against the railing. "Higher, did you say? It's funny you should mention the upper decks because I believe I saw something up there."

"What sort of something?"

"It may be a spirit, it may have been a trick of the sunlight." Vi shrugged. "I was about to do a little investigating from the bottom up. Care to join me? In the name of science, of course."

Peter motioned at her to lead the way and they headed toward the stern. He stumbled slightly as they went. If it were possible, she'd have thought he was drunk, but it had to be part of the effect of being on the ship.

The promenade circled an enclosed space with a series of porthole windows lining the wall. Vi stopped to peek inside and found a space with polished wooden floors with several tables arranged around the perimeter. No doubt, this was the gaming floor that Sam had told her about the night before. On this end, the ceilings were high enough to accommodate a stage with raised sconces for footlights and hung with red curtains. On the second story, a solid wall of windows let in the sun and lit the space, except for a wide balcony facing the stage. The space below didn't have any permanent chairs for watching the show, offering flexibility, but there was no mistaking the overhanging balcony. At night, the large room would need to rely on the oil table lamps and sconces that ringed the room.

Several of the Belles were inspecting their new performance space. Ceres did a few spins fit for a ballerina rather than a burlesque performer, and the others clapped and laughed. Even from the outside looking in, the energy of the room was light and eager, every one of them excited for the prospect of performing. Most of them were wearing the tight leggings burlesque was known for, both for the ease of movement and for showing off their comely attributes. Peter winked, then eschewed the window and pushed his upper half straight through the wall for a better view.

The sight of his disembodied rear end drew a chuckle, and Vi pushed her face against the glass to try to see more of the room. Her angle limited her view, but she was reasonably certain a well-stocked bar would be waiting at the opposite end. She would definitely have to investigate that further at some point.

Juno's graceful form swept into the edge of her vision with Jack and Diana trailing behind. The women on the stage all stopped their joking and went to the edge to receive instructions. As diverting as it would be to get a preview of the show, the Belles weren't her primary concern. Vi pushed away from the window and moved along the gallery.

"Vi, wait," Peter whispered, now whole and standing on the promenade. "I think I found what you saw. There's a chap in there who just waved me over."

She frowned. "You mean he's like me?"

"No, someone like me. You were right, there is another ghost on board." He jerked his thumb over his shoulder. "He's sitting at the bar and invited me over. What should I do?"

"What is he like?" Vi asked. "Are we dealing with something more like a wailer or more like you?"

"He's lucid enough and quite solid. In better shape than me, in fact. He could be here looking for you the same as Mary was. Then again, he could just enjoy the river. The only way to know for sure is to talk to him." The ghost pumped his eyebrows a few times in case she didn't catch the reference to their last conversation about fraternizing.

Apple Blossom's bell clanged its final warning. Behind them, the chug of the towboat's engine grew louder as it drew them away from the shore. She wouldn't be able to get off now whether or not the stranger was friendly.

"Go ahead and have a chat. But please, *please,* try to leave me out of it."

Peter rubbed his hands together. "Some reconnaissance then, is it? It's been a while, but I think I can still remember how to get more information than I give."

"Keep him busy, or at least away from me for the evening, will you?" Her mind flashed to Sam's eager smile. "I've been asked to dine with our good captain."

The ghost's eyes flicked between her and the wall, uncertainty wrinkling his brow. "Are you sure you don't want me to go with you? I don't have to go and talk to the other guy."

"Aren't you the one who wanted to be polite?" She smirked.

He crossed his arms and all but pouted. "Aren't you the one who scolded me for it?"

"I suppose you should consider this an apology." Vi made a show of shooing him toward the wall. "Now, you had better go or he may come looking for you."

"You are certain you will be all right without me?"

"Jealousy is a bad color on you," she teased, backing away and wiggling her fingers in farewell. She gave her next words a playful, maternal tone. "Play nice with your new friend."

Peter took a step to follow. "It's not jealousy, Vi. There is something off about him, not to mention that mate of his. I can't put my finger on it but—"

"You worry about your man," she said, heading in the direction of the knee boards connecting the two vessels. "And I'll worry about mine."

CHAPTER 7

The crew lodgings were on the hurricane deck of *Apple Blossom*, the second tallest part of the ship. On her way to find Bonnie, Vi passed a crewman affixing one end of a colorful string of flags to the front corner of the texas, while another pair waited on the roof of *The Piasa* to catch the other end. The two ships truly were acting as one now.

She and Bonnie were both given their own berths in the crew quarters, which was made up of a hallway flanked by cabins. The rooms were spare but clean, and one end of the texas boasted a lounge with a glass ceiling. The Belles were enjoying the larger staterooms below, but Sam was right about the breeze and the view. Her companion had already divided and stowed their scant belongings between their rooms and settled into a deck chair to enjoy the sight of St. Louis's sprawl as they made their steady progress out of port.

Vi flopped unceremoniously into a second chair. What she really wanted was a drink, but with the dead stranger sitting at the bar, the chair would have to do for now. She sighed. "I know all we've been doing for the last week is waiting, but I had not realized how anxious I was until we finally got underway again."

Bonnie kept her face turned toward the sun, but peeked at Vi from the corner of her eye. "How is Peter?"

"He's found himself a playmate, it seems."

The other woman shifted to see her better, face alight with interest. "Even with the water below?"

"This one does not appear to mind. I suppose he may be tied to something on the ship." Vi stretched her arms above her head and groaned contentedly before settling even deeper into the chair. "Or perhaps he just wanted to go on holiday. Being a ghost seems rather tedious; he may have just needed a change of scenery."

The young widow's voice was barely louder than a whisper. "It still must be better than just being...gone."

"I would not be so sure about that," Vi said, letting her eyelids droop. "I have met more ghosts than you, and in general, their dearest wish is for it to be over."

"Is that what he wanted?"

Bonnie did not have to say her husband's name for Vi to know they were no longer speaking of the stranger. "No," Vi admitted, gentling her tone. "Tobias wanted to make sure you were cared for. But he was also new at being a ghost. Even if he'd stayed with you until your last breath, he'd eventually be lost and alone, and ready to move on. He was actually one of the lucky ones."

"Lucky?" Bonnie's scoff rang out, disturbing a bird that was perched above them. It gave an aggrieved squawk and flapped away. Angry tears sprang to her eyes. "You're saying I should be grateful he went like that?"

Vi sat up and reached for her friend's hand, but she snatched it away. "You misunderstand me," Vi stuttered. "What I mean is that if he had to go, at least he did not suffer the way many ghosts do. And you both got to say goodbye." Her throat clenched. "I did not have that luxury."

The other woman rubbed her eyes to keep the tears at bay and sniffed ruefully. "We both know you didn't care one bit about the Colonel. You could not say goodbye because you left him. It isn't the same at all."

"You are partially correct. It would be most accurate to say that I loathed Edward." Vi chuckled, but the look on Bonnie's face sobered her again. She puffed up her cheeks and blew out a breath before continuing. "But I was referring to Patrick."

Bonnie's hands stilled. The anger melted away, leaving only a knowing sorrow. "Oh Vi, you didn't say goodbye?"

"It was wartime." She shrugged, a gesture of futility rather than indifference. "Hardly anyone did in those days."

"I'm so sorry. That must have been awful." The other woman wiped her hands on her skirt before giving Vi's gloved fingers a squeeze.

Vi had become accustomed to living a life without physical contact, but her heart swelled at the touch. She smiled wanly. "It was a long time ago, before any of my...talents surfaced. For a while after they did, there was part of me actually hoping that I would find his ghost. Now, I'm glad he wasn't one of the unlucky few. It means he is at peace."

As the ship moved downstream, they were joined by other craft moving in both directions. The occasional hoot of warning or greeting was exchanged, but on the whole, it was serene.

"I think he would want you to be happy," Bonnie said, gazing at the disappearing spires and water towers of the St. Louis skyline.

Vi let her eyes drift closed again, answering idly, "Yes, I suppose he would. Tobias would want that for you, too."

"Were you? In Cali, I mean, before what happened to Peter."

Her mind touched on all that she'd left behind—the saloon, the ranch, the freedom of anonymity. All hers, and all empty. "'Happy' is perhaps too strong of a word," Vi said after a while. "But I was…let's call it content."

"What more would you need to make you happy, then?"

She opened the eye nearest to Bonnie and squinted at her. "Why are you asking so many questions? Are you worried about what happens next for you? Because it's not easy, but—"

"For me?" Bonnie asked. "No, silly. I was wondering about your date with Sam."

Vi's second eye shot open. "What about it?"

"He's not with Minerva, and you said you two used to be sweethearts. Even a blind man would have noticed the way he looked at you. I thought maybe he was going to ask you to pick up where you left off."

The words hung in the air for a moment before forming a fist and striking at Vi's core. She jolted upright, straining to drag enough oxygen into her lungs. Pins and needles of ice prickled across her forearms and she almost didn't feel the weight of Bonnie's hand on her shoulder.

"Are you all right?"

"I need…I need to walk." Vi burst to her feet, shaking the sudden crush of tension out of her arms and through her fingers. Patrick's face flashed into her darkening vision, followed by her father's.

Even with the whole of both ships' bulks at her disposal, the world had become infuriatingly small. The water was too deep, too close. She didn't care where she went; all she knew was that she had an unyielding desire to be *away* from the smiling faces of the people she had loved and lost that now shouted for her attention. Her feet carried her a dozen paces before she realized that her companion had followed, but the other woman's voice penetrated the cotton-thick buzzing as she called Vi's name. She slowed her pace, though it had more to do with reaching the fore railing than any desire to talk. The men who had been working there were now blessedly absent, but the flapping of the banners they had hung no longer felt festive; they cracked like gunfire.

"I apologize. I didn't mean to upset you," Bonnie said. "I have clearly overstepped."

Vi concentrated on pulling in air through her nose and huffing it out of her mouth. "It's...it's not...your fault." She managed to push away the vision of Patrick, but it was replaced by her mother. Until her recent bout of this gripping anxiety in Sacramento, she'd been without it for years. This was the second episode in almost as many weeks.

"It was a stupid, insensitive thing to say."

"No," Vi wheezed. "This has happened before." She shook her head and steadied herself against the railing. As the world returned to equilibrium, Peter's face appeared behind her eyelids, not the misty white of his spirit flesh, but the velvety darkness of his living face and his penetrating brown eyes peering deep into hers.

"Please forgive me. I had it all wrong." Bonnie ran her palm over Vi's back.

She concentrated on the sensation, timing her breaths to the peak of each circle. "I think this happened...because you were right...but I can't. I just can't."

"It's okay. And you don't have to," Bonnie soothed. She let Vi catch her breath for a few more moments before giving her shoulder a squeeze. "No one makes Viola Thorne do anything she doesn't want to, right? You make your own choices."

Vi nodded, repeating the affirmation a few times in her mind to help make it feel true. When it came to affairs of the heart, she'd like to think she had control, though history had so far shown her that was an illusion.

"Besides, it may just be dinner with an old friend, like you've been saying," Bonnie continued. "I'm sorry I called it a date."

The only proven method of protection was to flee, to leave someone before they left. As the assertion took hold, the prickling feeling dissipated with each breath, leaving exhaustion in its wake. "I need to cancel. I can't let him bring it up."

"I can certainly vouch that you aren't feeling well. Do you want me to talk to him?"

Vi shook her head, both in negation and in an attempt to clear it fully. "No, I'll do it myself. I owe him that small courtesy at least. And the sooner, the better."

CHAPTER 8

The St. Louis cityscape had melted into the distance before Vi was ready to face him. Bonnie insisted on going with her, and after her episode, Vi really couldn't argue with her. From the way her friend nibbled at her lip and stole sidelong glances, it was clear that she wanted to ask more questions, but she thankfully did not press Vi for any more explanation.

Like her ability to speak to the dead, these occasional bouts of panic were something she'd preferred to ignore rather than examine. Of the former, she obviously had no choice but to let them happen, but she hoped the latter would simply go away with time. The idea of being one of those women sent away on a rest cure and patronized by a mentalist was nauseating, especially as the doctor would think her mad if she told the full truth of her circumstances.

When she checked the pilot house of *Apple Blossom*, there was a man reading the river. He told her she'd find Sam in the theater. She and Bonnie descended, then passed over to *The Piasa*'s main deck via the knee, this time opting for walking through the double doors at the bow rather than peeking through the portholes. When it was time for the show, this was the end where the audience would enter, and its triple-arched entryway had all the pomp and circumstance of a New York playhouse.

The bar and its gleaming bronze fixtures stood at the right as they entered. Peter and the other ghost watched them, but Vi kept her eyes directed toward the far end of the room. In her periphery, she thought she saw the unknown spirit gesture toward her with an exclamation of, "Do you see that? That's what I was talking about. It would be simple to—" before she tamped down her senses enough to completely ignore him.

From the momentary encounter, he did seem to be much more solid than Peter, as he'd reported. It was something to consider when she and her former partner had a chance to speak in private, so she pushed aside her curiosity and focused on the musicians sitting in a ring to the left of the stage tuning their instruments. Juno had a chair pulled up next to the pianist and was stabbing her finger at something on the sheet music spread across the stand. After the man took a pencil from behind his ear and marked it, Juno went to the edge of the stage and shouted something to someone waiting in the wings. If Vi had not seen her be the picture of poised elegance the night before, she would not have believed this frenetic woman before her was capable of such contained dignity.

Jack and Charles hurried into the room from behind, sweat dripping down their faces. They nearly knocked Bonnie over in their haste, but Vi stepped to her in time to pull her out of harm's way. Jack mumbled an apology but did not break stride on their way to the stage.

"Let's sit for a spell and watch," Vi said, moving to a round bar table. "And hopefully avoid being flattened."

Bonnie fussed with her hair as she took a seat. "We have only just gotten underway! You would think they were about to perform any moment."

Vi smiled as a wave of nostalgia broke over her. "There is fun in the frenzy. And it is an unfamiliar space where they are debuting new material in just a couple of days. Every moment between here and Memphis counts."

The stage hands reached the stage, and Charles shared a few words with the musicians. Juno stalked over, and from the way they shrunk away one would think she was a lioness rather than an actress. She gestured to something above the stage, and the two men hurried off to their next task. Vi's eyes traveled around the room, her stomach sinking when she spotted Sam sitting at one of the low tables near the footlights, surveying the scene with a relaxed posture and a satisfied smile.

A thin imitation of the chilly pinpricks washed over her. She tried reminding the needles that she was there to cancel her plans, but when the unfamiliar ghost leaned down next to her face, the true cause was clear. As hard as she tried to pull back, she couldn't block out the conversation between the two ghosts completely.

"Well, that's a nasty bit o' business, ain't it?" he said.

Peter stood at her other side. "Hells bells, Henry. Don't get so close."

Henry circled around and came at Vi through the table, putting himself nose to nose with her. She could still see the stage and people beyond, but it was as if she was seeing them through a pearly haze far brighter and thicker than any ghost she'd seen before.

"She can't see us, remember?" he said, bending close to her cheek. "I thought maybe this'n could, given the color of her shimmer, but obviously she can't."

Between her days on the stage and her time playing poker, Vi had the ability to maintain a stony visage in the face of almost anything, but he was trying even her granite resolve. She twitched her nostrils, then wound up for a sneeze in the hopes that he'd give her some space. Instead, the ghost continued to stare at her face with an expression full of intrigue. A much more transparent Peter came to stand behind him, motioning at the other ghost and silently asking Vi with his eyes if he should tell him the truth.

"I bet she could, though," Henry continued, "If'n she knew to plug up that hole. She's seeping like no tomorrow, but I'm getting something off her anyway. This one's got juice to spare. That gash'll just make it much easier for you."

"Me?" Peter squeaked.

"Well sure, you need a boost much more'n me. Just look at you. And here she is, practically gift-wrapped." Henry stood to his full if not terribly large height, leaving Vi to stare through his midsection. She didn't discern any marks to give away the cause of death until he turned his back on her. The knife did not follow him into his state between life and death, but the wound just inside his left shoulder blade told her the story. A violent death, more than likely steeped in betrayal. One would expect a much angrier spirit, but he seemed content if not absolutely elated.

Peter took a step away, pulling Henry along with him and flicking his eyes between her face and his. "No, I couldn't. It feels...invasive. Wrong."

"It's just like stealing a kiss, but this gal won't even know you did it." The other ghost crossed his arms. "You can't tell me you've never sneaked a peck afore."

"I'm still trying to wrap my head around all of this," Peter said. His next words had the air of repeating them for her benefit. "You're telling me that I can learn to siphon off the energy of any living person, and she's the most vulnerable because of that...injury."

"Yeah, and not just t' you or me, neither."

"You mean other ghosts? It's going to attract them?"

"Yes, though that isn't the only concern. We aren't alone here in the veil."

Bonnie jerked forward, applauding heartily. "That was beautiful!" she cried.

Vi startled out of listening to the ghosts and her practiced 1,000-mile stare. The fiddle player bowed his head in their direction, evidently the source of her friend's enthusiasm. Vi hadn't even realized he'd been playing, but she smiled and clapped politely as she mulled over Henry's words.

"Oh look," Bonnie said, waving to the far end of the room. "There's Sam. Now's your chance."

He had his hand raised in greeting from his place near the stage, leaving no question that he'd spotted her. Vi's thoughts returned to the task at hand, but she'd be pressing Peter for more information later.

She excused herself from Bonnie, and with far more resolve than she felt, walked over to where Sam was sitting. Thankfully, the ghosts didn't follow. This conversation was going to be hard enough without them talking over it.

"May I?" she asked, gesturing at a vacant seat.

"Of course!" Sam sprang to his feet and pulled the chair out for her. Once he'd resumed his seat he grinned. "Couldn't resist either?"

Her heart pattered for a moment as she thought he referred to himself, but when his eyes returned to the action on the stage, she breathed a relieved sigh. "Something like that."

"What do you think of my theater?" He gestured around the room, pride shining in his eyes.

"It's beautiful. And very clever, using a barge. I've never seen a room so large on a ship," she replied, then added, "On a river craft, that is."

"Spent some time at sea, have you? My, you weren't exaggerating! You are quite the traveler. You'll have to tell me all about it tonight."

"That is actually why I'm here," she said, struggling to keep her tone light. Had he always smelled this damn good? "I'm afraid I'm not feeling well. I do not think I would be good company."

"That's a shame. Too long away from the water can do that, though," he said, sympathy crinkling the skin around his eyes. The rippling in the stretch of aura around his right hand told her that he was about to reach for her, so she slipped her hands from the tabletop before he made contact. It was almost like trying to keep two magnets apart, but she mustn't succumb. She assured herself that with the two ghosts in the room with them, she couldn't take any chances. But even she had to admit that was only a half-truth. Vi was afraid of something quite different than the discovery of her powers. "We'll be docking at Chester tonight. Too dangerous to try navigating after dark. We could go into town and—"

"No!" Vi was on her feet before she'd even realized she'd stood. Sam recoiled as if stung, and she mumbled, "I mean, no thank you."

A loud and angry shushing came from across the room. Vi looked over to see Ceres snickering at her from her place on the stage, though Venus's face held a hint of apology for the behavior of their leader. Minerva scowled at Vi's proximity to her would-be beau, but it was Juno with a finger at her lips and daggers for eyes. Vi mouthed a silent "I'm sorry" before spinning on her heel to make her escape.

Sam followed. "Is everything all right?" he whispered.

She spoke over her shoulder, too embarrassed to meet his eyes. "I told you, I don't feel well."

"Slow down, won't you? Even if we aren't going to have dinner, there's something I wanted to talk to you about." His fingers rested on her shoulder and she reluctantly stopped to face him. "It will take just a moment and you may want to sleep on it. Please?"

Her heart thudded in her ears, but she allowed him to lead her back to the table. It felt like every step took an entire minute to complete, her hazel eyes carefully averted from his storm-gray gaze. Sam drew a deep breath and it shuddered out of him as they settled back into their seats. He smoothed his jacket of non-existent wrinkles. Vi fought down the wave of panic as he opened his mouth to speak.

With a shy smile, he said, "I want to put the act back together."

"You...what?" She stared at him full in the face, dumbfounded.

Now that he'd pushed the words out, he relaxed back into his chair. "You remember when we were kids, and we did that routine with the throwing knives? I thought it would make a great way to fill in between the Belles!"

Mortification burned a path up the back of her neck as she admonished herself for her stupidity. She had to be self-centered bordering on delusional to think he was going to make some sweeping, romantic overture after all this time. He misread her fit of self-loathing for a lapse in her memory and continued.

"You know, hitting targets, *not* hitting each other. That sort of thing."

She glanced up at the stage wistfully, her embarrassment and unexpected thrill at the prospect battling for supremacy. But just as quickly, the excitement receded.

"I can't," she said.

"I know, it has been a while," Sam said, holding up his hands. "But you were always better than me and I bet with just a little bit of practice you would be ready to perform in no time."

"That is not the issue."

She wouldn't even require practice; her skills were sharp as ever. Throwing knives was one of her favorite ways to relax on the ranch. Hitting a target was something she was good at, but unlike many of her other skills, it had little chance of damaging anyone in the process. But if she performed in public, there would be pictures, reporters, people who could recognize her, all of them dangerous and all of them far more likely if she were on that stage in such notable company.

As her mind spun in search of a plausible excuse, he leaned toward her. "I have a confession," he said, sending another thrill up her spine until he pressed on. "You can tell this ship cost me a pretty penny, I'm sure. In the old days, it only took a few months to recoup these kinds of costs, so I sunk all of my savings into a new venture when Pa retired. But now, everyone is keen on the railroad for moving freight."

The tinkling of the piano interrupted and they both glanced over at the flurry of movement. Ceres and Venus bobbed in tandem to the music as Juno clapped out the beat for emphasis. There was something else tugging at Vi, something besides the sound and action, and she struggled to pull her attention to Sam again.

His shoulders sank, shame creasing his brow. "If this thing with the Belles doesn't bring in enough customers, I could lose *The Piasa*, and all the money I already put into it. I really need the show to dazzle, you understand? So, when I got your telegram, I thought it was a miracle! The knife act is exactly the type of thing this crowd will eat up. What do you say?"

A sensation rippled across her back like an electric shock. Vi thought it was another bout of panic until her eyes were pulled back to the stage. The aether near the ceiling rippled from a sandbag a few moments before it came loose from its fitting. A cry leaped from her throat and she shot out of her chair, sending it clattering to the floor, but there was no way to stop the heavy mass as it careened to the stage and straight for the unknowing Belles in its path.

CHAPTER 9

Vi lay in her bed in her cabin, watching the scene unfold in a loop as if projected onto her ceiling—an endless cycle of the unearthly push against her, the bulging and rippling of the space around the rope and the twenty-pound load, followed by its free fall. Thanks to Vi's warning, the women had all managed to jump free, leaving the sandbag to land and burst against the stage. There was more than just the shock keeping Vi awake as the ship bobbed in the Chester harbor, though she was unable to put her finger on precisely what it was. She was about to examine the scene in her mind again when a soft knock interrupted her thoughts.

A luminescent head pushed through the woodwork before she had a chance to answer. "Ah good, you're awake," Peter said.

Vi pushed herself to a sitting position. "Henry is quite a character, isn't he?"

"Yes. Sorry about that. I wasn't sure what to do when you came into the room. What were you doing there anyway?"

"I was calling off my dinner date. Though after what happened, it probably would have been postponed no matter how I felt in the matter."

"It was a far more stimulating afternoon than I'd expected. I thought I'd get a chance to see a few pretty girls. But that was an exceptional show."

She shook her head in disgust. "I cannot believe the way I was shooed out of there. It is not like I do not have any experience tending injuries."

"They were hardly worthy of a battlefield-hardened hand such as yours," he said, looking around for somewhere to sit. In the cramped quarters, he only had the bed and a small desk to choose from, and he opted for the latter. "Just a few scrapes. They were seen to with a few bandages and brandies, much to Henry's delight. It's a favorite of his. We hovered there for quite some time enjoying the vapors, then he decided to go ashore once we docked. He invited me along, but I thought it was more important that I come here."

"What do you think? Is he going to give me any problems if he figures me out?"

Peter's bottom lip jutted out slightly as he thought. He shook his head. "No, he seems quite fine as he is. I am not sure he would even want to finish his unfinished business if you offered."

Her brows knit together. "Really? That would be a first."

"He's found a way to be quite happy as a ghost," Peter replied, his voice laced with envy. "He does what he wants, goes where he wants. And he's in no danger of falling apart and getting disoriented thanks to his little trick."

"What was all that about? He wanted you to do something with this?" Vi ran a finger across her cheek and held up the unnaturally iridescent residue.

"You know how you gave me a boost in Chicago? It seems to be the same principle, except that I don't actually need your permission. If I learned how, I could just take it from you, from anyone, really."

Henry's reference to a stolen kiss came back to her, and Vi was glad she hadn't bothered with a light. The way ghosts glowed, she saw Peter clearly whether or not she lit the candle. He, however, couldn't see the heat rising in her cheeks when she thought about the kiss he had stolen all those years ago. They'd both danced around the subject since his return as a spirit, but in many ways, that was the moment that had brought them to this one.

Peter continued, breaking into her reverie. "But having a hole in your aura is like cutting open an artery. You're practically dripping power wherever you go."

"That will be bad once we reach New Orleans." Her gaze wandered to the opposite wall and she contemplated the handful of stars visible through her window. "Entering in secret shall not do us any good if Mary can scent me the moment we come ashore."

"It's bad *now*," the ghost said, pushing away from the desk. "There are things, Vi. Things that are attracted to power like yours. They can feed on you without you even knowing it."

"Yes, I heard him say something about other things in the 'veil.'" She wriggled her fingers in the air and made a quiet but high-pitched warble. "Woooooh. Spooky stuff."

Peter scowled and began pacing. "You think he was lying?"

"If these things do exist, that is news to me." Her hands dropped back to the covers. "You would think I would have seen something by now if I am such a tasty treat."

"He said they are kind of like living shadows that are quite difficult to see. Even for ghosts. But is that a risk you are willing to take? He's been a ghost a lot longer than you have been seeing them. Maybe he knows what he's talking about." Peter stopped in his tracks. "You can find out if he's telling the truth! Just check your book."

"This again?"

"Think about it," he replied, perching on the foot of the bed. "Your ancestors have been recording all the weird stuff they've seen for generations. If someone saw something, there would have to be a reference to it there."

She took a breath to protest, letting it vibrate out through her lips. He had a point; with her aunt still in Chicago, the journal was her only source of knowledge. And if she really was vulnerable somehow, she would need to find some way to take care of it before she'd be able tend to her task once they reached their final destination. By way of agreement, she grabbed the box of matches on the side table and lit the candle before throwing off the covers.

Bonnie had been the one to stow her things, but Vi found the leather-bound book in a drawer in the desk. The cover hummed under her touch as she retrieved it and lay it open on the desk. The first page bore loopy lettering spelling *On Seeing the Unseen*. This was only the second time she'd seen these words, but there was something both familiar and unsettling about them. She reached back inside the desk drawer to retrieve a pencil and used the eraser to turn to the next page. Whether or not it held the answers she sought, Vi knew the less contact she had with the cursed thing, the better.

The first few dozen pages appeared to be in the form of a diary dating back to the 1600s and kept in the same scrawl as the writing on the first page. The handwriting shifted around the middle of that century to something angular and pinched, and she had to put her face much closer to read it in the flickering light of her taper. Peter looked on over her shoulder, the cold emanating from his body reminding her that the thin cotton gown was the only thing covering her body. She spared only a moment for embarrassment before reminding herself that he was no longer a man of flesh and blood and concentrated on the task at hand.

When the writing changed again, the entries looked less like a diary and more like an encyclopedia with larger letters at the top declaring the particular subject being recounted below. Some of them appeared to be terms worked out in Greek or Latin, while others were phrases like "The movement of objects by the deceased." Occasionally, some later writer had annotated things in the margins or inserted a loose piece of paper if they had more to add. She'd stowed the page with the damnable ghost trap diagram that had gotten her into trouble in Chicago in a similar way, except she unceremoniously shoved it behind the back cover. Vi had only done so on Peter's insistence; she would have been content to shred it and never look at it again.

A few of the sections also contained images rendered in ink or watercolor paint. She had intended only to search for references to the spirit-wound or things that would feed from it, but her innate curiosity slowed her hand as she came to one of these illustrations. It showed several figures, each taking up a small section of the two pages the renderings spanned and all of them surrounded with a different color. Many of them had a string of adjectives written below, but the one haloed in red was accompanied by two words: like us.

Vi pointed to the entry. "Henry said something else before. About the color of my 'shimmer'?"

"Well sure," Peter said. "You're red. Or rather, a sort of pink at the moment. But sometimes you look like you're made of molten rubies."

Her frown deepened. "That can't be. Ghosts are blue, and the living are all white, but there's no red. There's no, well, any of these." Her hand swept across the page and the bright illustrations.

"You mean, you don't see it?" He scoffed. "You're pulling my leg."

"No," she replied curtly. "I'm telling you this is all rubbish. We can't trust anything in here now."

Vi slipped the pencil under the front cover to close it, but Peter held it in place, the pale glistening of his spirit flesh shifting to his hand to give him enough strength. "And I'm telling you it's not. This is what *I* see when I look at the living."

She stared down at the picture, murmuring, "You see things I don't?"

"Fascinating! I had no idea. I just assumed it was the same for you."

"I've let you see what I see before."

"Yes, but that was when I was alive. After I died, I thought it was my shortcoming, or rather general "alive-ness", that had somehow muted what I saw through you. All ghosts see these colors though."

"And apparently, at least one of my ancestors." Vi ran her forefinger around the red aura of the painted figure.

"Or they consulted a ghost," he said, rubbing his chin. "But I suppose there could be some variation from person to person. Or perhaps it's something you can cultivate with practice?"

With the ghost distracted, Vi lifted the pencil and turn to the next page. "Let's just see if we can find anything about your living shadows first, shall we?"

The next section talked about haunted objects and buildings, followed by a few paragraphs related to strategies of communicating with ghosts who were too old or insubstantial and had lost the ability to speak. She turned the page again, and though she didn't find any reference to energy-eating creatures, she stopped there all the same.

"What is it?" Peter asked, bending closer. He elongated the word as he decided how to pronounce it. "Pro-noi-a...What does that mean?"

"I think it's the way I anticipate what people are going to do." She squinted at the page.

Pro-, meaning "before", and noia, meaning "thought." This is the term I've settled on for seeing the intentions of others before they happen. There can be either (or sometimes both) a visual and a physical reaction to the thoughts of the others, as if they project their intentions before them. I find that it helps my reflexes to be sharper than most, though it is certainly not infallible. If there is no thought behind the action, I do not seem able to sense it is coming.

"Huh. It's interesting," Peter said. "But why did you stop here?"

Her mind flashed to the creeping dread that had spread across her shoulders, making her turn and look at the stage before it happened, the ripples in the aether emanating from the sandbag before the rope released.

It was no accident.

CHAPTER 10

Chester, IL
October 17, 1871

Before her revelation, she and Bonnie had agreed to meet in the lounge on their deck in the morning for breakfast. After covering up the fading bruise around her eye and dressing for the day, the bleary-eyed medium made her way to the glass enclosure. In addition to her lightweight dress and sensible shoes, her ensemble included her holster and knife as a precaution against whomever had orchestrated the sand bag. The chances she would need to use it were slim, but the feel of the leather straps against her calf always gave her a sense of calm assurance.

Vi was not sure of the time, but the sun was high above the horizon and the ship well underway as she strolled along the promenade. The windows were open, and as she approached, the scent of coffee beckoned to her. She'd left off searching the book for living shadows after her realization, much to Peter's disappointment. Even so, sleep had been slow in coming after she'd sent the ghost off for the night.

When she passed the threshold, Vi saw empty cups and saucers spread around the room on low tables and upholstered chairs, the remnants of the crew who had already gone to their posts for the day. Both *The Piasa* and her tow lacked true cooking facilities, but there was a stove in one corner of the lounge. The pot on top was no doubt the source of the coffee smell. A picked-over tray of rolls and a few clean cups sat on a long table beside it. Vi swallowed roughly and licked her parched lips at the prospect of something to drink.

As expected, her companion was already there, a cup of something steaming before her and a thin book open on the table. The little brunette looked up with a smile when Vi entered, but her face fell as she took in her haggard appearance. "Rough night?"

"Indeed." Vi crossed over to the waiting coffee and carefully poured some of the liquid joy into a chipped cup. Despite the sunshine streaming in through the glass roof, there was a damp chill to the air. Adding a tipple of something a bit stronger to warm her belly wouldn't have gone amiss, but she'd have to do without.

"I found the library," Bonnie said. "It is more of a cupboard, really. I didn't find any Jules Verne, but I did find an issue of one of my serials that I hadn't read before." She held it out to Vi as she took the seat across from her. The cover showed a figure leaping from a window, his arms extending into black, bat-like wings and face contorted into a ghoulish leer.

"Charming." Vi blew the steam off of her coffee and shook her head in mock-reprimand. "You and your monsters."

Bonnie returned the book to the table and ran an affectionate hand over the cover. "It's just a bit of fun. And how else should I be filling my time? You made it sound as if we would be busy working, but no one has given us anything to do."

"I thought you wanted a holiday." Vi took a cautious sip of the brew, followed by a gulp after deciding it was safe to drink. "I suppose in all the hubbub, it slipped Sam's mind to give us duties."

"Of course," Bonnie said, her head bobbing. "What a terrible accident!"

Vi examined her from over the rim of her cup before taking a fleeting glance around the room to ensure their privacy. "I'm not sure it was."

"Terrible?"

"An accident."

When Vi finished recounting her conversation with Peter and what she'd found in the book, her cup was empty. Bonnie leaned on one elbow, her usual optimistic, fey face lined in thought. "Who do you suppose was the target? Juno?"

"It seems reasonable. The more I see her with the Belles, the more likely it seems that someone would have a problem with her and the way she runs things."

"But she may have been really badly injured, even killed!" Bonnie said. "Do you really think someone hates her that much?"

"It may not be a matter of hate. People do terrible things for plenty of reasons. I'd like to go down and talk to the girls and see what I can find out."

"I didn't think you would want to get involved. And it isn't as if Juno or the Belles have given you much of a reason to want to help."

"I'm not doing it for them. I want to know for Sam's sake. He has a lot riding on this and I don't want to see someone else's pettiness get in the way." Vi rose from her chair and waited for Bonnie to follow before leaving the lounge.

Vi supposed correctly that they would find the Belles in the main hall of the showboat already. This area had a much nicer setup than the crew lounge on the tow. Someone had brought out a samovar and put it on the bar to provide a steady supply of tea. Venus was filling a cup as they entered and Bonnie immediately went to her.

"Oh, you poor dear," Bonnie said, taking the cup and saucer from her and passing it to Vi without looking. She crushed the taller woman into one of her characteristic embraces. "You must have been so frightened!"

The Belle's glassy-eyed stare broke as confusion blossomed, and she looked to Vi for guidance.

"This is my friend, Bonnie Murphy," she supplied. "She saw the accident. Bonnie, this is Venus."

The little brunette pulled back and held the dancer at arm's length. "Don't you worry. We're going to find out—"

"Let me help you with this," Vi interjected, giving Bonnie a slight nudge with her hip—both to get her attention and to better reach the samovar—eliciting a squeak of surprise.

"Yes, thank you," said the copper-haired woman, stepping away and turning her attention to Bonnie. "And you can call me Enid. That's my real name. Venus is just for the theater. Diana's lucky. That's her real name and her stage name." Vi closed off the spigot and picked up a pair of sugar tongs, raising her eyebrows but not interrupting. "Yes, two lumps, please. Thank you. I don't usually drink tea. It makes me sorta jittery. But I didn't sleep much, though. Got to be sharp. Got to be ready."

Vi added the sugar and gave it a stir. As Enid took the proffered tea, the cup rattled against the saucer until she took a loud slurp and spilled it. If this was Enid calm, Vi would hate to see what "jittery" looked like.

"Did anyone figure out how it happened?" she asked.

"Nobody saw," Enid replied, wiping at the droplets of tea on her blouse.

"Have accidents like this happened before?"

"Juno runs a pretty right ship, and the boys are awful careful."

Vi handed her a napkin. "Jack and Charles, you mean?"

"Yeah," Enid said, smiling gratefully. "They take care of the setup and the rigging wherever we go. And nothin' like this's ever happened." She nearly jumped out of her skin when another voice joined the conversation.

"What about Daphne?" Ceres asked, strolling up to the counter and offering her hand to Bonnie. She retained her stage name for the introduction and her handshake was rather more forceful than proper. Unlike Enid, she didn't appear to carry any of the same pent-up energy or anxiety as a result of the accident.

With the cordiality complete, Vi pressed her to clarify.

"Daphne was before Enid's time," Ceres said, sipping her cup of tea and pulling a face. She reached across Vi for the sugar bowl. "She was the original Venus. Enid is her replacement."

"What happened to her?" Bonnie asked.

"A heel broke off her shoe during a performance back in New York. And broke her leg with it." Ceres's blue eyes flashed with something akin to amusement.

A nervous titter bubbled up from Enid. "That's not the same as a sandbag."

"All I know is it was an accident that shouldn't have happened," Ceres said, the spoon clinking against her cup as she stirred.

"Why do you say that?" Vi asked.

The dancer took another exploratory sip of her tea and sighed with satisfaction before answering. "We aren't big enough to have someone dedicated to just the costumes, so Diana and I help out with the sewing and such. We keep things organized. And I know there wasn't anything wrong with those shoes the day before Daphne fell, so..." She took another sip and let the veiled accusation hang in the air.

Vi leaned against the bar, her mind trying to fit the pieces together. If Ceres was right, this had been going on for a while. Then again, it may have just been an unfortunate accident; heels could break on their own whether or not Ceres believed it. Vi would need more information before she'd be able to come to any sort of conclusion. There were too many moving parts, too many people involved to get a real feeling yet. She took a breath as she formulated her next question, but wasn't able to speak before another voice ripped through room.

"You again!" Juno's clipped words came from the stage but were undeniably directed at them. Enid nearly dropped her saucer and Ceres winced. "This is a closed rehearsal," Juno barked. "Members of the company *only*."

"Sorry!" Bonnie called, giving Vi's sleeve a jerk. "I think we'd better go."

"Nonsense." Vi pulled her arm away as an obstinate grin split her lips.

Her companion looked from the grifter to the acerbic director and back again. "We can talk to them later. Let's just go."

"I'm sorry, haven't you heard?" Vi shouted back to Juno. "Sam asked me to join the show."

CHAPTER 11

"Is that so?" Minerva asked with a toss of her hair as she sidled up beside Juno. "And what makes you think you can just walk in and do that?"

Juno's reaction was far more measured, though there was a cold heat radiating from her as she said, "And your talent would be...?"

Vi stepped to a nearby chair and placed her foot onto the seat. With a flick of her skirt, she revealed the throwing knife strapped to her calf.

Bonnie whispered, "Vi, what are you doing?"

Minerva placed her balled fists on her hips. "Oh please, what are you going to do with that?"

Before the Belle had completed her question, Vi spun back and released the knife. It flew end over end in a tight circle, right through the gap between Minerva's elbow and her side. The knife came to a satisfying, thunking stop in the wainscoting.

As she stood stunned, the dancer's face went through a variety of shades before settling on an enraged crimson. She opened her mouth a few times, but words failed her.

Instead, it was Juno who spoke next, regarding Vi with far more interest than disdain. The anger from a few moments before had completely evaporated, leaving cool eyes twinkling with possibilities. "And you can do that again?"

"Absolutely."

Minerva finally recovered herself enough to screech, "What if you had hit me?"

Vi smiled slyly. "I make it my business never to miss my mark."

The leader of the troupe tapped her lips thoughtfully. "It's a good trick, but it's not an act. Not yet anyway."

"I can make it an act all right," she assured her. "For instance, let me introduce you to my lovely assistant." Vi made a show of presenting Bonnie to the room. The little brunette blinked owlishly a few times before letting out a nervous giggle.

Juno sniffed and held up one finger. She rotated it in the air a few times, but Bonnie didn't get the hint that she was supposed to spin until Vi took a shoulder in each hand and gave her a gentle nudge.

"Juno, you can't seriously be considering this," Minerva said, her voice equal parts acid and honey as she watched Bonnie complete her awkward circle.

"She'll do," Juno said. "Though you'll both need something more suitable to wear."

Vi stepped over to where her knife still quivered in the wall. "A target wouldn't go amiss either. I can't imagine Sam will appreciate it if I put too many holes in his shiny new theater."

Juno nodded and motioned Jack to her side. She gave him a few instructions, then turned back to her newest volunteers. "Diana is in the back right now finishing hanging up the costumes. Go and see her and take a look at what we have. This isn't a 'yes' yet, mind you," Juno added. "This is a chance for you to show me what you have to offer."

Bonnie started to thank her, but the head Belle had already turned her back and was making her way to the stage. She flicked her hand, and the rest of the dancers put down their teacups and rushed to follow. Minerva steamed at Vi for an extra moment before making a point of knocking into her as she passed.

"What changed your mind?" Bonnie asked. "And more importantly, why did you drag me into this?"

Vi couldn't tell how much of the second question was in earnest or jest. "You heard Juno, she did not want us hanging around. I will not be able to figure out what is going on if I don't have access to the room, now will I?" A wicked expression tugged at the corners of her mouth. "As for including you, it's easier to avoid hitting someone petite, don't you think?"

Bonnie spluttered, "I thought you said you never miss!"

"I don't," she replied. "But there is a first time for everything."

"That's not funny."

Vi held up her hand, her thumb and forefinger almost touching. "It's a little funny."

Bonnie sighed. "Let's go see about these costumes. Maybe I shall get lucky and nothing will fit."

The two of them walked down the aisle and mounted the short staircase next to the stage. They slipped into the darkness of the wings. Vi made out at least half a dozen different pulleys and levers in the gloom, some of them no doubt attached to sandbags like the one that had fallen the night before. Under the cover of darkness, it would be easy for anyone to loosen a knot without being seen.

A little farther on, light peeked through a gap between a door and its frame. They followed the light into a hallway. There was a matching door on the other side. The faint rustling of taffeta and silk hinted at what lay within.

Vi knocked on the doorframe before entering, sending Diana wheeling around to see who was behind her.

"Sorry," Vi said. "I did not mean to startle you."

Diana relaxed. "It's fine. I just get a little jumpy when I'm alone back here. I can't shake the feeling that I'm being watched."

Bonnie pushed the door the rest of the way open to allow her and Vi to step into the room. Before they'd interrupted her, Diana had been hanging a variety of costumes in one of two wooden wardrobes hulking in the corners. An array of shoe and hat boxes were stacked on the flat surfaces, which included a long table lined with mirrored glass. A few elaborate headdresses stood out from the general mess, the silk flowers adding a strangely organic touch to the many carefully crafted frills. Much of one wall was occupied by a carved wooden screen for changing clothes and keeping at least a modicum of privacy.

In another corner, a dressmaker's dummy displayed a breathtaking silver gown nearly dripping with beadwork and lace. The hem had pins in it, but it appeared more or less complete but for this finishing touch.

Vi jerked her thumb at the dummy. "Perhaps it is just your model who is watching you?"

"That's lovely!" Bonnie said, wandering closer to the gown.

"Thank you," Diana replied. "After all the work I've put into altering it, it had better be. Enid is shorter than our last Venus and hemming around all those beads is a real hassle. I have been working on it basically around the clock since we boarded. And it's a good thing, too. Now Juno wants it ready by Memphis."

Vi stepped over to a crimson outfit that caught her eye. She ran her thumb over the tight, even needlework. "Do you make them all?"

"Me and Ceres, yeah. Though I'd much rather be performing." Diana sighed, her face drifting in the direction of the stage where the other women were all in the middle of rehearsal. Her eyes regained focus and she smiled at Vi. "What can I do for you, ladies?"

"My friend and I are hoping to join the show." The blond woman's thin brows knit together, and Vi added hurriedly, "We're no dancers. But I do have a talent for knife-throwing, and my friend here is very good at standing still, if you catch my meaning."

"A knife act?" Diana gasped. "How exciting! I saw one, once. Are you going to strap her to one of those spinning wheel things?"

Bonnie blanched. "To *what*?"

Vi shook her head. "No time for anything so elaborate, I'm afraid. Which means we need the costumes to do a lot of the heavy lifting. Do you have any recommendations?"

Diana twined her fingers in thought, then gestured at the nearest wardrobe. "All of the outfits that are already being used in the show have a label. Just look for the strings on the hangers and you'll know they are already taken. These are for the Belles, both in and out of the main show, and the other is for the rest of the company." She gave Bonnie an appraising look. "You and me are about the same size, I'd bet. I've got a cute little blue outfit that might work for you. It was from the last show. No one's using it right now."

She rummaged for a moment before pulling out something that was indeed a lovely shade of blue. Bonnie's eyes grew wide as she took in the skirt which managed to be both fluffy and miniscule at the same time. "What role was *that* for?" Bonnie squeaked.

"I was the Moon," Diana replied wistfully. The edges of her expression curdled. "I hated that role. They had me up above the stage, dangling over everyone on a swing for most of the show. I got to sing a little with the chorus, and I had a few lines, but overall, definitely not my favorite role." She held the garment out to the other woman. When Bonnie didn't immediately take it, she shook it at her, before finally shoving it into her hands.

"I suppose that makes sense," Vi said. "Given your name. Goddess of the Moon and the hunt and all that."

The dancer made a noncommittal sound as she stooped to find Bonnie some shoes. "Diana is my real name. I was just lucky that it also belonged to a goddess." With her quarry in hand, she turned back to Bonnie, who had the dress at arm's length and a terrified glint in her eye. Diana gently took one shoulder in her free hand and turned the other woman toward the screen. "You'll look great. And I'll have some tights for you as well, if it fits."

Bonnie squeaked as she ducked behind the screen. Vi started to peer into the various boxes and cartons on the makeup table, cooing appreciatively over the quality of the wares. "The Belles must be doing quite well."

Diana snorted. "Don't believe what you see here. The things I didn't make, Juno brought with her from a previous company. We're barely scraping by."

A prickle spread from the base of Vi's skull and trickled down her spine. She took a deep breath, attempting to home in on the source of the sensation, but she didn't have to wait long. Henry slipped noiselessly into the room, the blue flame of his aura dancing just a few feet behind Vi's back. He stopped short when he spotted her, then took a few hesitant steps closer.

"Is that so?" Vi asked, doing her best to distract herself from the spirit. Inside the next box, she found a mass of black hair. The strands of the wig were coarse and straight, more than likely horsehair rather than human. Vi dipped at the waist, pulling the wig over her own coiffure before tossing her head back and letting the onyx locks fall over her shoulders. As she leaned in to check herself in the mirror, the ghost leaned perilously close. In her reflection, she saw faint traces of her strange wound, and the ghost was looking at it with an expression that was far from gentlemanly.

Vi spun around, blurting, "What do you think?"

Bonnie's head poked out around the edge of the screen. "I hardly recognize you."

The ghost took notice, giving a lecherous waggle of his eyebrows before he stepped toward the screen.

"I'm not much of a fan of wigs myself," Diana said. "Too itchy. But it looks good with your skin tone."

Vi took a hurried step between the ghost and her scantily clad friend. "Can you think of anything that would suit me?" she asked the dancer. "Perhaps something red?"

The spirit didn't bother to stop, but simply passed through Vi's shoulder on his way. Her body grew cold where they touched, which she'd expected and braced for. But then her skin became warm, as though it was kissed by the summer sun. The ghost lurched away, his luminescent eyes growing wide and startled.

Vi couldn't keep her expression neutral any longer and she met his gaze. Henry stabbed his finger at her. "You *can* see me! I knew it!"

CHAPTER 12

Before Vi reacted, there was a soft knock at the door. Diana excused herself, unwittingly walking right through the ghost and his incredulous gaze. The dancer opened the door a crack and exchanged a few words with whomever stood on the other side. After a titter, she turned back to Vi saying, "I'll just be a few minutes. Help yourself to whatever you like and we can see about getting it fitted properly when I come back."

Vi waited for her footsteps to fade. "Yes, I can see you. I can see you trying to get an eyeful," she hissed.

Bonnie squeaked. "What? Who? Is that Peter?"

"No," she sighed and pinched the bridge of her nose. "It is the other one."

"You know Peter?" The ghost asked. "That sly devil. He never let on!"

"That is because I told him not to. I have enough on my plate without dealing with anyone else's unfinished business."

There were a few rustles and bumps from behind the screen as Bonnie emerged and looked around for the culprit. The stranger jerked his thumb at her. "I take it she can't see me though."

"No, that displeasure falls only to me," Vi replied. "But now that we're talking, spend a lot of time around the ladies' changing room, do you?"

Henry hooked his thumbs through his ephemeral suspenders. "It passes the time. And it doesn't really do any harm, does it?"

As Vi was generally a passenger on that same train of thought, she didn't correct him. Bonnie, however, went red in the face and spluttered in his general direction. "That is disgraceful behavior. You should be ashamed of yourself!"

Henry did not appear the least bit disgraced as Vi looked the ghost over from head to toe. The white fog of his body swirled thick and bright, his stance far steadier than Peter had looked since they boarded. "How long have you been dead? If you don't mind my asking."

"It's hard t' keep track," he said, running his hand over what had once been a stubbly chin.

"You don't seem too worse for the wear. I know I didn't expect to see another ghost on the boat. I practically had to drag Peter aboard."

Bonnie paced over and rested a hand on a patch of Vi's bare skin to allow her to see him as well. "Oh my, yes! You seem just fine."

Henry inclined his head in greeting, then gestured at the gash in Vi's aura. "Speakin' of worse for the wear... you should really take care of that."

Bonnie followed the line of his hand and let out a squeak. "Vi! What on Earth is that?"

Vi cursed silently, but aloud she said, "It is nothing."

The other woman took the medium's face in her hand and moved it around to get a better look. The eerie blue gleam reflected in Bonnie's pupils as she tutted. "And how long has this been going on?"

"It is a little souvenir from Chicago." Vi jerked her chin out of Bonnie's grasp. "It's been bleeding off and on like that since we left."

"That is not like any blood I've ever seen. It looks kind of like what ghosts are made of." The little brunette lifted her hand and replaced it again, testing what she saw. Her frown grew deeper. "Why didn't you tell me?"

Vi studied her hands and mumbled, "I thought it would get better. I did not want you to worry."

Henry interjected, his tone irritatingly condescending, considering she'd caught him skulking around the dressing room. "Oh, it is not goin' t' get better. Not on its own, that is. You're bleedin' pretty freely now, and the runnin' water isn't goin' t' help you any more'n it does your friend. Though I already told him how t' overcome that particular difficulty."

"So I've heard." Vi crossed her arms and leaned against the makeup table. "You've found a way to take energy from the living."

He waved away her concern. "Not much and not often. Most people don't even know it's happenin'. That's part of the beauty. Though I'd understand if'n you didn't believe me, that's what brought me down here. As lovely as you ladies are, I was startin' to feel a little...thin. And that Diana, well, she's somethin' special."

"There's a difference?" Bonnie asked, her outrage morphing into curiosity.

"Let me put it this way. Potatoes can keep you alive, but wouldn't you rather have a nice slice of peach pie if'n you had the chance?"

Vi frowned. "I thought it was a matter of quantity, not quality. Peter's told me that he gets stronger being around me in particular, that I give off an excess of some kind. But you're saying you *taste* things from people?"

"In a manner of speakin'. You can feel the difference between the dead and livin', I'm sure. It's along the same lines. Though it takes a while t' have a pallet as refined as mine."

Bonnie voiced Vi's feelings for her. "That's ghastly!"

The ghost snorted. "It is what it is. Don't kill the messenger," he added with a wink. He turned his attention back to Vi. "You're practically hemorrhaging power, and you really had no idea?"

"It is not as though I have the sniffles. There are no symptoms."

"You sure about that?" Henry arched a thick eyebrow.

Vi scowled. "Why do you know about any of this? You could not have figured it all out after you died."

"I was part of a special division during The Rebellion," he said, grinning. "It was my job to know. Though I never expected to put any of it into practice so soon. Considering your prowess, I'm surprised we didn't meet back then at any of the Spiritualist meetin's."

"Were you a medium, too?" Bonnie asked.

Henry ran this thumbs along his suspenders before letting them snap noiselessly against his chest. "No ma'am. I was a serial dabbler. I trained as a chemist, but I had my fingers in all kinds of pots. My work toward the end was more of a theoretical nature. But we did have several mediums in our employ."

Vi mulled this over for a few heartbeats before feeling another bout of sensation wash over her. Through the wall, she detected Peter approaching. Though it was his shape she thought she recognized, it could very well be some other quality she hadn't appreciated before now. Mary and Cassandra had felt different from one another when she'd encountered them on the train, but she'd chalked that up to the level of rage and malice each possessed. If other feelings and forces shaped an aura, that would prove to be a useful trait to explore.

Peter's head passed through the door and he took in the scene. His eyes flicked between Vi and the other ghost, his face awash with uncertainty about how to proceed. "Oh, there you are, Henry. What are you doing here?"

"The jig is up," Vi said. "Everyone's been introduced."

"I did not tell him, Vi. I swear!" Peter passed fully into both the room and conversation. "Though I suppose I did not do a good job of keeping him occupied, either."

Vi crossed to the wardrobe and took out the red dress. The gold beads on the bodice were not as elaborately sewn as the masterpiece on the dummy, but she suspected they would positively glow in the limelight. She removed it from its hanger and strode to the wooden screen. "How about you keep him away while I try on this costume and we call it even. Besides, we have much more important matters to discuss. Namely, this business about stealing energy from the living."

Henry made a rude noise. "As you clearly demonstrated, it wouldn't have to be the livin'."

She flopped the dress over the top of the screen and stood on her toes to see the ghost. "Meaning?"

"Just now! You took from me without so much as a by-your-leave."

"What's he talking about?" Peter asked.

Vi scowled and rocked back on her heels, out of sight. "I assure you, I did nothing of the sort." She sounded far more confident than she felt, but the memory of the heat spreading across her skin at his touch shouldered in to bring her doubt. As she pulled her day dress over her head, she sensed the ripples of Henry pacing on the other end of the room.

"And I assure you, you did. It's easier with the livin', at least for me. Ghosts are just balls of free-floatin', lightly packed energy. There isn't much of a barrier between us. However, ghosts can see each other comin'. The livin' on the other hand, they sit nice and still and never even know the difference. A person might feel a little light-headed, but that's hardly the crime you're makin' it out to be. But you, you could gobble me all up and no one'd be the wiser!"

Peter rubbed his chin, puzzled. "I thought she put off energy, not collected it."

"Under normal circumstances, sure. But with that thing depletin' her stores," Henry said, grimacing at the cerulean ooze on Vi's face, "she has to make it up from somewhere. Touchin' solid ground helps, but it won't cure her."

Vi pulled the red dress from its perch and waved her hand over the screen to catch their attention. "'She' is right here, remember?"

Henry stopped pacing. "When I first saw that injury, I'd assumed that's *why* you were on this tub headin' south in the first place."

She slipped her arms through the bottom the dress and out the top, but paused to ask, "What do my travel plans have to do with any of this?"

"There've been rumblings, rumors. There's somethin' going on down south. Some kin' of massive surges. Somethin' happened in Chicago recently, too. I tell you, I have seen more comfortably solid ghosts in the last month than I've seen my whole life. Death," he corrected. "I thought you were goin' down there to take advantage of the free pick-me-up. And you're not the only one. There are...things that cross over to this plane. Things you can't see, but they think the livin' and the dead are a tasty treat. You'd best be careful, or one of them might pick up your trail. A psychophage--that's what I call them anyway--it'll make that little leak into much more than a trickle."

With her costume now in place, Vi came out from behind the screen to take a gander in the mirror. Unlike Bonnie's rigid dress, the red skirt hung in loose pleats around the middle of her thighs. Vi had a smaller chest than whoever it had been made for, but overall it fit quite nicely. She straightened the wig and tucked a stray piece of her own hair back under the netting. "That sounds like something mother ghosts would tell their naughty little dead children to make them behave better."

Bonnie gave the ensemble an appraising look before nodding her approval. "What is that about a ghost bedtime story?" she asked. Vi filled her in and took up her place near enough for the other woman to make contact. When Vi finished, Bonnie turned to Henry and asked, "But ghosts can see them, these psychophages?"

Henry turned his regard to her and ran an appreciative leer over her petite form and even more petite ensemble. Bonnie fussed ineffectually with the tutu. When she realized the dressing corner was free, she hurried to the screen to get back into her regular clothes.

"Yes," Henry replied, watching her as she went. Peter flicked his ear and he continued. "They're closer to bein' like us than they are to bein' like you folk, I suppose. And we only scratched the surface when it came to detectin' anything beyond our own sphere of existence. It was all theoretical when I was workin' on all this, but I believe now more than ever."

Vi twisted to see the back of her dress in the mirror. "What do they look like?"

"Well…" The ghost rubbed the back of his neck, an expression of chagrin on his face. "If'n you want t' get technical about it…I haven't actually seen one. But I don't gotta see one myself to fear them."

"Why haven't I heard of this before?" Vi demanded. "It's not as though I am a complete novice."

"Most spirits don't stick around long enough to see them, I guess. And it seems safe to assume those that do rarely make it through the encounter. We can't fight the phages any more'n the livin' can fight off a ghost who has doin' damage on their agenda."

Vi's hand rose unconsciously to the tender skin on her throat, the memory of the angry spirit and her own impotence at Mary's hands far too fresh.

Peter reminded her, "And it isn't as though you are over-fond of making polite conversation with the dead. It's usually in and out with you, if you acknowledge them at all. You should really finish reading Pru's book."

At the mention of the odious tome, Vi glared at him, but didn't address the suggestion.

"I do not know what book you're talkin' 'bout, but do you read German?" Henry asked. "There's a fellow named Reichenbach who's doin' some fascinatin' work on—"

"We've got far more immediate problems than my choice of reading material." Vi brought Henry up to speed about her suspicions surrounding the previous evening's near-miss. Bonnie had rid herself of the frothy blue getup and was emerging from behind the screen by the time she finished.

"Is that why you are back here playing dress-up?" Peter asked. "You were the one who said you wanted to lie low from here on out. And now you're going to be in the show. That's a terrible risk."

Vi tossed some of the ebony locks of her borrowed hair over her shoulder. "But you see," she said, her words thick with a non-specific but clearly Eastern European accent. "I vill not be dees 'Vi' you speak of. I vill be Anastasia, meestress of zee blades." She snatched up another wig from the box and tossed it at Bonnie. "And my lovely assistant Natasha vill be helpink me. Vee are very beautifuel and meesteerious seesters."

Bonnie giggled. "Do you expect me to talk like that too? I'm not sure I'd be able to keep a straight face."

"Nah," Vi replied, returning to her customary Yankee voice. "The lovely assistant is more of a silent partner. I can do enough talking for the both of us."

"That's an understatement," Peter said with a smirk. Then his smile slipped. "I still say it's a gamble."

"And you know how I feel about gambling," she said, quirking her eyebrows. Peter harrumphed, evidently not enjoying Vi's attempt at levity. She continued more somberly, "I want to help Sam. This show ship is his life. And I don't want to let some petty jealousy get in the way of his plans."

Bonnie made a pretty wrinkle of her button nose. "Would jealousy really lead someone to ruin the show? And to hurt one of the Belles?"

Vi held up her fingers and ticked off the items as she spoke. "The three main reasons behind any crime are love, money, and power. The offshoot being that someone covets someone *else*'s love, money, or power. Even though there were plenty of Belles on that stage when it happened, I suspect Juno was the target. She's got the power, and not much in the way of love or money. I think someone in the show is gunning for her." Vi slipped back into Anastasia's accent. "But fear not, my dear seester, zee only crime happenink on my vatch is vhen I steal zee show!"

CHAPTER 13

Juno approved their costume choices, then dismissed Vi and Bonnie from the hall to work on their act. Tensions were high after the incident the night before, and she did not want new people underfoot. It was a reasonable request, given the circumstances. But it also meant Vi would not be close enough to the action to be of any real aid if anything else happened.

With a bottle of pilfered whisky under her arm, she and Bonnie left *The Piasa* and returned to the deck chairs on the towboat. They would need to decide which tricks to do and build some kind of story line to carry the knife act, but Henry's words about energy transfer buzzed too loudly in her ears to concentrate. Vi did not need to fake her headache or wooziness and begged off for a few hours rest. Though she would not give Peter the satisfaction of an "I told you so," she had to see what the family diary had to say before she'd be able to focus on anything else.

When Vi was safely ensconced back in her own berth, she stowed the bottle on her bedside table before blowing out a puff of air and heading to her desk. The book lay right as she left it, half-obscured by a handkerchief in the bottom of a drawer. Vi snatched it from its resting place before she talked herself out of it.

Her head swam slightly as she crossed back to her bed, and Vi worried for a moment whether she would even be able to keep the buzz of memories at bay well enough to read in her current condition. She braved running an index finger across a portion of the exposed spine, and something distinctive and strong bubbled to the surface. In light of Henry's talk about "flavors" of energy, she concentrated on the different sensations one by one.

For the first time, Vi could clearly detect that the memories all had a different kind of essence, like a waft of perfume or specific key signature, but composed of something completely different than scent or sound. Though she had not planned on doing anything besides reading about the transfer of energies, this particularly memory somehow both reassured her and gently demanded she notice it at the same time. Perhaps if she gave this one some attention, the strange whispering of the book would quiet long enough to find the reference she sought.

So after a fortifying swig from the bottle, Vi tore away the handkerchief and placed her hand upon the cover of the book. An aetheric wind swirled around her, gripping at her core and urging her to allow herself to be swept up in its current. Vi swallowed the lump in her throat and acquiesced. Though on some level she knew her physical body remained perfectly still, something grasped the heart of her spirit body and wrenched her toward the floor. Her hands shot out on impulse, but when they should have hit the wood, they simply passed right through. The rest of her followed suit until she found herself standing on what the logical part of her brain told her had to be the ceiling of the suite below her, but it was, in fact, the glossy, colorless granite of the floor within the memory.

Vi took one steadying step forward as she regained her equilibrium before she peered into the darkness. The murkiness itself had weight, like a curtain that could be lifted, though not by her. The floor she was no larger than a few paces wide in each direction, but somehow she could also sense that the distance above her was impossibly high.

In a blink, a figure stood before her. The woman was older than Vi by a decade or two. She wore a plain, dark dress and white apron. The rough fabric could have come from that moment in time, but something about the cut of the garment and the cap on her head spoke of another era. The eyes peering at Vi from under a distinctive brow were bright and intelligent, and most surprisingly, blue. In Vi's admittedly limited experience walking through memories, there had not been even a trace of color to be found. This figure, on the other hand, had the eyes of the dead, and was using those eyes to bore a hole right through Vi. Their gazes locked for several heartbeats as Vi waited for a scene to unfold as it normally did. When the figure spoke directly to her, Vi nearly jumped out of her skin.

"Cat got your tongue?" she asked.

Vi looked over her shoulder to find the woman's scene partner, but found only the blanket of velvet dark behind her. When she returned her glance to the figure, she was smiling. Vi prodded herself in the chest and raised a questioning brow.

The memory sighed. "Yes, you."

"Oh...um. Hello there," Vi replied lamely.

"You must be Viola."

"How do you know my name?"

The figure's grin widened. "Your auntie told me all about you. I was not sure when to expect you, but I am glad you are here." Her tone was friendly, but also somehow flat. As if she were not quite whole. Vi found it unsettling.

The grifter grimaced. "She failed to tell me anything at all about you, I'm afraid."

"Please, have a seat and we can discuss it."

The figure gestured to the space behind Vi. When she looked at it this time, there was a simple wooden stool waiting for her. Vi settled in, and immediately the strange not-quite-memory was similarly seated, though much closer than before. This memory eschewed the normal laws of time like the others Vi had seen, which did not make the way she was breaking the rest of the rules any less unsettling.

The colorless woman laced her fingers in her lap. "My name is Alice."

"Are you one of my ancestors? A ghost?"

"Yes and no," replied Alice, her tone clinical and detached. "Alice Thorne was your ancestor, but I am not Alice Thorne. I am a construct. She began the process of creating me, and others followed. I am her voice, her shape, and some of her memories. But I can also access all of the other memories left here." She unclasped her hands and brought one up to her collarbone. "I am the caretaker. What can I help you with?"

"I would not wish to bother you," Vi said, gesturing to the darkness around her. "You seem as though you have your hands full as it is. And I rather enjoy reading on my own, so perhaps another time?"

Alice regarded Vi with her unsettling eyes, her smile never wavering. "I am also intimately acquainted with every entry. It is my job. My reason for being." She gestured at Vi's stool and the living medium reluctantly took her place. "What can I help you with?"

Vi placed her elbow on her knee and her chin against her fist. She hadn't planned to do more than just do a little light reading. If Alice's claims were true, she probably would speed up the process. "All right, I'll bite," Vi said. "I need to know more about how the energy exchange between the living and the dead works."

"Can you be more specific?" The caretaker cocked her head to one side. The blackness behind her gently churned, as if the gesture had disturbed it.

Vi mulled over her conversation with Henry. "Can it be dangerous to the living?"

The darkness swirled faster, the eddy growing taller than Alice. She rose and stepped toward the whirlpool, her eyes glowing brighter every moment. "Yes."

Without moving, Vi found herself closer to the opening, as if the floor itself had contracted. She took a step forward and her foot fell onto an expanse of floor made of rough-hewn wood.

The sepia room in the memory was washed in morning light, making the white walls gleam. Vi shielded her eyes against the contrast, and when she brought her arms down again, she found the remains of a heatless fire in the hearth and a straw mattress on a rustic frame. A lump under the covers told her a body lay upon it, and a ghost sat beside it. At first glance, Vi assumed it was the woman's own spirit taking a final look before departing. However, as Vi stepped forward, it became clear that the person on the bed was only a child.

The ghost stroked the girl's pale hair as she hummed. Vi crossed to the bed for a better look and spied a weak glimmer where the dead and the living touched. A contented smile spread over the ghost's face as her spirit flesh grew brighter and brighter.

"Stop that!" Vi demanded a moment before remembering she could do no more than watch.

The muffled sounds of shouting voices came to her from the other side of the door. She was going to go investigate the scuffle when the door burst open and a now familiar form stomped through it. Alice, the once-living Alice, bustled across the threshold in a storm of shawls.

Another woman followed, her face lined with worry. "Do you really think you can help her?" she asked, clinging to Alice's ample sleeve.

This Alice had the flat, brown-gray eyes of a memory, which she narrowed as she examined the room. When the ghost felt the weight of her gaze, it stopped humming and the happy swirl of her spirit body froze.

Alice nodded to the distraught mother. "Yes, I can help her. But you have to leave. *Now.*" She took the other woman by the shoulders and ushered her out.

Once the door was latched shut, Alice faced the bed. The ghost had left her prey behind and floated a few inches above the floorboards, her once sweetly smiling mouth twisting into a ghoulish leer. One claw-like hand reached forward, and the rest of the spirit followed.

Though Vi knew she didn't face any real danger, the expression on the ghost's face was enough to make her put as much distance between them as the small room allowed. With a final glance at the child, she pressed her back against the far wall to watch the scene.

Alice, on the other hand, did not seem the least bit disturbed by the ghost as she retrieved a hunk of chalk from her pocket. "Hello, Jane. You have been rather busy as of late."

Hearing her name gave the ghost pause. "You know me?" she rasped.

Alice knelt down to the floor and swept the chalk in a wide arc. "I was not certain I was correct." She drew the other half of the circle, and Vi craned her neck to better see what she was up to. "But I had my suspicions when the Smiths started falling ill."

"They deserve my wrath!" Jane howled, her spirit flesh darkening like a thunderhead. "You do not know what they did to me!"

The chalk rose and fell as Alice drew a series of lines. Vi recognized the shape of the ghost trap she had put to catastrophic ends in Chicago and shuddered. Alice glanced up at Jane before returning to her task. "I know enough."

"Then you understand? They must pay."

Alice used her free hand to point at the little girl on the bed. "*She* was not involved. She's innocent."

"Yeah!" Vi added. "Keep your hands to yourself."

The hem of Alice's dress moved in time to the aetheric wind that Jane's rage was kicking up. The ghost shook her head violently, clutching it in confusion and rage. The next time Alice exhaled, it was accompanied by a puff of steam. Vi was impervious to the cold, but from the look of things, Jane was pulling all the energy in the room toward her. Tiny streaks of lightning brightened the ghost's body in places, and Vi would swear she'd grown a head taller.

Jane's voice rose to a shriek. "The loss of her will be my true revenge! They deserve that pain!"

The ghost barreled towards Alice just as she dusted the last of the chalk from her hands. The ghost passed freely into the snare, but slammed into the far side of the barrier as if it were a brick wall. She wailed and scratched at the invisible threshold.

"This has gone on far too long already," Alice replied. "I may not be able to undo the damage you did to that sweet child's brothers, but at least I can stop you from doing her any more harm."

To both Vi and Alice's surprise, Jane's desperate cry morphed into a hideous cackle. Alice blanched as she rushed over to the child's bedside muttering, "No, no, no!"

Vi glanced down at the tiny body lying on the bed and let out a gasp when she realized the child was no longer breathing. Alice shook the little girl, angry tears springing to her eyes. After a few moments, she put the corpse to rest and tucked the blanket around her chin as if she were only sleeping. Vi tore her eyes from the dead girl as the sound of raised voices came from the other side of the bedroom door.

"You were too late," Jane snarled.

Alice whirled on the trapped ghost. "You fiend. She was just a child."

Someone pounded an angry fist against the door. "Let me in. You have no right to keep me out!" shouted the man on the other side.

The little girl's mother pleaded, "Jeremiah, stop! Alice is just trying to help."

"Like hell she is," he replied. There were a few muffled groans and slams against the door before it gave way. Jeremiah stormed past Jane and over to the bedside. Alice rose as he approached and he pushed her roughly aside. "Do not lay a finger on her."

Alice steadied herself with the patch of wall right next to Vi, then turned to face the mother. "I am so sorry. I did not make it in time."

The other woman crumpled to the floor, her wail of anguish drowning out Jane's ecstatic laughter. Jeremiah clutched the body to him, made even tinier in contrast to the grown man's hands. His face shot up to Alice, eyes burning like hellfire. "You did this. This is your fault."

Vi hardly had a chance to wrap her head around what she'd just seen when her body shot backwards as if pulled by a string. When she opened her eyes again, she was back on her stool in the black room. The Alice before her held Vi in a steady, blue gaze, her expression serene. "May I help you with anything else today?"

"That was you?" Vi asked, bringing her surprised breathing under control.

"Alice Thorne was your ancestor, but I am not Alice Thorne. I am a construct. She began the process of creating me, and others followed. I am her voice, her shape—"

"And some of her memories, yes." Vi held up a hand to stop her from continuing. Evidently, this construct only had a limited supply of responses.

Her blue eyes shone in the dark room as she gave Vi the same, vacant smile as before. "May I help you with anything else today?"

"What happened to you, er, that Alice? Did she get out of there safely? Jeremiah looked mad with rage."

The construct did not even blink despite the words that followed. "Alice Thorne was tried as a witch five days later and drowned by the townspeople. It was in those five days she made me before passing the book on to her niece, Meredith."

Vi cringed. The memory had not only revealed that ghosts were able to take enough energy to kill the living, but confirmed Vi's fear that the living would always react poorly in the face of what she could do. Just like Vi, all Alice wanted to do was help. And all that impulse got her was an early and watery grave.

Alice's head cocked to the side again and the murk eddied in response. "Would you like to see her death? Meredith was present and recorded it for posterity."

Vi gawped at her. "What? No. Of course not."

The construct straightened and the swirling stopped. "May I help you with anything else today?"

"No," Vi replied, rising. "I think I have had quite enough for one day."

CHAPTER 14

October 19, 1871
A few miles south of the mouth of the Ohio River

The apple never saw it coming.

It soared through the air, and as it reached its apex, Vi's blade sliced into its flesh. If she hadn't hit the core, the knife would have sailed clear through. Then again, Vi always hit the core.

Bonnie took a few steps back and caught the apple. The sticky spots on the deck showed that not all of her attempts had been quite so successful. Still, after a full day of practice, she was getting the hang of being Vi's assistant. They would be able to audition for Juno soon in order to gain access to the cast and crew, but for now, they were out in the fresh air working out the kinks. Vi was happy for any chance to distract herself from what Alice had shown her.

"I wonder if we could talk the juggler into helping us out," Vi said, holding up her hand to receive the impaled fruit.

Bonnie tossed it over, the weight of the knife's handle making it spin awkwardly and not quite on target. "He would probably be a whole lot more accurate."

"You are doing fine. No, I was just thinking of the showmanship. I feel confident I could hit three in quick succession. But I think catching three in a row would be quite difficult for anyone but a consummate professional."

An unexpected voice interrupted Vi's musing. "You would need more than one knife for that," Juno said as she emerged from the patch of shade she had been enjoying. "I cannot recall any other knife act that only had one."

"Well, they are a rather specialized piece of equipment," Vi replied, pulling the knife free from the apple. She chomped into it and gestured over the expanse of river to her left, munching as she spoke. "And as you can see, there are not many opportunities to shop."

Juno wrinkled her nose. "Even so, what I am seeing here is not yet an 'act.' I have a rather high standard for my shows."

Though nothing else untoward had happened since the sandbag fell, Vi did not want to give up her backstage pass for keeping an eye on the show. She knew the solution to the problem, but had also been rather hoping to avoid it. It appeared that was a luxury she no longer had. With a sigh, Vi swallowed her mouthful of apple and said, "I know where to get more."

"Good," Juno replied. "See that you do, and perhaps—*perhaps* you shall be up to snuff by the time we reach Memphis." With a dramatic sweep of her skirts, she turned and left them alone once again. Even though her words weren't kind, Juno had recovered some of her aplomb since shoving off in St. Louis. It improved the group's morale in general, but probably "too little, too late" for her if someone were really targeting her.

"Where on Earth are you going to get more throwing knives?" Bonnie asked, retrieving a rag from the railing and wiping the remaining juice from her hands. "Surely not in...wait, where are we again?"

"Hickman."

The collection of buildings that passed for the town were ranged on a hillside. It was a good place to stop and pick up the bare necessities, but it certainly was no bustling metropolis.

"But I am not going to buy the knives," Vi continued. "I am going to borrow them. Sam was the one who gave me the idea to propose a knife routine. He must have his set here or he would not have suggested it in the first place."

"I have not seen our good captain around much. Not since the accident."

"Indeed. He has probably just been on the *Apple Blossom* instead. All of the steering happens from there. That doesn't leave much 'captaining' to be done over here."

"That did not stop him from being on board the first evening, if I recall. Though I suppose there was some incentive," Bonnie said, playfully tossing the rag.

Vi caught it with her free hand and wiped the juice from her blade. "Then you will also recall that I turned down his invitation. I think he may be avoiding me."

"How will you have the chance to ask?"

"We're tied up here for a little while yet. Perhaps I can catch him on shore before we push off again."

Bonnie took the rag back and shooed Vi with it. "Well, then get going. I need a rest in the shade for a while or I may just melt."

Vi put her foot up on a deck chair and put the knife back into its sheath. As she made her way down the stairs to the main deck, an unexpected shiver ran up her spine. It must be the exertion that made Bonnie feel so warm, because Vi was certain the days were getting colder despite traveling ever southward. The leaves along the shore were well past their brightest and best, many of the trees already skeletons.

Warm or cold, Vi was definitely thirsty as she stepped onto shore. She and her assistant had put in several hours of practice already that day. There were not many storefronts to choose from in this little backwater. She was disappointed to see there was not anywhere in sight for a lady to grab a quick tipple.

Instead, her eyes fell on the general store, which might have something sweet to offer even if it was not precisely the type of refreshment she would have preferred. This was probably for the best, given there was plenty of practice still in store for her.

Vi stepped up the wooden steps, but the sound of familiar voices around the side of the building made her pause. She slunk around to the corner and rested her back against the wall to do a little eavesdropping.

"We should really be getting back," whispered a woman. It was definitely one of the Belles, but Vi couldn't be certain which one.

A male voice answered. "There's time. At least, time enough for a kiss?"

The woman laughed, followed by a suggestive silence. Apparently, she agreed. After a few seconds, she said, "Happy now? Let's go." The floorboards creaked, but her steps were halted.

"Not nearly as happy as I would be if we didn't get back on."

"What are you talking about? You know I have to finish the tour."

The man huffed a frustrated sigh. "You don't need them."

"Of course I do. We both do."

"She needs us a hell of a lot more than we need her."

This time, Vi clearly heard the kiss, followed by the woman giggling again. It probably was not Minerva and Sam, based on the conversation, and she took some comfort in that. And obviously it was not Juno on the other end of those lips. Vi inched her way closer to the corner and attempted to surreptitiously peek around it.

"At the very least," the woman said, "we need to go back to New York. She won't pay anyone until we do."

"I can't believe you talked me into that," the man said. "I'm not accustomed to someone else holding the purse strings." Vi recognized the same bitter tone Charles had used at the dinner in St. Louis.

"It is not all that long to wait. Just be patient."

"It's hard to be patient when all I want to do is marry you."

Vi jolted with shock when the door to the general store swung open. She covered her mouth, but her sound of surprise had already escaped. The stranger emerging gave her a quizzical glance. Vi smiled her most innocent smile and inched back away from the corner. The man held the door ajar for her, so she bowed to politeness and stepped up to the threshold. As the door closed behind her, Vi caught a glimpse of Charles as he came around the side of the building, his eyes narrowed in suspicion.

The door closed and a little bell above it announced her presence. The shopkeeper popped out from behind the customer he was helping to greet her, but returned his attention to the man before him. It took Vi's eyes a moment to adjust to the shade of the interior, but soon she realized it was Sam standing at the counter. Her heart leapt into her throat. She reminded it that it had nothing to fear and sidled up next to him just as the shopkeeper finished counting out the tin cans.

"...and twelve. So, those, plus the coffee and the bacon, and the fuel of course, brings us to six dollars. Is that all for you?"

Sam glanced at Vi under his lashes, then answered the other man. "Yes, that will be all. Have the wood brought over to the towboat. I can take the rest myself." He reached into his pocket and pulled out a few bank notes.

The shopkeeper nodded and started sliding the cans into a burlap sack.

"Need a hand?" Vi asked.

Sam hesitated, but only for a moment. "Yes, thank you."

"I am supposed to be working my way down the river, after all." She softly knuckled his shoulder, turning his body to a slightly more open position. "Seems like I should at least carry a few cans."

He smiled, though his eyes were tight. "From what I hear, you are already working."

"Oh, so you heard about that?" Vi asked. "I suppose it is hard to keep anything from reaching the captain's ear."

"Yes, word does get around." He cleared his throat and shifted his gaze to the sack. "Though you have got yourself a different partner than I expected."

Vi feigned helplessness. "Juno thought Bonnie would be good on stage. And who am I to argue with her expertize?"

Sam chuckled, and his face finally relaxed. "If I recall correctly, you can argue with just about anyone."

The shopkeeper finished putting together their load, and they each took a sack with a nod of gratitude. They walked out the door and back into the daylight, passing a wagon half-filled with wood.

Vi jerked her chin at the load. "This is a good little shop and all, but I can't imagine this is a normal spot to refuel. Not a vessel the size of yours."

"No, not with Memphis only a day away. But we are going to be running overnight tonight, and I want to make sure we have a surplus."

"Overnight? Why in such a hurry?"

A flash of anxiety crossed Sam's face and his voice became tight. "I want to get into the next port with plenty of time before the performance. We have got to make sure people know the Belles are in town and there is gambling to be done, or what is the point?"

It wasn't an altogether unreasonable thing to do, but his expression made her wonder. "Won't it be dangerous, though? I thought we would avoid moving around too much in the dark."

"The river does start to meander a lot more from here on out," Sam capitulated. "Which is why I plan to be on the prow with a pole all night to keep us from hitting a snag."

Vi patted the sack she carried. "Ergo, the coffee."

The gravel beneath their feet gave way to the muddy bank. Sam reached for her sack as they approached the ramp, but Vi smirked and raced on ahead.

Sam followed, shaking his head. "You always were stubborn."

As she took in his grin, Vi realized both her chill and her thirst had diminished. There was something so familiar and so comforting about her old friend. He knew her, the old her, the her before any of the insanity that now defined her life. Despite having turned down his earlier advance, Vi found herself wishing they could spend more time together, even it was just as old friends.

Before she realized she had done it, Vi asked, "Would you care for some company this evening?"

"I would not want to impose."

"No imposition at all. As I said, I am supposed to be earning my keep on this trip." She smirked. "The least I can do is keep us from sinking along the way."

They headed for the stairs and made their way to the sunroom and the closet that served as the larder. Vi finally relinquished her bag and arched the kink out of her back.

Sam eased the door closed, and when he turned back, he had a canister of coffee in his hand. For a moment, he was every inch the shy boy Vi had known in her youth. "Well, I suppose I will see you at sunset?"

"I have one more tiny favor I need to ask," Vi said. "Have you got your knives aboard?"

"You cut me out of the act, and now you want my gear?" The words could have come from anger, but the grin on his face told her he was already over the slight.

Vi batted her lashes dramatically, her voice dripping with honey. "Pretty please?"

"I have things I need to see to." Sam shook the coffee can by way of explanation. "But you go ahead and take whatever you need from my room. It's number twelve. And the kit should be in a drawer."

Vi clicked her heals and saluted. "Aye-aye, Captain!"

Chapter 15

Even though she had his permission to be there, Vi still felt as though she were a trespasser going into Sam's room without him. Of course, she would feel awkward about being in his room if he had been present, but for very different reasons.

The room was larger and more lived-in than her own cabin. The window allowed enough of the mid-morning light to enter that she saw Sam had made his bed that morning. A spare pair of boots was tucked beneath it, the heels perfectly lined up. He had a shelf of books and few other personal items around the room.

Vi looked from item to item, unsure where to begin. Though he had indicated the knives would be in a drawer, there were several drawers to choose from. The desk would be the least intimate place to rifle through. She tried the top drawer first, but all it contained were some charcoal nibs and stray pieces of rough paper. The next drawer was far more crowded—a chain with no pocket watch, a few ledgers with prior years scrawled on the front, a ring with a dozen keys—but still no leather case. When she tried the third and final drawer, it wouldn't budge. Upon further examination, she found a lock. Though the key was likely on the ring she had just found, Sam probably would have mentioned that the knives were in a locked drawer if it were relevant. So, Vi moved on to the dresser next.

Nestled among some spare trousers, she found what she was looking for. The trifold leather case was even softer and more worn than the last time she had seen it. Four throwing knives lay within, strapped into place to keep them from coming loose in the carrier's pocket. Sam's blades were about the length of the tip of her finger to the heel of her hand, with cork handles a few inches long. They were slightly longer and had one edge more curved than what she was accustomed to using, but they were balanced for throwing and it shouldn't take her long to acclimate to them. In some ways, a whole lifetime had passed for Vi since she and Sam had taken turns practicing tossing them into spare crates in the alleys behind the theaters where their mothers performed. In reality, it had only been fifteen years since she had become competent with the blades, and even less time since she had been with Sam last.

Vi smoothed down the clothes in the drawer and considered the task she had volunteered for that evening. With luck, they would not encounter any dangers in the night. On the other hand, she did not feel like she had been all that lucky lately. There was only so much she could do to help if she clung too hard to propriety. She pulled out a pair of Sam's pants and a faded denim shirt before pushing the drawer closed. When she stood, she spied a black cap that had seen better days. If she was going to play at being a river rat, she might as well have the whole ensemble.

Vi balanced the cap atop her coiffure and stepped out the door, nearly bowling Ceres over in the process. When they collided, the load in her arms fell to the deck.

"Apologies," Ceres said, bending to grab the shirt before it fluttered all the way to the railing. "I was not paying attention."

Vi picked up the knife case and double-checked the straps. She gave Ceres a glance of what lay inside before snapping the case shut again. "Quite all right, though it is a good thing these are securely fastened."

"How is your act coming?"

"Better, now that I have more to work with." Vi gathered everything into a tight wad except for the hat which once again sat at a comical angle on her head.

Ceres laughed. "Don't tell me that you thinking of wearing *that* for the show. I know Juno has some rather modern views and all, but I do not think you would fit in very well with the rest of us."

"Oh, it will be tights for me as well. The rest of this is for another task. I shall be trying my hand at polling this evening with our good captain. Shall we?" Vi motioned at the other woman and they fell in step together.

"Better you than me," Ceres sighed. "I need my eight hours of sleep or I am a complete harpy." She took a quick look around and lowered her voice. "By the by, that was quite a number you did on Minerva. She's still seething and saying she *nearly died* to anyone who will listen. A word to the wise, she holds a grudge like no one else I have ever known."

Vi's thoughts shifted to the unfortunate Daphne and the broken shoe. "Thank you for the warning. I will try to...tread more lightly going forward." The dancer did not make any particular reaction to the oblique reference to footwear. That could mean she did not catch Vi's meaning, or she did not share her suspicions. Or perhaps she was just holding her cards close to her vest. They continued together along the deck in silence until Vi pressed for more. "And how are the Belles? Has everyone recovered after the accident?"

"We had one rocky day of rehearsal. But I think everyone will be ready for the performance tomorrow."

"And Juno?"

They arrived at the sunroom and Ceres paused at the door. "What about Juno?"

"She seemed on edge before the sandbag nearly flattened her." Vi shrugged one shoulder, feigning nonchalance. "I was just concerned. I was a nurse, for a time. Old habits die hard."

Ceres sighed. "It hasn't always been that way. When this all started, it was mostly a lark. The best job I'd ever had. Now, well, let's just say there are definitely days I wish I had gone with my sister to New Orleans when she asked me. But one can never tell which day will be a good one and which will be a bad one."

"Will you see her when we arrive? Your sister, I mean."

Ceres's eyes sparkled. "Yes, and I can't wait. It has been far too long. Now, I really must get that spot of lunch I came up here for, and then back to rehearsal. I'm looking forward to seeing what you and your friend can do."

The dark-haired woman nodded her farewell and stepped into the lounge. She had elected not to have her meal with the rest of the Belles below; perhaps this was one of Juno's 'bad days.' Vi's stomach grumbled, reminding her that she also required sustenance, but she did not want to continue the conversation lest her line of questioning became too transparent. The key was not to seem too eager with any of them or they might start talking about it.

A few of the crewmen were also within, but they more or less ignored the dancer as she entered. From the way they diverted their eyes from the beautiful woman, Vi suspected Sam or even Bulloch must have warned them against fraternizing. This made it all the more likely that she was right about hearing Charles's voice at the general store, but she still did not know which Belle he'd been meeting in secret.

As Vi continued on her way around the sunroom to her cabin, *The Piasa* was making its way out of the Hickman harbor and onto the wide expanse of river. From her place on the hurricane deck, she saw the drastic shift in the landscape clearly. To the north where they had just come from, bluffs and rocky outcroppings dominated the view. They had passed boulders as big as houses for the past day, like enormous building blocks strewn by a giant, naughty child. Now to the west, forested plains and farmland predominated. The Ohio River had added its waters to the Mississippi a few miles upstream, and they were well and truly entering river country. The stretch of water would be both wider and deeper from here on out, but also wilder.

Hopefully, *The Piasa* would be able to tame it on the overnight run.

CHAPTER 16

Once Vi showed Juno the set of knives, she agreed to let Vi and her partner into the 'inner sanctum' to continue building their act out of the wind, but only on the condition that she would not disrupt the Belles as they rehearsed. She and Bonnie cleared a space on the gaming floor to use as their own mock-up of the stage and give them a feeling for how much space they would have to work with.

"And then, you do like so," Vi said, crossing her hands over her belly before raising her arms high into the air. As she reached the apex of the gesture, she flipped over hands to make her palms faced the ceiling. Vi turned to two o'clock and ten o'clock, bobbing her head at the imaginary audience and grinning.

Bonnie stifled a giggle. "You are really good at that."

"Anastasia knows, is all in the wrist," Vi replied, rolling the 'r' and repeating the flip of her palm. "Now you try, Natasha."

"I am going to look foolish," Bonnie warned.

The younger woman did her best, but her body lacked the tension to really sell the flourish. She was not committing to the action enough to sell it, which actually made her look more foolish than if she would just give it her all. Vi was about to demonstrate again when a scraping sound at her back caught her attention.

"I have a delivery for you."

The voice came from behind a scenery flat. Except for the fingers visible on both sides, it appeared to be floating of its own accord. Once it was settled on the floorboards, Jack's head popped out from one side. The painted target was at least seven feet tall.

"This will do nicely," Vi said. "Thank you."

"Yes, very kind of you," Bonnie added.

He leaned against the edge. "The boss says jump, so I jump. 'Sides, the stage here is smaller than the last one. We had extras." He rapped his knuckles against the wood and smiled. "Sturdy enough for you?"

"Let us put it to the test."

Vi went to the table where Sam's knives waited in their sheaths and retrieved one of the blades. She whipped it at the target and hit dead center. The knife wobbled a little, but stayed embedded in the wood without falling.

"See?" Vi said to Bonnie with a wink. "All in the wrist."

Vi felt a weight on her and followed the sensation to the stage. Minerva was glaring in her direction, but when she was caught staring, the dancer went back to pretending to fawn over Juno's character.

"Anything else I can do for you?" Jack asked.

"Yes, actually. I believe we have everything worked out for the act. There are a few more things that would help us." Vi explained the other set pieces they would need and he and Charles's roles in bringing them on at the right time.

He nodded along to her description. "That shouldn't be a problem. Leave it to me."

Something over Vi's shoulder caught the stagehand's attention, and he hastily excused himself. Vi tried to thank him before he left, but he had already taken off at a trot toward the main door of the hall. Bulloch's face flashed through a series of porthole windows as he made his way down the promenade outside. There were few things in the world that would send her anywhere near the first mate, especially not at speed. Jack, on the other hand, would have things to discuss with him. There was nothing quite so chaotic or rewarding as putting on a show. At a glance, everyone had more or less recovered from the scare with the sandbag, and if Pru's book was right and there was a perpetrator behind it, they had decided to lay low for the moment. Or even better, she could hope that it was a onetime affair, and having failed, whoever it was thought better than to make a second attempt. She retreated from her thoughts of impending danger and found Bonnie practicing her flourishes again.

"Better."

Bonnie slumped. "I am not sure I will ever be able to do it like you."

"You do not have to do it like me." She smirked. "You just have to do it like you."

"*I* don't get up on stages in front of people," she replied, scrunching her face in disappointment. "If this is going to happen, I am going to need to be someone other than myself. I will need to be you."

"Or Natasha." Vi chuckled. She drew her fingers in an upward arc across her lips to remind Bonnie to smile. "Careful what you wish for," she said through the gritted teeth of her fake grin. "Being me is not all it is cracked up to be."

Bonnie beamed and did her rotations to the invisible crowd. "I would much rather be you."

"Why?"

Bonnie dropped her arms to her sides when she finished, and her forced smile dropped with them. "You are a lot braver than me, for one thing. You are more like a hero in one of my books than I will ever be."

Vi glanced around them, and though no one was obviously eavesdropping, she lowered her voice anyway. "I was in hiding when we met, remember? Does that sound like bravery?"

"You had your reasons," Bonnie said. "Though you still have not come clean with me about precisely what those reasons were."

"Sure I did." Vi drew closer, motioning at her friend to keep her volume in check. "I was tired of being an errand girl for ghosts."

The little brunette narrowed her eyes, one corner of her mouth rising. "That may be one reason, but I do not believe that is the only one. You promised to stop protecting me, remember?"

Vi pinched the space between her eyes. "We do not have time for this right now. We really need to keep practicing."

"That was not an answer." Amusement pulled the other corner of Bonnie's mouth to match the first.

"But it is the truth," Vi sighed.

The petite woman took a step back and repeated the showy gesture with more confidence. "What's next?"

"I believe it is time to put some holes in our target, don't you?" Vi crossed over to the bull's eye and pulled the knife free.

"Vi, when this is all over…"

She stepped away from the target and motioned at Bonnie to take her place in front of it. "Yes, yes. I will tell you about...the other thing."

"Actually, I had a different request."

"Oh?"

"Could you...ugh, you are going to think me silly." Bonnie put her hands to her cheeks to hide the flush. She shut her eyes, but fought through her embarrassment to say, "Could you teach me how to fight?"

Vi cocked her head to the side. "You were serious about that?"

The other woman opened one eye and peered at her. "Yes," she squeaked.

"Whatever for?"

Bonnie huffed out a breath and dropped her hands. "This will come as no surprise to you, no doubt, but I would benefit from some toughening up." Vi was on the verge of agreeing, but her friend's next remark stopped her short. "Things might get messy in New Orleans, you said so yourself, and I would like to be able to defend myself if need be."

Vi's insides grew leaden and cold at the prospect of putting her friend into a position to need to use her fists. Being a traveling companion to wile away the long hours was one thing, but to actually put her into the path of the dark forces at work down South was another. And that was if they made it there without being spotted by anyone else from Vi's past.

She swallowed hard and stepped over to where the rest of the throwing knives were waiting. "And knowing that, you are still sure you want to come with me?" she murmured.

"Well, I am certain I do not want to go home." Bonnie took her place in front of the target.

Vi smiled wanly. "There are many other places besides home you could go rather than running headlong into danger with me."

"But few as exciting."

"I will make a deal with you. We get ourselves through the performance in Memphis, and afterwards we'll split a bottle of something and I will lay out my whole story for you. And *then* you will decide if you want to come all the way to New Orleans or get off in Baton Rouge. If you decide to stay, I will teach you some things about defending yourself. Deal?"

Bonnie beamed and held her hand out for Vi to shake. "Deal."

CHAPTER 17

When night fell on the river, the cries of eagles and titters of song birds were replaced by a chorus of crickets. One of the musicians was playing a banjo somewhere on board, but it wasn't so much a song as picking along a few bars at a time while he figured out a tune.

As Vi leaned against one of *Apple Blossom*'s railings while she waited for Sam to come down from the pilothouse, the green and gold flickers of fireflies danced among the trees on the shore. The breeze fluttered across her borrowed clothes, sending a shiver down her spine. Vi snugged the cap lower, now sitting comfortably on her head after trading in her pinned up coiffure for the plaits she most often wore on the ranch. She toyed with the tufted end of the braid, a few strands still glinting red in the lamplight even though most of the henna had already faded away. Vi wondered idly if she should secret away "Anastasia's" wig on her way off the boat in order to help conceal her when they reached New Orleans. Then again, if what the diary said about the color of auras was true, it probably would not be much of a barrier to those who would be looking for her.

The sky still held a rosy glow, but a few stars had already made their appearance in the wide expanse of darkening sky. The only problem with telling someone to meet them at sundown was that what constituted sundown could vary from person to person.

Vi sighed and turned her back to the scene to lean against the railing the other way for a while. On the deck above, the warm shimmer of candles and lanterns lit up the windows. Down on the main deck, a single lantern hung from its fitting above the cargo hold, casting just enough light to make the shadows among the crates deeper. Vi reached to her back pocket where Sam's knife case protruded. She did not have her bullseye, but throwing the knives would help to pass the time.

Vi squared off ten paces away from one of the Belles' crates, presumably now totally emptied of its cargo. The knives could not really do any damage; they were made for show and not for deep penetration like the one she kept on her for defense. All the same, better to use an empty one just in case. She pulled out two of the knives and set the case down at her feet. One she gripped by the hilt in her left hand, the other she held by the tip of the blade and readied herself for the throw.

Before she let it fly, Peter stepped around the edge of the crate. She was surprised to see him, not because she did not think he would come and check up on her and Sam, but because she had not sensed him coming. The ghost's outline was blurry, his body insubstantial and barely shining. When he lifted a hand in greeting, he moved as if there were weights tied to his arm.

Vi's brow knit with concern. "Peter, are you all right?"

"I admit, I have been better. The water must be quite a lot deeper here."

Guilt tightened her stomach. The whole point of this quest was to put Peter to rest, not make him even more uncomfortable. "I'm sorry. Is there anything I can do?"

"Could I stay here a while with you? I was hoping that I could get a little boost."

"Yes, of course."

He stepped forward, his own brow now crinkling as he looked at her face. "Unless you are not feeling up to it. The deep water must be affecting you, too."

She puffed out a sigh. "I am fine. Honestly, you are worse than Bonnie. She's been fussing over me whenever we are not practicing."

"She cannot even see what I see," he reminded her. "And once we reach New Orleans, you can be sure I won't be the only one who notices. Henry cannot be the only ghost who has figured out how to siphon off energy from the living."

A flush of vicarious guilt and remorse washed over Vi as the vision of the dead child flashed through her mind.

"That is a bridge I shall cross if I come to it," she lied. There were few things Vi was more certain of than that she would never be anything like the vengeful ghost of Jane. "But we still have several days before that becomes an issue. I prefer to focus on what is in front of me."

He snickered. "I do happen to be in front you, Thorne. May I?" Peter raised his hand but did not reach out to the wound on her cheek until she nodded. As if wiping away tears, he traced the line of her cheekbone with the knuckle of his index finger. Instead of saltwater, he came away with fingers glowing with energy. His breath hitched, but when he exhaled, there was relief written on his face. Peter's spirit-flesh brightened and solidified. "Much better."

The intimacy of the gesture and their proximity made the knot in Vi's stomach squeeze tighter. She cleared her throat and took a half-step back. "Happy to help."

"Speaking of helping your friends, have you found out anything interesting about the sandbag bandit?"

Vi chuckled. "That cannot be what we are calling him. Or her."

"One of the girls?"

"If Juno was the target, it sounds like it could have been just about anyone. But as far as I remember, they were all on the stage with her or busy at the time. Right now, my money is on Charles."

"Because of what he said at the dinner?"

"And because of a clandestine rendezvous I stumbled on." She filled Peter in on the conversation she'd overheard in Hickman.

He bobbed his head. "Yes, then, suspecting Charles does seem reasonable."

"Unless, of course, I was wrong from the start." Vi squared off from the crate once again and held her blade at the ready. She set her sights on the forehead of the girl grinning from the Midas poster.

"Viola Thorne is saying she was *wrong*?" He snickered. "This is a day for the history book."

The blade flew end over end, coming to a stop right in the middle of the woman's brow. "I am starting to doubt whether what I felt was real." She readied the second knife, keeping her gaze fixed on where she wanted it to go rather than meeting Peter's eye. "What if what I saw in the diary is just making me paranoid?"

Peter mulled over her words until after the second blade was sitting beside the first. "Have you ever been wrong before when it comes to your pronoia? With the flashes of menace, that is."

Vi bent to retrieve the other knives. "Back in Sacramento, I had a kind of attack of nerves. It felt like someone was watching, following me from the post office. But no one was there." When she risked a sidelong glance, she found a wide grin on Peter's face. This is why she rarely confided her singular problems in others; no one else could understand. Her neck grew hot as embarrassment washed over her. "What is so amusing?" she gritted, raising the third knife.

"If you are talking about recently, then someone *was* watching you."

His words made her falter and the blade hit a foot to the right of its target. Vi faced him fully, one hip jutting out and her free hand balled at her waist. "Care to elaborate?"

Peter brought his thumb to his sternum. "Me."

"You?"

"I told you, I had been in town for a few days. But you hadn't gone to pick up your post yet. I wanted to be there when you finally opened your letters to get an idea if you understood my warning. You did not do it right away of course, so I kept on your heels. Then you got distracted by that damned horse."

"I got distracted by someone trying to *steal* my horse. There's a difference," she replied with a chuckle before shaking her head. "You always did have a problem with Smithy."

"I'm still convinced you never would have married the Colonel if it wasn't for that silly animal." Peter's grin faltered. "And you did ride him right out of my life and off into a new one all on your own."

Vi stepped back toward the crate. She took a deep, steadying breath and tossed the final knife. This one flew true and landed beside the first two blades. The woman on the poster went right on smiling despite the new hole in her head. Vi related to the hole, if not the smile.

As she walked over to retrieve the knives, Peter asked, "What, nothing witty to say?"

Vi reached up to steady the vibrating handle. "This does not seem like a good time."

Her voice had barely raised above a whisper, but he heard her the way he always managed to hear her. "Ah, come on. You do not want me to tell you to stop... beating a dead horse?" he called back, stretching out the final words to demonstrate he was joking.

She chuckled, pulling the blades free. "Well, I suppose there is no sense closing the stable door after the horse has bolted."

"What about putting the cart before the horse?"

"Or..." Vi returned to his side. "Looking a gift horse in the mouth."

His eyes danced. "Which brings us back to what we were discussing before we decided to...hold our horses? It sounds to me like *your* gifts have not failed you yet. Ergo, the sandbag could not have been an accident."

"There was one more time." Vi hesitated, unsure of what kind of reaction to expect. But now that she had begun, she might as well finish. "When we first got on the boat. You were downstairs getting to know Henry. I was talking with Bonnie about Sam—"

"—and I told you he was bad news, did I not?" Peter asked, crossing his arms. "You should trust that feeling."

"I have not felt threatened any time I have actually been with him, though. Just when I was afraid he might say something," Vi replied. "It is possible I felt something from someone else and the timing was simply unfortunate."

The ghost stroked his chin. "Yes. Perhaps that is possible."

"Which is a good thing. Because Sam will be here any minute. I am helping him keep watch tonight."

"Then I suppose that means I am helping keep watch on *him* tonight."

She sighed, "Fine."

"Really?" Peter eyed her suspiciously. "I expected more of a fight from you."

Vi lined up her next throw and let all four knives fly in quick succession as she replied. "I am trying this new thing these days where I do not keep secrets from people. Especially not my partners."

"Does that count retroactively as well? I can think of a secret or two I might want an answer to."

CHAPTER 18

Before she formed a response, another voice rose up over the twilight serenade.

"Vi? Is that you?"

Sam emerged from the cargo area carrying a lantern. As Vi and Peter had been talking, the last of the warmth of the setting sun had disappeared. The light Sam carried painted him gold, a stark contrast to Peter's form made of mist and moonlight.

Vi gave Peter a heavy glance to ask for his silence before waving at Sam. "Guilty as charged."

"Sorry to have kept you waiting. As you surmised, the crew was not altogether happy about doing this run at night. I had to have words with Bulloch." Sam handed her the lantern and gave her an appraising glance. "I think I recognize those clothes."

She grinned. "What do you think? Am I fit for the engine room next?"

"You do not want to be anywhere near that boiler, trust me. But the role of riverman does suit you. And your other role, how is that coming? I assume you did not only steal clothes from my room. Are the knives up to your exacting standards?" he teased.

"It took a little time to get reacquainted." She gestured at the tattered poster beside her. "But as you can see, we are cooperating nicely."

Sam squinted into the darkness. When his eyes fell on the knives still stuck into the crate, she had expected him to be impressed, maybe even a little proud. Instead, his face drained of color and his mouth settled into a stern line. "You shouldn't be using my cargo for target practice."

"I thought as they were empty, there was no harm to be done. The Belles have all of their props and costumes backstage, don't they?"

His scowl remained for a few breaths, but his face soon softened. "No, no harm done. But please do not do it again. All right?" She nodded, following him into the corridor between crates. He passed her the lantern. "We need to get a few poles. Bulloch tried to insist he and another crewman should do this, but to tell you the truth, I am looking forward to a nice, quiet night on the river."

Vi's mind flashed to the conversation her first day aboard and Bulloch's muted, dishwater gray aura. "He is an odd sort, isn't he? Opinionated."

"To put it mildly."

"How did he come to be your first mate?"

Sam pointed to the poles strapped to the ceiling and Vi held the light higher. "We have not known each other long. Perhaps in time, things will become easier between us." He dragged over a short stepladder, then took a closer look at the assortment of wooden tools.

Vi noted the evasion but did not press him. Running the ship was his business, and if he did not want to answer, she did not need to pry. As Sam worked the poles free, she helped him guide them to the deck. When he came down the ladder, he bundled the poles under his arm and dragged them out into the open. They were both about twenty feet long, but one had a hook on its end and the other had a flat head for paddling.

"Are the engines not fast enough for you?" Vi joked, tucking the other end of the load under her arm to keep them from scraping the woodwork.

"If this was still just some lumber barges tied together, that would be the only choice." They crossed the knee board and made their way to the front of *The Piasa* around the starboard walkway. "Now, I will use it to probe the waters ahead, and you will light my way."

When they reached the prow, Sam propped the paddle against the railing and held out the other pole for Vi to take.

"Sounds easy enough."

She affixed her lantern before pushing the pole out over the water. The light itself weighed several pounds, and the pole bowed and refused to remain still. She let the back end rest against the deck and placed her foot on it to lend the weight of her body to the task. The oil lamp cast its yellow light onto the river, illuminating the whorls in the current but no obstacles. The quarter moon occasionally made an appearance between the bows lining the shore, and a splash of stars added their pinpricks of light to the fireflies.

They were standing close together. She glanced down and saw that it would only take a few more inches before their bodies would touch. He shifted his weight to his other foot, drawing minutely nearer. There was a gentle pull in the space between them, like the opposite of the aetheric wind that told her a punch was coming. This breeze urged her closer. An unexpected thrill shot across her skin at the thought, and she struggled to push it down. Sam had said he was looking forward to a quiet evening, but now, the silence became stifling.

"So...." Vi made a completely unneeded adjustment to the lantern pole and inched away. "Um, your father. When did he retire?"

"When the war started. He did not want to risk being on the river, and he worried about having his ship commandeered, so he sold it and split the profits with me."

"And you? Were you in the war?"

"I joined up, just like most of my friends. With my experience on a riverboat, I was mostly doing supply runs, especially once Memphis was captured and turned into one big hospital, so to speak. They were always in need of supplies and I had the experience to help get them where they needed to go." Sam's eyes never left the water, but he patted his right leg, the one with the limp. "It didn't keep me out of the line of fire, though."

"And to think, we could have crossed paths."

He twisted to face her. "You were in Memphis?"

"Some of the time. You know how I left New York to be a nurse—"

Sam grinned. "How could I forget? I was devastated." He rested one arm against the railing and leaned closer.

"Hey," Peter grumped. "Watch it, buddy."

Vi had nearly forgotten the ghost was there listening, and his unexpected exclamation made her startle. She cleared her throat and turned away to make another useless adjustment to her grip. "Well, I ended up there. For a while at least." Vi felt Sam decide to reach for her even before his arm moved. She blurted, "That is where I met Patrick."

He straightened again and returned his gaze to the water. "Your husband, I take it?"

"Yes. He was injured in the line of duty." This was a true statement, but Patrick's duties had not been the stuff of regular soldiering. Vi was instantly taken back to the image of him obstinately attempting to get out of his cot and assuring the doctor that he was fine despite the bullet wound in his arm. Peter was there, too, doing his best to keep his partner from taking a swing at anyone. Vi had been the one to convince him to stay put and get treatment. "I patched him up. And later when he asked me to go with him, I did."

"Back to the front?" Sam marveled. "I would want to keep the woman I love as far from danger as possible."

The statement did not surprise Vi in the least. It was how most men would feel. But Patrick had never doubted her ability or her mettle. It was the reason she fell for him so fast and so deeply.

"It was *my* choice," Vi said. "Though we were not necessarily in the thick of the fighting all of the time. Our duties were rather more...clandestine in nature." Peter coughed a warning, and he was right. She was already saying too much. "But enough about the war. What happened for you after the fighting stopped?"

"I was hired to captain a vessel out of New York again, taking cargo to the lakes." He sighed. "But then with all of the new railway construction, things never really went back to the way they were. People can get their goods west much faster on a train."

"Ah, that is why you decided to move your operation to the Big Muddy." She used her hat to gesture out over the water before flopping it back onto her head.

"And why I came up with this floating theater scheme."

"It looks like I am not the only one who decided to follow my parents' example. You managed to pay tribute to your mother and your father in a single act."

Sam grimaced. "Well, we have not had our first performance yet. I think it is too early to say it is a success. Let's wait to see what kind of a crowd we can draw first."

Peter stepped up to Vi's side. "You know, this does not all quite add up. If business was so poor, how did he afford a second boat?"

It was a fair question, especially given how fine *The Piasa*'s accoutrements were. If all he needed was a stage, that could have been done with far less of a flourish than the full three stories he had commissioned. Not to mention pushing a barge the size of the floating theater up and down the river would take extra fuel. This was not the kind of question one generally asked in polite company, but Vi weighed her curiosity and their years of friendship against the status quo and proceeded, albeit, in a veiled way. "How long do you think it will take to make up your losses?"

Sam's eyes rolled skyward for a moment as if he were doing math, then he returned his gaze to her. "It is hard to say. The Belles should be a pretty big draw. People in these parts could use a good laugh. And when it comes to the gambling tables, well you know what they say about the house always winning."

"Unless of course you are dealing with card sharps."

"I am not the naïve boy who used to take you out for shaved ice, you know." He brought his thumb to the middle of his puffed up chest. "I know a sharp when I see one. I will be able to ferret them out before they do too much damage."

Vi chuckled. Given he was currently in the company of a practiced grifter and was none the wiser, she had far less confidence in his skills than he did. "Perhaps when I am not performing, I could help you with that as well. Walk around the floor, keep an eye on things?"

"Before tonight I would have said no. But now that I know you ran headlong into the fighting, I suppose I should trust you can handle yourself with a few drunks and gamblers."

Peter interjected, "He doesn't know the half of it."

"I own a saloon," Vi said to Sam. "My whole business is built on drunks and gamblers. There is even a little stage there. It is really not that different from the conditions here at all. So tell me, business owner to business owner, how much did this setup set you back?"

Sam pulled his watch from his pocket and squinted at it. "We could be talking about a whole world of things, and you want to talk about that?"

"He's evading," Peter said. "Not a good sign...."

"Why won't you tell me?" Vi asked, locking him in the same stern gaze she had used to put Patrick squarely in his cot without further argument.

"Because I had to take out a loan. Happy now?" Sam said, an edge of bitterness creeping into his voice as he pointed to the grand entrance of the theater. "I have this ship, but for all intents and purposes, I am a pauper. Every cent I make has to go back to the loan. And the sooner I can pay them back, the better. The terms of the loan were...less than favorable."

"Why didn't you just say so?"

"I wanted you—" The words caught in his throat and he started again. "That is to say, I did not want you to know. To think less of me."

"I do not care how much money you do or do not have." She rested a hand on his shoulder. "You are my oldest friend."

His gray eyes locked onto hers. He murmured, "Would you ever consider...something more?"

CHAPTER 19

Vi was unable to fight the panic that washed over her face as the world tilted. At first, she believed it was her own mind's reeling that made her stumble. When she heard the creaking of the decking, she realized it was more than just another attack of nerves. Sam staggered against the railing, the watch in his hand jerking free and flying into the river as he attempted to stay upright.

The lantern pole swung with the force of the impact. Vi almost dropped it, but managed to keep it from splashing into the river.

When her eyes met Sam's again, all of the hope had been chased away by distress. "Swing it over to starboard!"

Vi shifted her position and dangled the light to her right. The front corner of *The Piasa* on that side was a few feet higher than where they stood. Voices raised in alarm from the second ship, relaying orders to cut the engines.

"Bring that light in," Sam commanded, every inch the captain again. "I'll get another one lit and meet you over there." He pointed to the corner and rushed through the doors of the theater.

Vi made her way across the sloped decking. Footsteps pattered, then thundered from the direction of the towboat. More lantern light was added to their search for the problem as Bulloch and two other crew members joined her at the rail.

"We've run aground," Bulloch said.

Vi squinted at the shoreline. Everything was black, but there had to be at least fifty feet of water between the ship and shore. "How is that possible?"

Sam returned, setting down his lantern before hastily kicking off his shoes and rolling up his pant legs. "Must be a sand bar. We will have to go out and try to push her free." He lifted himself up and over the railing and reached a foot into the water. It was moving fast, but his foot hit something solid after only a few inches. Sam stepped out onto the obstruction and waded out to the highest point of the ship.

With a nod, Vi tried following suit along with the other crewmen. Before she could get the second pant leg rolled, Bulloch caught her roughly by the shoulder and spun her to face him. "Not you, girly. Don't you think you've done enough damage already?"

Vi scoffed and recoiled, putting a pace between them. "How is this my fault?"

"I told you. Women on board a ship are a distraction, even if you put on a pair of trousers. And this distraction might have cost us *The Piasa*." To the men he called, "I'm right behind you."

The sense of ownership the first mate had for the ship rankled, but it was also understandable. Blaming her, on the other hand, was ridiculous. Vi stabbed her hand at the dark expanse of water concealing the sand bar. "It is a natural phenomenon. You cannot possibly say this is on me."

"Oh yeah?" Bulloch replied, inclining his bulk over her in an attempt at intimidation. When Vi didn't flinch, his scowl deepened. "And what were you two doing when this happened?"

An unexpected heat crept up Vi's neck and into her cheeks, chasing away the chill of the night. "Not that it is any of your business, but we were just talking."

"It must have been a helluva conversation," he sneered. Another handful of crewmen approached, but slowed when they saw their first mate and his menacing posture. "What are you waiting for, an invitation? Your captain needs your help. Over the side!" Bulloch roared at them. He turned his attention back to Vi and yanked the lantern pole out of her grip. "And I suggest you get yourself out of the way and out of my sight." Bulloch stomped off, summarily dismissing her before she could protest.

While the men heaved themselves over the rail and into the water, she stood all but frozen in her anger. The only thing that moved were her hands balling into fists and releasing.

"Vi," Peter said gently. "Maybe he's right."

"What?" she hissed.

He put his hands up defensively. "Not about it being your fault. That was out of line. But they do seem to have it handled. Perhaps you should leave this to the professionals?"

The rage whooshed out of Vi with her next breath, replaced by exhaustion and the cold. She gave him a tired nod and headed for the tow, hands buried in her pockets and heels scuffing in frustration. When she reached *Apple Blossom*, she remembered the knives she'd left behind. Both the cargo and the leather case had shifted when they'd run aground. The moonlight was barely enough to see by after the flashes of lantern light had left spots swimming in her vision, but she managed to find the case a few feet from where she'd left it. Thanks to the tight lashing, the crates had only shifted an inch or two after hitting the obstacle, all except for the one where the knives waited for her. It did not strain against the ropes, as if it had not felt the force of hitting the sand bar at all.

Peter leaned against the crate. "Come on, Vi. It is late. And unlike yours truly, you need to sleep. Don't forget, you have your big debut tomorrow."

As if on cue, a yawn pushed up from her belly, traveled up her throat, and escaped. Peter pointed at her gaping mouth to prove his point, and she nodded as she indulged in a long stretch. "I am just putting these knives to bed, then I shall follow suit. But will you stay here for me and make sure they do not, in fact, need an extra hand?"

"Not much I can do for them."

Vi pulled the knives free and slipped them into place. "You can come and get me."

"Anything for a *friend*." The stress he put on the last word confused her at first, but then she remembered the conversation he'd been eavesdropping on right before they'd hit the snag.

"Sam *is* just a friend, Peter. And I do not intend to be anything more. Not to anyone." Her voice dropped to a whisper. "Not again."

The ghost may have had more to say, but Vi didn't give him the opportunity. She disappeared into the dark, hoping tomorrow would prove to be brighter.

CHAPTER 20

October 20, 1871
Memphis, TN

Sam had gotten a lot of things right about the layout of *The Piasa*'s theater, but the dressing room was not one of them. Though the mirrors and dedicated lights were a great touch, there simply was not enough space for many people to get ready at the same time.

Juno had approved Vi and Bonnie's act that morning when they did a test run, but as they would not go on until the break between the first and second acts of Midas, they were relegated to the hallway for the time being. They could have taken their costumes back up to their rooms, but Vi wanted to stick close to the Belles now that the show was about to start. If it really was one of them behind the acts of sabotage, no doubt their flare for the dramatic would compel them to strike when an audience was present.

"Do you think we will have to stay in Memphis for a while to do repairs after last night?" Bonnie asked.

"We hit a sand bar, not a boulder, so hopefully there was not too much damage done. This tub was made by lashing individual barges together and putting a floor on top. I did not see any particular splitting last night, but it was also quite dark." Peter hadn't returned in the night, which may have meant that the crew had not needed an extra hand. Or perhaps he simply did not wish to speak with her.

"It would be good to get off and walk around a spell. It seems like a nice place. And as large as the ships are, I need a change. And who knows when I will be back this way again?"

With the deep waters of the Memphis harbor beneath her feet and pulling the energy out of her, Vi wholeheartedly agreed. "Perhaps we can have ourselves an outing after the show or tomorrow morning before we shove off. I cannot imagine Sam will want to do another nighttime run." She pushed off from the wall and jerked her thumb at the nearest stage door. "I want to go take a look at the rigging, just to ease my mind. Would you keep an eye on things here for me?"

Bonnie agreed, so Vi walked over the threshold and into the wings. The red curtain was drawn across the front of the stage. Over the tinkling sound of the piano, she heard the sounds of the people mulling around. The musician was warming up the crowd and would be followed by the juggler. Midas had three acts with a break between them for the others to perform.

There were gas footlights on the outer edge of the stage, but until the curtain went up, it would remain quite dark there. Though there were some set pieces and other flats that would come in from both sides of the stage, the rigging was all located on stage left. Vi carefully made her way across the darkened stage, guided by a single candle flame shining on the other side.

The candle belonged to Jack, who had pulled up a chair and was dealing out a hand of solitaire on a low table. He doffed his cap when she approached. "Shouldn't you be getting dressed?"

"Trust me, I would love to. But at present, the room is all elbows and taffeta."

Jack snickered. "I can imagine. Diana was complaining about it, too. So, just enjoying the extra space back here, or can I help you with something?"

Vi stepped over to the line of ropes and pulleys. There was one for the curtain nearest to the audience, and six more spaced a foot or so apart. Just like on the deck of a sailing ship, the extra lengths of rope were coiled in neat piles below each pulley to avoid tripping and tangling. Everything appeared in order. Vi shook her head. "No, thank you. Just looking around."

"You're worried about another accident," he stated flatly. "It's all right. I don't blame you. But when that happened everyone was running around like headless chickens. During the performance, I never leave this post. You are safe with me. My own baby sister will be out on that stage, after all. I won't let anything happen."

"Thank you. That does give me comfort," Vi replied. "She is not my sister, but I would not want anything to happen to Bonnie. I am the one who roped her into this."

"I've been looking forward to your act. I saw you practice some, but it's different seeing it all together. You just concentrate on your aim, and I will take care of the rest."

Vi bobbed her head and headed back across the stage. The noise from the other side of the curtain was growing louder as the audience filled the seats near the stage and in the balcony. The gaming tables and bar at the back of the room were no doubt also getting some attention. She imagined Sam in his captain's uniform, walking among the patrons and doing his best to hide how nervous he must be. For his sake, she hoped all of the seats would be full, though for her own part, she had more butterflies in her stomach than she had expected. Every confidence game was a performance of sorts, but she had not been in front of this many people in quite some time.

When she reached the center of the stage, Vi froze. A tangible trickle of anxiety crept across her shoulders, and it had nothing to do with stage fright. There were no telltale waves of sensation coming at her from any particular direction, just the creeping dread that someone was doing something threatening. It was faint, almost like a residue rather than an active thought, but the malice was unmistakable.

Vi tried to push her awareness further, like a bloodhound scenting the air. But when her sphere of sensation went much past an arm's length, her head swam. She sucked her energy back and the bout of dizziness subsided some, but she was still unsteady on her feet. In the darkness, Vi made out the shimmering blue of the gash on her cheek seeping steadily. With the constant drain on her stores, she did not have enough excess to make a real search. She would have to rely on her eyes if she was going to figure out who was plotting something.

When she returned to the hallway, the Belles were just clearing out of the dressing room. Juno was playing the titular Midas, a comical pair of false muttonchop whiskers obscuring her face and a crown on her head. Their version of the myth was satirical, so she was wearing a cropped imitation of a jacket and waistcoat over a faux paunch and a monocle over her right eye to give the impression of a banker. Ceres was playing Dionysus, and the two blondes were her nymphs, at least in the first act. They were all adorned with the wax fruit and silk flowers Vi had noticed her first time in the dressing room. Enid was in her first costume as Midas's daughter, the elaborate gown waiting patiently on the dressmaker's dummy for later.

In a deep and resounding imitation of a king, Juno announced, "The curtain rises in five minutes."

"Did you take a peek?" Enid asked, her eyes shining with anticipation. "Is it a good house?"

"I did not look, but it sounds pretty full out there."

Ceres blew a drooping leaf out her eyeline. "Are you feeling all right? You look kind of peaky."

"Not going to pull out, are you?" Minerva gave Vi an exaggerated pout. She turned away to tuck the offending piece of Ceres's headdress back into place.

"I'm fine, thank you," Vi replied, keeping her scowl in check. To Bonnie, she said, "Shall we?"

The Belles filed toward the stage door, but Enid caught Vi by the shoulder as they passed. "Just have fun out there. That's all that matters. Well, not all that matters. Entertaining people. That matters, too. Oh, you know what I mean." She tittered. "There I go again! Have a great show."

Minerva leaned out from the stage door and called, "Yeah. Break a leg."

Though the expression was common—wishing someone 'good luck' was said to have the reverse effect—Vi suspected the dancer would probably prefer she fell off the stage. When Vi and Bonnie entered the dressing room, the first thing she did was to check her shoes. They seemed solid, but that did little to allay Vi's fears, especially after the bad feeling she'd gotten on the stage. If it had been emanating from Minerva or one of the other women, they had managed to hide it well. Of course, they were actresses; making people believe they felt one way when they really felt another was how they kept themselves in bread and butter. Vi hoped her own special talents would be able to see through them if needed, but with the way her head was swimming, she couldn't be certain of anything.

Vi slipped off her regular clothes and shivered in the coolness of the dressing room. She was also desperately thirsty, but there was no water in sight. It would have to wait until after she finished. With a sigh, she pulled on the red and gold outfit, the shining beads catching the lamplight. Once she had on her tights and boots, Vi finished it off with black leather belt looped loosely around her waist. She affixed a stiff leather pouch that would allow her to have her hands free even if she needed to carry the knives around the stage. Their customary case held them tightly, but she needed them loose to do what needed to be done.

As Vi and Bonnie dressed, they reviewed the order of the tricks. Vi would introduce them, then they would walk through some demonstrations to show the knives were real and sharp enough to cut. She would hit a few apples, then put Bonnie against the board and throw the knives around her.

"Then applause, applause, applause." Bonnie fussed with her tutu. "I bow, you bow, we bow, and off we go. And then, finally, off with this get-up."

"Perfect." Vi put her Russian spin on the word, intent to keep it and the occasional dropped word here or there going until after they took their bows. "We will bring the house down, da?" She took a final look in the mirror. The black eye had all but disappeared, so she had only required a light touch of makeup today. "And do not forget. You must make gestures larger than life. Back row must see everything we do."

Bonnie pinched her cheeks to give them some extra color. "It's so much to remember! And only for a few minutes. I cannot imagine keeping everything the Belles have to do straight. I'm glad I do not have to speak at all."

"Do not worry. All will be well." Vi's assurance lost some of its power when she knocked into a chair on her way to the door.

The little brunette's brow crinkled. "Are you certain? Ceres is right, you do not look well."

Though Vi's stomach was in knots and her head still didn't feel quite right, it wouldn't do Bonnie any good to know that. If she lost confidence and flinched while Vi was throwing, that would present its own kind of danger. Until after the performance at least, she had to keep up appearances for both their sakes.

"As you say, is much to remember." Vi flashed her friend a smile that was far more confident than she felt. "Now, on with the show!"

CHAPTER 21

Once they were backstage, Vi and Bonnie watched some of the Midas show from the wings. They split up in order to be ready for their entrance from either side of the stage when the time came. Vi stood behind the edge of the curtain, careful to keep from being seen.

The first act had Midas wining and dining Dionysus, and the crowd was eating it up. Juno's false belly and over-the-top impression of an aristocrat made them laugh and clap nearly every time she spoke. Even with the silly costume, she could command a room like the best dramatic actress. Based on the hooting and whistling, Ceres and the "nymphs" were also greatly appreciated. Their song, sung to the melody of "Hard Times Come Again No More" but with the lyrics changed to fit the plot, ended the first act. They brushed by on their way off stage, Enid giving Vi a thumbs up on her way.

Vi caught Bonnie's eye from across the way and held up one hand to count down their entrance on her fingers. When her fist closed, they both walked out onto the stage, arms wide and bright smiles on their faces before the applause had a chance to fully die.

As she and Bonnie reached the middle, the limelight burst to life, showering them in a pure, white beam. The audience were just dark lumps a few feet below, except for the ghosts who were clapping and cheering appreciatively along with the rest. They glowed with their own light, though Peter was a few candles worth darker than Henry and less distinct.

Vi called, "Ladies and gentlemen." She put her hand above her eyes as if shading them from the sun and bent deep at the waist as she pretended to search the crowd. When she straightened, she continued with a wink. "Or should I be saying, lads and gambling men?" This earned her some chuckles and raised glasses.

Vi cued the fiddle player with a nod, and he started up a dramatic song from his place on the floor just in front of the stage. Adding the music had been Juno's last-second idea, and Vi had to agree it added an air of danger. They hadn't actually had a chance to practice with the spotlight or him playing yet, and they both pulled at her already stretched concentration.

For a moment, she forgot what came next, then turned back to Bonnie with a flourish. "This is my beautiful sister, Natasha. She is lovely creature, da?" Bonnie stepped forward and dipped into a deep, almost kneeling bow just as Vi had showed her. She popped back up, her arms held high. The men hooted and pounded on the tables. The other woman blanched slightly at the eruption of sound, but her face settled into a saucy smirk. She was enjoying the attention even if she wouldn't admit it.

"And I, druz'ya moi," Vi continued, tossing in a few of the only Russian words she actually knew to help sell her accent. "I am Anastasia. Mistress of the blades."

From the wings on Vi's right, Jack rolled out a black box on wheels with Sam's knives laid out on top. She had her own knife strapped to her calf, both as part of her costume and as a surprise for later. Charles rolled out a matching box laden with a bowl of golden apples from Bonnie's side of the stage.

Vi picked up one of the knives and held it up for all to see. "These blades, they were my father's, and his father's before him. He wanted son, but...he got Natasha and me instead. Poor man. Though I am not too disappointing, nyet?" She gave a little shimmy and got her own set of catcalls.

As Vi's eyes adjusted to the lighting, the blobs in the crowd were turning into humans again. She did a quick scan for Sam and found him taking a place against the wall on her side of the audience, laughing and clapping along with the rest. He was only a few feet from Peter, who scowled at him for temporarily blocking his view. Vi knew he wouldn't mind the ruse about the knives' origins; every good act needed a story. But she was relieved to see he did not appear outwardly cross with her about the previous night. In private might be another matter, but at least she could put aside that fear for the moment.

"I loved to watch him use the blades. He was my hero, so big and strong." Vi lifted her arms and flexed. "And brave. Oh da, Father was brave. He would do like this—" Vi stepped behind the box, placed her left hand palm down, then spread her fingers wide. With the knife in her right hand, she gently placed the tip in the gaps as she continued. "And with the blade he moved so fast, it was like blur. I asked him, nyet, begged him. Father, Father, please teach me how to do this. But would he teach me? Nyet."

Bonnie put on a pretty pout and traced tear tracks down her face. She was doing such a great job of making her gestures 'larger than life' as she'd been told, Vi almost laughed with pride. Instead, she mimicked the gesture and the crowd booed the fictional father for his heartlessness.

"So, I try teaching self. Without fatherly guidance, I may not do so good. Let us try." Bonnie made a show of looking scared, knees knocking and everything. Vi stabbed the blade between her fingers, slowly at first, then moving it faster and faster between the gaps. In reality, it was a trick she'd picked up during the long cold nights in the field, but she and Bonnie had agreed that the family angle was a good one to use for the story if they were already posing as sisters.

After she finished and the clapping stopped, Vi said, "Now, maybe some are thinking 'Blade is dull.'" She casually flipped the knife into the air and caught it again by the handle. "You are thinking, 'This is just pretend.'" Another flip. "'There is no danger, Anastasia.'" Flip, catch. "'You are bluffing.'" Flip, catch. "But I never bluff."

This time when she tossed the knife into the air, she sent it higher. Vi caught it by the tip and threw it straight into the side of the wooden box. It rattled on its casters and rolled a few inches. The crowd took in a short, gratifying breath of surprise.

She leaned toward the audience, her hand at the side of her mouth to give an aside. "Well, unless is cards. But bluffing there has different danger." A few of the gamblers at the back of the room shouted their approval. Vi added a cheeky, "I will be with *you* shortly."

"Can't wait!" a man shouted back, and the audience laughed.

Vi looked at the beaming Bonnie and had to admit, this was going even better than she'd hoped. She picked up another knife from the top of the box and continued flipping and catching it as she continued her story. "So, I show my father what I can do with knife, and you know what he say? 'Women should only use knife for cooking.'" Bonnie took an apple from the bowl and held it out for all to see. "The problem? I am terrible cook. We must throw out anything I do."

On the word 'throw,' Bonnie tossed the apple high into the air. Vi finished the line just as it peaked and let the knife fly. The skewered fruit landed in Bonnie's hands, and the crowd cheered. She pulled the knife out, set it down beside the bowl, and took a big bite of the apple before throwing it up in the air again. Vi timed her next throw so she'd hit the bite mark.

Bonnie displayed it to the crowd by strutting across the stage to even louder applause. While she did, Vi picked up her last blade and retrieved the one from the box, then countered Bonnie's movement to pick up the knife she'd left by the fruit bowl. As Vi approached stage left, dread rippled across her skin. She glanced up, but saw no danger coming from above. When she stole a look into the wings, she saw Charles observing the act with rapt attention, but nothing to cause the feeling. Vi looked to the sea of dark shapes that made up the crowd. Anyone could be out there with any number of bad intentions.

Bonnie must have seen Vi's distraction, because when she turned back, the other woman had followed her gaze. Vi painted her grin back on and gave a minute shake of her head to tell Bonnie nothing was wrong. She put the blades into the pouch, handles out. They knocked gently against each other, but the bag was deep enough to keep them from falling out by mistake. Though she needed them loose in order to draw them out quickly, no sense losing a toe in the process.

Jack emerged from the opposite side of the stage with their target. It stood taller than him, but was lightweight and rested sturdily on two perpendicular boards. The target had a few chinks and scuffs from their time practicing, but likely all the audience saw were the concentric circles painted in red and white. The pair of performers each took up a position on either side of the target, Vi gesturing high and Bonnie gesturing low. Bonnie had left the first apple behind on the other box as she passed and handed Vi the final blade.

"Our father, he was very strict man." Vi added the knife to the collection at her hip. "Especially with my sister. He would tell us, 'Children should be seen and not heard.' Which as you can see, Natasha has taken to heart."

Bonnie mimed locking her mouth shut and tossing the key over her shoulder with a little kick of her heel, which drew a few snickers from the audience.

Vi repeated her gesture of making an aside and used a stage whisper to say, "Which means when I ask for help with target practice, she can't say no."

The violinist knew this was a cue to ramp up the intensity of the music, and he vigorously climbed up and down the scales as Bonnie gave an exaggerated, theatrical shrug before standing before the bullseye. She put her arms straight up over her head. With her back flush against the target, the back of her stiff skirt was pushed down, but the front remained sticking out to either side. Vi took a few paces back, brandishing two blades in her left hand. She faced the target, then sent a pair of knives sailing into the wood to the outside of each of Bonnie's knees, followed by another pair above the edges of the costume. Vi retrieved the knives while Bonnie did a little spin and flourish, then they repeated the trick using Bonnie's outstretched arms. The audience roared louder and louder with each set of throws.

As Vi approached the target a second time to pull the blades free, a shiver ran down her spine. Her head swam and she reached up to the top of the flat for balance. The act was almost done; she just needed to keep herself together for another minute or two. Afterwards, she could rest and try to banish this infernal dizziness. Her tread was unsteady as she swapped places with Bonnie, who readied herself for the next set of throws.

Bonnie stood back while Vi threw the first knife into the target at shoulder height. The lovely assistant stepped up, turned her back on the blade and arched it until the back of her neck rested against it. Vi took a steadying breath, then threw her second knife. It hit the target near her partner's belly. The next one thunked into the wood near her chest. Vi lifted the final blade and let it fly. It hit the target, but landed far closer to Bonnie's bared throat than she had intended. The other woman's eyes grew to the size of teacups as she stepped away and looked at the shape left by the knives. She did not have the stage sense to keep her shocked face turned away from the audience. To distract them, Vi stepped up to the edge of the stage.

"Do you have brother or sister, sir?" she asked, pointing to a random man in the crowd.

"Yeah, I got a brother!" he slurred back.

"I bet you want to slit his throat sometimes, too, da?"

The audience laughed, and Vi turned back to her assistant. She mouthed a silent apology, then flashed Bonnie an exaggerated grin and gestured at her to copy it. The little brunette followed suit, but the smile looked every bit as forced as it was.

As Vi returned to her spot, she picked up another apple from the bowl. She tossed it to Bonnie, who caught it and placed it on top of her head. She put her arms up in a circle like a ballerina, her eyes tight with worry.

The voice of her aunt Prudence drifted into Vi's mind. "You must be a clear, still pool."

She took two steadying breaths in through her nose and out through her mouth, and the image of her hot spring materialized. On the third breath, she lifted her right leg to balance on just one foot. Rather than overtake her, the dizziness ebbed as her foot lifted higher.

The crowd waited in hushed anticipation as the violin music crescendoed. Vi lifted the first knife, catching a glimpse of Bonnie's worried expression one more time before she closed her eyes and threw. She released Sam's knives in quick succession, and based on the hollow wooden sound, she was hitting her intended spots on either side of Bonnie's torso.

Vi reached down to her final blade, the one sheathed on her calf, and slipped it free as she stepped into a deep lunge. She released the smaller, sharper knife underhand and braced herself.

The music stopped just as she let go, or else she pushed it from her mind.

All she heard was a sickening wet sound when the blade hit something other than wood.

The audience gasped.

Then they fell silent.

CHAPTER 22

Vi froze, too terrified to look up and see what she had done. Terrible visions of her knife embedded in Bonnie's gut, her chest, her neck, flashed before her tightly shut eyes. She took two shaking, impossibly long breaths.

The room exploded with applause.

Vi's head shot up and she found the knife embedded in the flesh of the fruit rather than her friend. Relief flooded her body, rendering her limbs numb and heavy. The blade had passed clear through the apple, and when Bonnie stepped away, it remained pinned to the spot. She bent down to take Vi's hand and help her to the front of the stage for them to take their bows. The room was on its feet, hooting and hollering–all except for Peter, who was making his way toward her with worry creasing his features.

The performers finished blowing kisses and curtseying before retreating to their original sides of the stage. In the darkness of the wings, Vi nearly collided with the next act about to take the stage. The ventriloquist's dummy made a rude noise at her as he and his human hurried to center stage. She couldn't really blame him; she wouldn't want to follow the show she and Bonnie had just put on either. Nothing like a hint of real danger to make the heart pound, and hers was a timpani at the mercy of Hadyn.

Vi put a hand against the wall to steady herself, and Peter passed through it a few moments later. "What happened out there? You were all over the place."

"Thankfully, not too far off my mark," she replied.

"I do not mean your aim. Though I am sure our young friend will have some choice words for you on that account." He snickered, but immediately sobered. "No, I mean your color. You seemed fine at first, a little dim but mostly fine. Then it was like it was being drained away."

Vi looked over her shoulder and back to the stage. "I felt something. A threat. Like I was being watched. But if I try to home in on it, this stupid thing goes haywire." She put her hand to her cheek to stem the flow of energy, and her palm warmed as she reabsorbed some of what she was losing.

"To be fair, you *were* being watched. By an entire room full of people."

She shook her head. "No, this was like that day in Sacramento we were talking about."

"There were also two ghosts watching. But when I was watching you both of those times, I didn't mean you any harm. Your extra sense perceived me as a threat, but you know I'd never hurt you."

"That is true," she replied, though at the time back in Sacramento she absolutely had been fearing his retribution.

"Besides, Juno is the target, right?"

"That is the prevailing theory anyway." The audience's laughter cut into the conversation, bringing her back to attention. She moved toward the stage door. "Speaking of which, where is our fearless leader?"

"I have not seen her since the act break."

When Vi reached the threshold, she peeked around the doorframe and found the hallway empty. "Did you notice anything strange when she was on stage? Anything to indicate who might want to hurt her?"

"No. Well, not exactly...."

"What does that mean?"

His smile was sheepish. "Look, maybe it is just because of what Henry said, or the deep water, or just that your attack of nerves is contagious. But I may have seen a shadow."

"A shadow," Vi said drily, glancing around pointedly at the darkness that surrounded them.

"One of Henry's shadows," he clarified.

"You mean that ghost story for ghosts?" she scoffed. "You have been on the water too long. There was no mention of them in the journal, remember? And what would one of them want with Juno anyway? Is she a tasty treat like Diana?" She nearly spat the words out as she thought about Henry's dressing room antics.

Peter murmured something, but too quietly to make out clearly.

"What?" she asked. Vi threw her hands into the air to stop him before he could speak. "Actually, no. I do not have time for this right now. I need to go make things right with Bonnie and make sure Juno is safe. You go back out to the audience and see what you can see from there."

Vi stomped off through the door, angry with herself more than anyone else, but too exhausted to keep her venom in check. Peter was always eager to believe everything. You'd think after their time with the Pinks and working the river he would be more cynical, more like her. But he had never lost his sense of wonder, not even in death. Part of her was jealous of his propensity toward faith, but that was the part that was also preoccupied with keeping all of the Belles alive and Sam in business.

She was already halfway to the dressing room when she thought she heard Peter's voice again. "I did not see it with Juno." It was a whisper, but she somehow clearly heard it, as if he breathed it right into her ear from ten paces and a wall away. "I saw it near you."

This gave Vi pause, but the dressing room door opened and the Belles came pouring out. Juno had exchanged Midas's waistcoat for a long, flowing dressing gown. The two nymphs were now a maid and a butler, and Enid had swapped her plainer costume for the impressive gown. Their happy chatting died down slightly when they saw her, a few of them exchanging concerned glances.

"Is she in there?"

"Yes," Ceres replied. "And she seems kind of shaken."

Vi nodded and gathered her courage as she waited for the dancers to pass. When she walked in, Bonnie was taking her frustration out on her costume, twisting it around roughly to get to the buttons.

"Here, let me help you," Vi said.

Bonnie stopped her struggling long enough to shoot a glare her way, then turned around to give Vi access to her back. Vi worked the buttons in silence.

"What has gotten into you?" Bonnie seethed, sliding the costume down and stepping out of the crinkled pool of fabric. "The applause go to your head? Decided to add some danger?"

Vi had only seen Bonnie angry once before, and that was after her late husband had showed up unexpectedly. Even under those circumstances, she had seemed more like a petulant child than the enraged woman who stood before her. The young widow had been through so much in just a few short weeks, and she was hardening every day.

Vi swallowed around the lump in her throat. "I owe you an apology, I—"

"You're damn right you do." She picked up the dress and shoved it onto its hanger in the wardrobe. Her hand went to her throat, rubbing at the wound that had almost come to pass. "You could have killed me."

Vi took her friend by the shoulders. "It was a mistake. I did not do it on purpose."

The little brunette twisted out of her grip and pulled her regular dress on over her shift. Tears glistened in her eyes as she whispered, "You promised. You promised me you do not make mistakes."

A nervous chuckle escaped Vi before she stopped it. "We both know I make plenty of mistakes."

"Not like that, you don't!" Bonnie leaned both hands against the makeup table.

Vi scrambled to recover from her ill-timed attempt at levity. She put her hands up in surrender. "Mea culpa. You are completely right. I did promise. And I am so sorry. You have to believe me, I would never try to hurt you on purpose."

Bonnie's body deflated as her rage was replaced by disappointment. She looked into the mirror and her reflection regarded Vi. "You were drunk, weren't you?"

"What? No, of course not!" She pulled out a chair beside her friend and sat down, but despite putting herself into the path of Bonnie's diverted gaze, she refused to look her in the eye.

"I have myself to blame, really. I should have seen it," Bonnie sighed, shaking her head and gazing at her own reflection. "You were bumping into things, distracted. I never should have gone out on that stage with you."

"What happened is decidedly *not* your fault."

Vi had become accustomed to fighting the impulse to touch people, and she hesitated before trying to take her hand. When she finally reached for it, Bonnie ripped it from her grip. The rejection was like a knife to the gut.

"Don't! Don't you dare."

"Bonnie, I swear to you. I have not had a drop all day." She cleared her throat. "Something did happen and I was not at my best. But I promise, truly promise, nothing like that will ever happen again."

"No, it definitely won't," Bonnie replied. She turned to scowl down at Vi. "I quit."

Vi nodded. "Of course. I completely understand. We will tell Juno it was a onetime thing."

The sound of muffled applause came from the direction of the stage. It was time for the second act to begin, and Vi was no closer to figuring out what was happening than before. She shot to her feet, and her head swam again.

"I have to go. There is someone—" Her mind flashed to Peter's warning. "—or perhaps something near the stage that I have to take care of. I will explain everything later. I promise. But right now, I have to go and see if I can stop whatever it is from happening."

"By all means, do not let me keep you," Bonnie replied caustically.

Vi considered telling her everything right that moment, but the other woman made pointed shooing gestures that precluded any further discussion. So, Vi headed for the stage once again, mumbling, "Once more into the breach."

CHAPTER 23

Vi didn't realize she was still wearing her flashy red and gold costume until she had already made it back to the wings, but there was no time to worry about the relative ridiculousness of her appearance until after the danger had been averted. Worry gnawed at the pit of her stomach as she peered out onto the stage. Juno as Midas was lying on a settee feigning sleep. Ceres, still in her vines and flowers as Dionysus, leaned over her and gave the faux muttonchops a comical tweak before turning to the audience.

"The king was so good to me, I desire to give him a gift. He told me his dearest wish is for all he touches to turn to gold. I would want everything to turn to wine, personally." She paused for laughter. "But if he wants gold, I shall give him gold."

Ceres reached into a pouch hidden within the folds of her costume and produced a powder that sparkled like gold dust in the stage lights. Vi slunk a few steps behind the scenery to be closer to the prostrate Juno just as Ceres sprinkled the powder over her.

Juno let out an enormous snore and snuffle before turning over on her settee as Ceres continued her monolog. Juno was of course completely awake, and when she caught sight of Vi lurking between the flats, she held her with a glare that could melt ice. She mouthed something that looked like "What are you doing? Get out!"

Vi shook her head, returning a silent, "I can't."

The temperature of Juno's expression rose to boiling. Judging from the heat behind her eyes, it took all her strength not to get up and wring Vi's neck right there in front of everyone. Juno pretended to stretch to hide her face as she gave Vi an exaggerated but mute, "Get. Off. My. Stage."

"And now," Ceres said with a hint of mischief in her voice, "I must away with the dawn. When the good king awakes, he will get his just rewards."

She swept off stage left while Enid entered from the right. The pianist played the opening bars of "Beautiful Dreamer" as she took her place at center. The intricate white lace of her dress had been starched within an inch of its life and it blazed in the halo from the footlights.

A wave of ill-intent washed over Vi and she slipped to the next flat. Juno would be lying there on that couch for the entire song, an easy target for another sandbag. Whether or not she bilked her employees or ran the troupe with an iron fist, she did not deserve to be flattened. Vi craned her neck to search the darkness above, but if there was any kind of counterweight ready to fall, she couldn't make it out with her eyes or her extra sense.

She was about to move again when a sweet, lilting voice rose up over the piano music. Enid's pure and effortless tone captured Vi's breath as she sang.

Beautiful dreamer, wake unto me,
Starlight and dewdrops are waiting for thee;
Sounds of the rude world, heard in the day,
Lull'd by the moonlight have all passed away.

For all her awkwardness and somewhat gawky appearance, there was no question now about why Enid had been brought into the troupe as a replacement rather than promoting one of the other performers. Vi was not keen on hyperbole, but she'd be quite comfortable saying the young, freckled lady sang like an angel. Vi blinked away the distraction and returned to the task at hand.

When she got close enough to Juno that she was sure she'd hear, Vi whispered. "You are in danger."

"What are you talking about?" Juno hissed.

Vi tried to find the words to explain, but at the same time, Enid crossed to the settee and stood over her "father" to finish the verse. Vi held her breath, terrified the audience would catch sight of her now that their eyes were directed her way.

Beautiful dreamer, queen of my song,
List while I woo thee with soft melody;
Gone are the cares of life's busy throng,
Beautiful dreamer, awake unto me!
Beautiful dreamer, awake unto me!

When Enid turned back to cross to the front of the stage, Vi answered Juno. "I think someone is trying to hurt you."

"Now?"

Vi's extra sense burned across her shoulders, but remained directionless. Her eyes darted once again to the ceiling. Still no sign of danger from above. But the anxious prickling grew stronger. Whether because her stores of energy were depleted or her pronoia was somehow on the fritz, she simply could not get more specific. She just nodded in reply to Juno; better safe than sorry.

Enid was at the front corner of the stage, gesturing to the audience to pull them even deeper into her thrall. It was a short song, and Vi hoped that once Juno was up and moving again, she would make a more difficult target.

Beautiful dreamer, out on the sea,
Mermaids are chanting the wild lorelei;
Over the streamlet vapors are borne,
Waiting to fade at the bright coming morn.

"I am fine," Juno murmured. "You need to go. NOW."

The panic seared into Vi's back, biting as deep as an asp and spreading its venom. Tears welled in her eyes, and she realized she was gripping the edge of the scenery flat to keep upright. Whatever was going to happen was going to happen soon.

"Just trust me," Vi all but gasped as she attempted to steady the vibrations of her touch on the painted flat. "You will need me."

Enid made her way across the front edge of the stage, moving once again to center as the final verse began. Vi stole a glance at the enraptured audience, forlorn, gentle smiles settled on the faces of even the hardest river man.

Beautiful dreamer, beam on my heart,
Even as the morn on the streamlet and sea;
Then will all clouds of sorrow depart,
Beautiful dreamer, awake unto me!

The chanteuse arrived at center stage and took her final step right up to the edge to repeat the last line and put the song to bed (as it were.)

Fire shot down Vi's spine and she knew with an unforeseen and utterly terrible certainty that Juno was not the one in danger. The world tilted as her stomach dropped, blurring her view of Enid's fateful final step forward.

Vi didn't see what happened immediately, but the flames rushed from either side of Enid to cover and consume the hem of her gown. Enid let out a scream and stepped away from the naked flame of the footlight, but with the fire now surrounding her, there was nowhere she could step to be out of its path. The blaze devoured the lace overlayer, whooshing its way to her waist as she raised her hands up into the air in mute horror.

As soon as the world stopped spinning enough for Vi to move, she pushed over the scenery flat and staggered to the front of the stage. The people in the first few rows were on their feet, some clawing their way away from the fire and others standing stock still in shock. Vi knew at a glance that there was too much fabric and nothing near to use to tamp it out. When she reached Enid, she dug her fingers into the gaps between the buttons at the singer's waist and ripped the top few layers free. She grabbed one side and yanked with all of her strength, sending Enid in a mad spin as the flaming lace came free.

After Vi bundled up the smoldering fabric, she threw it to the ground and stomped on it until all that was left was a pile of smoking rags. The audience was all rushing for the exit at the back, shouting and shouldering past each other as they fled. Sam was doing his best to shout over the din that the situation was under control, but no one was interested in heeding him.

She turned to find Enid had dropped to the stage and Juno was at her side, patting out the last few tendrils of fire. "What are you waiting for?" Juno screeched to the wings. "Drop the curtain!"

Jack startled out of his shock and went for the lever. The heavy velvet drape cascaded down to the stage, cutting them off from the cries of the crowd and plunging them into darkness.

CHAPTER 24

October 21, 1871

The Memphis papers used headlines such as "Mayhem on the Mississippi" and "Jeze-Belles Jinxed?" They reported varying numbers of casualties depending on how many copies they were hoping to sell, but in truth the entire audience got out more or less unscathed. Enid, on the other hand, was another story.

Most of the damage had been restricted to her dress, but her legs had also gotten a few nasty burns before the fire had been completely put out. Unlike the incident with the sandbag, when Vi offered her assistance as a former medic, Juno took her up on it. After Jack had carried Enid to her room, Vi cut away what was left of her tights. She cleaned her wounds as best as she could with what was on hand, settling for wrapping her injuries in strips torn from a bedsheet. She would need more and better supplies if she were to properly treat the injuries, but it was already well past closing time for the stores in town.

Vi visited Enid first thing the next morning. It was not as early as she had intended, but Vi was so drained after everything that had happened the night before, she slept until the sun had crept far above the horizon. She missed breakfast completely, and even though she was not happy about this newest "accident," she was not sorry that the incident was successfully delaying part two of her discussion with Bonnie.

Peter stood outside the cabin as Vi gently turned Enid's leg this way and that to assess the damage. The red-head sucked against her teeth, but to her credit, she never complained about the pain. Most of her injuries were superficial and would not require much special care, but she had a few angry, crimson and white blisters that would need a poultice.

Vi set Enid's left leg back down on the covers as gently as possible. "It may not feel like it, but you were lucky. This is not anything we can't take care of here on the ship. Unless of course you would prefer to go to the hospital?"

Enid twitched the thin cotton sheet back over her exposed flesh. "Have you dealt with burns before? I trust you of course. Of course! But this is all quite worrying. A dancer needs her legs!" she tittered before sighing. "Will it take long before I am back on my feet? I do not want my clumsiness to delay the Belles too much."

"I have some experience with burns, yes. But if you want to see a proper doctor, I want you to feel that you can. Juno will understand. No amount of clumsiness should deny you medical care."

"I feel so stupid," Enid said, settling deeper into the mattress. "I never should have gotten close to the edge like that. I am still getting used to stages and footlights."

Vi rubbed her chin. "This kind of thing has happened before?"

"Not to me, thank goodness, but yes. I have heard of this kind of thing before." Enid winced as she shifted. "It's the starch, you see? It makes clothes nice and stiff. It makes whites even brighter. But it does make things more likely to burn."

"I had not realized laundry could be hazardous," Vi replied. This was the first she'd heard of the phenomenon, and if it weren't for the sinking feeling, she'd had throughout the show, Vi may have even believed this explanation. And of course, even if the starch was to blame, someone had to have added it. "Certainly something to keep in mind the next time you do the washing."

Enid tittered. "Oh, I never do my own washing anymore. Not since joining up with Juno. And I definitely never touch the costumes. I am all thumbs when it comes to sewing. Diana is the real talent there. Oh no! She must be so upset about what happened! She spent ages on that dress, and there I went and ruined it."

"It was not your fault," Vi said, echoing her words to Bonnie just half a day earlier and reminding her of the groveling she had in store for her.

Her full night of sleep had helped restore Vi enough that she felt the tingle of Henry approaching at twenty paces. Peter was at his side, mumbling something to him about staying out of sight while Vi did her examination. The second ghost replied, but she didn't make it out clearly. Her first impulse was to feel annoyed at his presence at such a delicate moment; for all she knew he had come to prey on Enid while she was vulnerable. As she remembered Henry's former profession, her spirits brightened.

Vi got to her feet and gave Enid an encouraging smile. "I will go in to the apothecary right this minute and get what I need to fix you up. We shall have you up on that stage again in no time. You just rest for now."

Enid thanked her as she headed out the door, but before Vi was able to get more than a step past the threshold, she was surrounded by most of the Belles and Jack. Minerva was noticeably absent, though it was possible she had been there earlier and simply grown tired of waiting. The two ghosts paced a short distance down the walkway to give her the space she needed in case one of them were to touch her.

"How is she?" Juno asked, her white-knuckled hands clasped close to her heart. She appeared far older and more tired than Vi would have guessed possible.

"She will be fine," Vi assured her. "Nothing to worry about."

The dancers let out a collective sigh of relief.

"Is there anything we can do?" Ceres asked.

"You can keep her company while I go into town." Vi flashed a glance to the ghosts, and Peter nodded his understanding. "Keeping her mind off the pain is one of the best services you can provide. That and a spot of breakfast, I'd wager."

Juno squeezed Vi's arm and thanked her before she pushed open Enid's door. Vi headed down the walkway but waited until Ceres and Diana passed by on their way to get the other dancer some tea before she spoke to the ghosts. She watched Diana's back recede with narrowed eyes, all too aware that she was the engineer behind the dress. That did not necessarily mean she was the one who had sabotaged it, if in fact it had been sabotaged at all. But between her access to the costumes and her absence from the stage when the sandbag fell, she was now at the top of Vi's suspect list–though Minerva's apparent lack of concern was also worth noting.

Vi rested her back against the wall near where the ghosts were waiting for her and let out a relieved puff of air. "She is very lucky."

"And you're sure she'll be all right?" Henry asked.

The earnestness in his expression surprised Vi, and her brows knit together. "Yes. She will be in pain for a spell, but she will be able to walk around with the bandage on without any problems."

The ghost sighed. "So glad t' hear it. She's quite a nightingale, that girl. I'd hate to see her wings clipped so young."

"I did not take you for a lover of music." Vi smirked. "I rather thought your appreciation of the Belles ended with their legs."

"They have many fine qualities," Henry replied, bouncing his eyebrows mischievously.

Vi rolled her eyes and turned to Peter. "Does he know?"

"Yes, I told him about the pronoia during the show."

Henry's face fell. "It's hard t' believe anyone'd do that on purpose."

"Enid thinks it was a just an accident involving an over-starched bit of lace, but I am not convinced. Which is where you come in. I need your help figuring out if there was anything else present that could have caused her to light up like a bonfire last night."

"You can count on me, Vi," Henry replied. "I'll come along when you go in t' town and tell you what you'll need. Providin' there's any lace left t' test, that is."

Vi waved vaguely in the direction of the upper deck. "Yes, I have a scrap of it in my room."

Peter interjected, his glowing eyes narrowed. "And you think now that Enid is the target, not Juno at all?"

"It would appear so. She was on stage both times something bad happened." Vi wagged a finger and shifted her voice to a cold, imperious tone to imitate her aunt. "And as you know, there are no such things as coincidences."

He snickered. "That was eerie."

"Would you please stay and keep an eye on things? I would feel a lot better knowing that someone is looking out for her." Peter opened his mouth to protest, but she knew his thoughts before he voiced them. "Someone I *trust*."

"Fine. Say 'hello' to Memphis for me," he sulked. Vi nodded her gratitude and motioned to Henry to follow her to the stairs. Just before she began her descent, Peter called, "And if you are feeling generous, pick up a cigar for me."

At the bottom of the steps, Henry gave her a quizzical look. "You smoke cigars?"

"Not as such," Vi replied. "But Peter does. Did. Does." When the look of confusion deepened, she continued, "He cannot smoke them himself of course, but he does still enjoy mingling with the smoke."

"Huh. That's clever. I'll have t' give it a try sometime."

"I am both surprised and gratified to hear you have not figured out all of death's little pleasures on your own. If Peter is willing to share, I can smoke it for the two of you and that can be my thankyou for this little errand."

They rounded the bend to the next set of stairs and descended to the main deck. It stood deserted, save for the cargo. It seemed like an oversight not to have someone at least keeping watch on the crates. Perhaps the crew assumed no one would think to risk thievery for fear of the unfortunate ship's bad luck rubbing off on them.

Before she had made it all the way to shore, she spotted Bulloch, his head bent in conversation with someone near the end of the plank. He was nodding in curt bursts, and no matter how she strained to hear, she couldn't make out what he and his companion were saying. When he caught sight of her approach, he straightened to his full height and regarded her with suspicion.

"Where do you suppose you are going?" he asked.

Vi lifted her chin. "I have been charged with the care of our young singer. An excursion to the apothecary is in order. Do you or your friend have any idea where I might locate one?" On the last sentence, she raised her voice and smiled sweetly at the turned back of the man she assumed was a local.

"Why didn't you just tell one of the others what to get for you?" Bulloch growled. "We will have to shove off at some point, and if you all aren't aboard, I can't be held responsible." From his tone, she believed he would not only live up to the threat, but revel in it.

"Which others would that be?" Vi asked, raising her brow but keeping the perturbation out of her voice.

The first mate crossed his burly arms, the forearms bare save for the thick carpet of hair. This time she could make out the tattoo she had been expecting to see, one bearing the name of a Rebel naval ship. "I can't keep track of you all," he replied. "Just be back in an hour, if you think you can manage it. Cap'n wants to get underway and out of scrutiny before too long."

Vi gave him a mocking salute before brushing past him. Bulloch returned to his prior conversation, but not before mumbling something unflattering about the brazen state of womanhood these days.

"You ought to be more careful," Henry warned, falling in step beside her. "Something tells me that one isn't shy about using his belt to do the talking for him."

"He would not dare. Even if I were not a friend of the captain, I am still a passenger." A sly grin split Vi's face. "Besides, I could drop him like a sack of potatoes if the mood struck me."

He looked back over his shoulder at the first mate and doubt crossed his face, but he had the good manners not to contradict her. Instead, he remarked, "So, you have experience as a nurse, I gather?"

"Yes. You were not the only one to serve in the army." Vi spied the sign for an apothecary a few storefronts away and quickened her pace.

Henry nodded sagely. "I see now where you get your steel spine."

She hid her unease with a shrug, remembering how easy it had been to walk away from her duty. Though of course, she had not walked all that far in the end. The things Patrick had recruited her to do were part of the war effort, if somewhat adjacent. "It did not last long. But I know more than the average person. Enough to come in handy from time to time. Now, what am I going to need to check this lace?"

CHAPTER 25

Henry gave her a short list of supplies, including iodine and a pair of tweezers. As she neared the door, a familiar blond head bobbed into view. Minerva was waving farewell to the couple behind the counter. With a genuine smile on her face for once, she really was a beauty, but her mouth took on a sour tilt when she caught sight of Vi. The expression faded almost instantly, replaced by concern as she met Vi and her invisible companion just outside the shop.

"Have you seen Enid yet this morning?" Her hands twisted the top of the small paper sack in her hands. "Is she going to recover?" The display seemed sincere, and Vi gave her the same reassurances as she had the other dancers. Minerva's left hand still clutched the bag, but the right one rose to her collarbone. "Oh thank god."

"I did not realize you were close," Vi said archly.

The blond woman pulled a face. "Honestly, I can hardly stand her. Talks too much for my taste. But the show would be absolutely devastated without her." She glanced at the bag in her hand and shuffled her feet in her the direction of *The Piasa*. "I should really get back. Goodbye."

"Well that wasn't the least bit suspicious," Vi murmured to Henry, sarcasm dripping from her words like candle wax. "Do you think she meant it? I hear she is a champion at holding grudges."

"Based on what I've seen of the show, she's not wrong. The others are fine actors, a'course, and they're good for a laugh. But Enid might be pulling in crowds someday all on her own."

Vi pulled open the door to the apothecary. "That does not mean she is safe from envy. What do you suppose was in that bag?"

"Let's hope our little experiment'll shed some light."

In a few minutes, Vi had a little paper sack of her own with the supplies Henry had requested, as well as something to treat Enid's burns. She stepped out onto the street and turned her face fully into the sun to soak it in. For the first time in several days, she felt more rested, alert, and equipped to deal with whatever was coming her way.

The ghost looked her up and down, but not with the same kind of hungry leer she'd seen him use to appraise the fairer sex before. "Coming ashore agrees with you."

"It appears I still have not gained my sea legs, or I suppose 'river legs' as it were." Vi set off in the direction of the ship with a bounce in her step and a tune on her lips.

Henry shook his head, his voice rising over Vi's whistle. "That's not it. You can draw energy from the ground again now that you're touching it. In fact, it's a shame that Peter didn't come along with us. He would've benefitted from a chance to draw in more energy himself."

He reached out to prod the gash in Vi's aura and she batted at his ephemeral hand. "Stop that!" Vi received a few sidelong glances from her fellow pedestrians and she gave them a nervous chuckle as she gestured to the empty air. "Bee." For the ghost's benefit only, she mumbled, "Or make that gadfly."

After the other people and their judgmental murmurs passed, Henry pointed at her reflection in a shop window. "Just look."

As Henry said, the gash on her cheek had narrowed significantly, almost as if it were a wound that was doing its best to scab over. If it were a real wound, she'd be able to stitch it closed to aid the healing process, but she doubted even the best stocked apothecary would have the right kind of needle and thread for a hole in the spirit. Most of the time, Vi repressed the sight of her own aura, but she flexed her special senses enough to see she shone about half as brightly as the rest of the living.

"You should feel steadier, for a time at least," Henry said. "Maybe your second performance will go better than the first."

Vi scowled as her thoughts shifted to Bonnie and her completely justified anger. "I do not expect to have another chance." She took off once again down the sidewalk.

"Pity," the ghost said, loping alongside. "I thought it was a great start."

"The start was not the problem," she grumped. "The ending on the other hand...."

They were only a block away from the riverfront now, but the sound of raucous laughter drew her attention. Her gaze snagged on a nearby tavern, and her mouth all but watered at the thought of a nice tipple to delay her return to the ship. That was the notion that got her feet moving, but it was *who* she saw through the window that carried her inside.

Bonnie was seated at a table with the Belles' accompanists and a few of the variety act performers. They were almost all men, and all sitting rather close together. It was the kind of scene that no one would bat an eye to see Vi in the middle of, but the young widow was oddly out of place. Or rather, she appeared completely at ease, and that was the odd part.

"Bonnie?" Vi asked, stepping up to the table.

"Oh Vi! Hello Vi! It's Vi, everyone," Bonnie exclaimed, her words slurring together.

"Oh my," Henry said. "I think I will leave you to it and meet you back at your room." He beat a hasty retreat toward the riverfront, eschewing the door in favor of passing straight into the next building.

In something that was meant to be a whisper but fell short by several decibels, the little brunette said to the assembled showmen, "She's the one I was telling you about."

Fear jolted up Vi's spine, but she kept her mouth smiling as she regarded the juggler and ventriloquist in turn. "And what has she been telling you precisely?"

"That you were s'posed to come into town with me, but I di-didn't wait. So, they said they'd keep me comp'ny," Bonnie replied. She rose from her chair on legs as unsteady as a fawn's. "And, I said that you really like whiskey, but I had never tried it. Until now!" Her voice grew shrill with delight on the last word and she giggled as she reached for her glass. Finding it empty, she pouted.

"I think that is enough for you," Vi said gently, but seeing the petulance beginning to gathering on Bonnie's brow at her words, she added a hasty, "for now. Just for now."

Bonnie hiccupped. "Dis is fun. I see why you like it."

When her friend began to list, the pianist rose to steady her, but Vi wrapped a protective arm around her waist. "I have her, thank you. And you should all head back to the ship as well. Bulloch only gave me an hour, and it is almost up."

The assembled performers all rose to their feet and flagged the barkeep to pay their tab. Vi helped Bonnie to the door, and the little brunette started to hum something equal parts happy and off-key. She interrupted herself to remark, "They were nice."

Vi patted her head. "Yes dear, they seemed very nice."

"You're nice, too," she said, then corrected. "Sometimes."

She shifted Bonnie's weight and gritted, "I am many things, but I am not sure 'nice' is one of them."

"You sure you don't need help?" asked a young, male voice. The juggler jogged to catch up with them.

"Haven't you helped enough?" Vi hissed. "It is not even noon."

"*Hey*. Hey, Vi." Bonnie stabbed her index finger into Vi's sternum, her voice as serious as the slur allowed. "Be *nice*. 'Member?"

The man rubbed the back of his neck and looked at Vi through his pale lashes. "I did not mean any harm, ma'am. I promise. I would have looked out for her and gotten her back safe. We were just having a little fun."

"Yes, I picked up on that," Vi replied. The annoyed, maternal bent to her tone brought her up short, but in for a dime, in for a dollar. "Quite a lot of fun."

"Now, ma'am, you can't right well blame a man for doing what a pretty girl asks him to do."

"Thaz true," Bonnie interjected. "And I asked for whiskey."

Vi sighed knowingly. "Yes, I suppose you did." To the juggler she murmured. "But there are quite a lot of pretty girls for you to chase on *The Piasa*, aren't there? Perhaps one of them, who is not my young friend here, would be interested in sharing a drink with you in the future?"

"What, the Belles?" he scoffed. "Even if that wasn't against Juno's rules, which it definitely is, most of them are spoken for."

"Is that so?" Vi asked, her mind going back to another shopping trip and the sound of Charles's entreaties to one of the dancers.

The lanky youth nodded. "Well, sure. Ever since we hitched up with the captain, Minerva only has eyes for him. Ceres has a beau back home in New York. I don't see Enid stepping out any time soon. And Diana and Charles have been sweet on each other for as long as I remember." His eyes grew tight and he leaned in closer to Vi, his voice lowered. "But you didn't hear that from me, got it?"

"I take it that is also against Juno's rules?"

"You bet. Don't let the tights and the bawdy tunes fool you. Juno keeps a closer eye on them girls than a mother superior!"

They reached the gangplank and the impatient form of Bulloch as the juggler laughed at his own joke, and Vi mulled over his words. There was no love lost between Charles and Juno, that was clear even before she found out about the moratorium on fraternizing. Those were both extremely strong motivators for a young man in love. However, the voice on the other end of the clandestine conversation, presumably Diana, was loyal to Juno and accepting of her methods. Diana had also voiced her support in the dressing room that first day. Vi chuckled as she realized she now had the answer to the question of where the dancer had disappeared to during their fitting.

"Wasso funny?" Bonnie asked, bringing Vi back to the present.

Vi steered them to one of the benches on the first level of *Apple Blossom* and unloaded her charge. "Oh nothing. Just putting the pieces together, I think."

The other woman smoothed out her rumpled dress and smacked her lips. "I'm thirsty."

"For water, I hope," Vi replied. "That should help make you feel better."

"Better? I feel great!"

Vi eyed her friend. "How many drinks did you have, pray tell?"

Bonnie cocked her head and started to count on her fingers, but when she lost count the second time she just shrugged, grinned, and batted her eyes. Apparently, her friend was copying more than just Vi's choice of alcohol today; that was one of Vi's signature gestures. So was the scowl that creased her face next.

"You might feel great now, but you won't for long. This right here is the fun part, but trust me, it does not last. You need to have some water and a nap."

Bonnie's mood shifted immediately. "You don't get to tell me what to do. 'Member? I quit."

"We may not be doing the show anymore, but this is advice you should heed." Vi crossed her arms and jutted out one hip. "Trust me, I have had my fair share of hangovers and it is not something you want."

"No, no, no. I didn' jus' quit the show," Bonnie said, rising shakily to her feet as angry tears sprang to her lashes. She reached out and pushed Vi's shoulder hard enough to make her twist at the waist. Surprise more than anything else made her stumble a little at the contact; the other woman was acting on instinct rather than intention and her action hadn't stirred the aether at all.

"What has gotten into you?" Vi yelped.

"Forget the show." Bonnie closed the distance between them, this time shoving Vi with both hands. "I quit *you*."

CHAPTER 26

Vi was prepared for the blow this time, though not the sting of the words nor the violence of the feelings they drew from her. The other woman moved to push her again, her features tight with rage and despair. Too shocked to act, Vi let her do it.

"Hey, you there!" Bulloch roared, appearing from nowhere. He stared daggers at Vi, but as Bonnie pushed her again, it became clear Vi was not the instigator. The first mate laid a meaty paw on the little brunette's shoulder and spun her to face him. "What the hell is going on here?"

"Nothing," she snapped.

He crinkled his nose, reacting to the stench of alcohol on her breath. "I think it's time for you to go sleep it off."

"Fine!" Bonnie twisted out of his grip and backed toward the staircase. "We are *done* here anyway." An angry sob distorted her final word, and she took off for her room.

Vi slumped onto the bench, her mind far away from her body. Emotions rose and fell within her—anger at being abandoned, guilt at what she had done to prompt it, sorrow over the prospect of losing her only living friend, and the utter certainty that she deserved every single bad thing that came her way. Against all odds, Bonnie had wanted to come with her, even knowing about her bizarre abilities. And now, Vi had found a way to push her away.

Bulloch's voice reached into her thoughts, and Vi glanced up at him, numb.

"I told you, didn't I?" He crossed his burly arms. "Making trouble. *Fighting* of all things. I tell ya, this trip can't be over soon enough. Then I can be rid of all you ridiculous tabbies!"

Vi barely registered him as he stomped away and remained glued to her place until well after the ship had shoved off. It was Peter who finally awoke her from her reverie.

"Vi?" He knelt in order to look up at her down-turned face. "I just came from Bonnie. The poor thing is distraught! I know you wanted me to look after Enid, but I heard her sobbing. I think she needs you."

Her scoff rang out over the water. The ghost shifted to sit beside her, but Vi kept her eyes on her hands. "I am the last thing she needs right now," she murmured. Vi recounted her trip into town and its aftermath.

"Well, as you said, she was skunked." Peter leaned against the seatback and spread his arms. "Once she's sobered up, I am sure she will change her tune."

"I'm not." She rubbed her hands down her face, stretching her cheeks. "Booze tends to make people more truthful, not less." Vi released her face and sighed. "She's better off without me anyway. She always was."

Vi mistook the coolness against her shoulders for a draft at first, but realized Peter had wrapped his misty arm around her. With the effort written in the flare and swirl of his depleted spirit flesh, he gave her a gentle squeeze. "You know, just because a woman runs out on you, it doesn't mean she doesn't want you to follow her." He snickered. "Present company excluded, of course."

She smirked. "I suppose I am not a typical woman in more ways than one."

"Oh, my dear, you didn't just break the mold. You crushed it into dust!"

The term of endearment made her breath hitch. Though he had used it sometimes when they were partners, he hadn't called her anything other than 'Vi' or occasionally 'Thorne' since his death. Her shocked numbness receded, and her eyes grew hot.

Misreading her reaction, Peter added a rushed, "No, no. It's a good thing!"

"I did, you know."

"Did what?"

She wiped at her tear and turned to him with a sad smile. "I wished you had followed me. Especially at first."

Peter passed his arm through her, sending a deep chill through her body. He angled away to better look at her full in the face.

"But how could I?" He gawked at her. "You disappeared."

"You still found me."

His foggy body darkened with agitation. "Yes, but you gave no indication—"

Vi raised a hand to silence him. "I am not saying I *expected* you to follow me. Only that I missed you. And...and I am no longer certain I made the right choice." She let the next tear fall unhindered, but turned her face away as she whispered, "I am starting to think I have never made the right choice once in my entire life. Everything is my fault."

Silence filled the next few moments, and she feared he would simply walk away and leave her to her misery. The frosty sensation touched her back again. "It was not all bad, though, was it?" Peter asked, leaning close to her ear. "It sounds like you were happy in New York. And we did good work together with the Pinks, right? Plus, before you joined 'Trick and me on that foolhardy endeavor, you were saving lives."

Peter's use of the nickname for Vi's late husband brought the ghost of a smile to her lips. She sniffed and wiped at the tear track down her cheek. "I would hardly classify a stitch here or there as saving lives." Guilt gripped her insides and tried to strangle the words she fought to release. "And can that possibly make up for the lives I ruined? For Chicago? For you?"

"I don't know, Thorne. If anything, it sounds as though your life only went downhill after you met me."

Her head shot up and she gazed at him with wide, wild eyes. "What an awful thing to say. Of course not!"

"I believe that means that everything is, in fact, my fault."

"That is simply not true," Vi insisted. "I made my own choices every step of the way."

"So did I. So does Bonnie."

Vi flopped back against the bench in frustration. "She did not though, not about the show. I made her do it and she almost got hurt. And for what? So I could play at being an investigator again?"

"She could have refused." Peter jerked his thumb toward the upper deck. "And let us not forget poor Enid. There may be lives at stake here, too."

The mention of the wounded singer reminded Vi of her earlier errand. She searched around them for the parcel she had dropped when Bonnie was pushing her around. It rested near the foot of the bench, and she bent down to retrieve it with a groan. "You know, all I wanted was to do something *good*, something useful. No, not just useful. Useful and *mundane*, with no ghost assassins dogging me, or books that whisper when I touch them. After Sacramento, I was starting to think I was not capable of anything normal. I thought I would get to the bottom of this whole silly affair with the Belles and maybe I would be able to look at myself in the mirror again. Now, I know that ship has truly sailed." Peter raised his brows and looked pointedly at the water surrounding them. He snickered at Vi's accidental pun and she fought a chuckle of her own. "Stop it. You know what I mean."

"You want to solve this thing? Let's do it." The ghost sprang to his feet. "You have what you need to test the fabric. Why not go and find out whether or not your pronoia can be trusted?"

"You were listening to the part where I said I did not want to have anything to do with supernatural problems, correct?" she sulked.

"As you have so elegantly illustrated, there does not seem to be any way of escaping them. You left any kind of normal life behind years ago. And you would not even know there was a puzzle here if you did not have your abilities. Why not use every weapon in your arsenal to solve it?"

She pursed her lips while she mulled over his words. During the war, they had definitely used any method at their disposal to carry out their missions. Whether or not she knew the origin or had a word for it, her pronoia and uncanny accuracy had always been present and helping her accomplish her goals. Consulting a chemist was the next logical step. Did it really matter that the only one she knew happened to be dead?

"When did you get so wise?" Vi rose, her whole body buoyed by Peter's enthusiasm.

"I have always been wise." He bowed his head slightly and bade her to lead the way with a twirl of his hand. As he followed, he added, "You are simply becoming wise enough to listen."

On the way to her cabin, Vi considered stopping by Enid's room first, but Henry had promised it would not take long to find out if starch was present on the lace. She was forced to pass by Bonnie's room on her way to her own and gulped down her anxiety as she approached the door. The walkway was blissfully silent, and Vi hoped that even if she was angry, Bonnie had heeded the advice to sleep away her stupor.

Next door, Henry waited as promised. He greeted them from his place stretched out on her bed before stepping up to the desk with a giddy grin. Vi upended her bag, scattering the small bottle of iodine, a pipette, and a pair of tweezers for herself, and the bandages and salve for Enid. The glass container was a dark orange color to keep the iodine from degrading. She took it by the cork and held it up to the light of her window. "So, what do I do?"

"Where's the sample?" Henry asked.

Vi opened her top desk drawer and pulled out the scrap. It was singed along one edge and was barely large enough to cover the palm of her hand, but considering how little of it was left after it caught fire, she was lucky to have even that much. As she held it out for Henry to see, he was nearly vibrating with anticipation. "It is just a little fabric," she said. "Nothing to get so excited about."

"As you can imagine, I haven't had much occasion for chemistry in a while. I loved my work." He rubbed his hands together. "We'll need a little more light first. But then all you need t' do is add a few drops of the iodine t' the sample."

She lit a candle and put the piece of lace into the pool of light. Using the pipette, she drew some of the iodine out of the bottle and dropped it onto a corner of the lace.

"What am I looking for?" Vi asked.

"The color should change. Starch turns black in the presence of iodine."

She leaned down to get a closer look, her nose wrinkling as the strong scent of iodine infiltrated her nostrils. Not only did the sample remain white, the iodine beaded on the surface. The presence or absence of starch would have given one possible and even an innocent explanation for what had transpired, but the complete lack of it pointed to more nefarious intent.

Vi stepped out of the way to give Henry a better vantage point. "What does that mean?"

He rubbed his chin. "Put it near the flame, but don't let it touch. I want to see the reaction up close."

Vi used the tweezers to pick up the lace and held it near the candle. As it got closer to the heat, the surface showed signs of shifting, as if the fabric was melting. A few moments more and there were tiny, watery pools forming on the edge closest to the flame.

Henry nodded and rubbed his chin again. "Now, put it into the fire."

She obliged and the fabric caught even before she had dipped it fully into the flame.

"Aha! It's some kind of paraffin wax," Henry said. "One with an extremely low meltin' point."

Peter moved to get a better angle over the other ghost's shoulder. "Wax? How does that work?"

"Basically, someone turned that poor girl's dress into one big candle." Henry pointed to the one on the desk. "The wax melts and releases a flammable gas. It burns and melts more wax, releasin' more gas. In this case, the cotton lace acted as the wick."

"That isn't normal, is it Vi? Even in the theater?" Peter asked.

She shook her head, then blew out the last of the burning fabric before the fire reached the tweezers, and more importantly, her fingers. A stream of gray smoke rose from what was left of the lace.

"No," she replied darkly. "This was definitely sabotage."

CHAPTER 27

"Someone woulda had t' do this in advance," Henry said.

"Yes," Peter replied, "but the real question is, how far in advance?"

Vi set the blackened lace down on the desk. "I disagree. I think the real question is, how could no one have noticed?"

"When Enid did her costume change, she had maybe fifteen minutes between acts."

"She did it in less than that," Vi said. "I saw her in it right after I finished. And she was already backstage and in the dark for the whole ventriloquist's set."

Peter furrowed his brow. "Surely it did not happen then?"

"No," the other ghost agreed. "It woulda taken a long time t' rub the wax into the entire lace layer. Maybe even hours."

Vi had already come to the same conclusion, and she rested the tips of her fingers together as she laid out her suspicion. "Who wasn't on stage when the sandbag fell?"

The ghosts thought about it for a moment, and Peter answered. "Diana."

"And who spends hours on end working with the costumes *and* knows exactly where people are on stage at all times?" Vi asked wryly.

"Diana!"

She tapped the side of her nose and turned to Henry. "I guess your peach pie is not as sweet as you thought."

He scoffed. "I don't believe it. Auras don't lie, and the color of hers says she's a gentle soul."

"Whoever has been working against the Belles never did anything direct. Nothing overtly violent," Vi said. "Maybe that *is* her being gentle."

"And maybe the indirectness and subterfuge is why your pronoia got so confused," Peter speculated. "Someone waiting for someone else to stand in the right spot is not at all the same as you dodging a punch coming right at you."

Vi had assumed her problem seeking out the direction of the threat had been her wound, but Peter's theory also had merit. Of course, the two ideas were not mutually exclusive. His other claim about seeing some kind of malevolent shadow hanging about seemed farther from the truth than ever.

Henry clenched his teeth and crossed his arms. "Or perhaps she is innocent, or if not wholly innocent, she was not working alone."

"Now *that* would make a whole lot of sense." When the pair of ghosts regarded Vi quizzically, she shared what the gossipy juggler had told her. "There really is only one way to find out if she, or Charles, or both of them were involved. It is time I had a little chat with the seamstress." Vi headed toward to door.

Peter stepped into her path, face drawn with worry. "Do you want us to come along?"

"I have this well in hand." She crossed the threshold, but grabbed onto the jamb to stop herself when Peter spoke again.

"What are you going to do?"

Vi leaned herself back into view and grinned. "The best way to confront an indirect criminal is with the direct approach. I am simply going to ask her what she knows and go from there. And though I am warming up to the notion of using my abilities to aid me, I would rather not send her into a fit of hysterics if she catches sight of you by mistake."

Henry interjected, motioning to the forgotten supplies on the desk. "Aren't you forgetting something?"

She snapped her fingers in recognition and moved back to the desk. After she blew out the candle, she gathered up the bandages and salve for Enid. "A perfect excuse to figure out where our dear arsonist is at the moment." Vi chuckled.

"Now who's getting excited?" Henry asked wryly. "Morbidly so."

"I am simply happy to be putting this whole shady business to rest." Vi's grin widened as she slipped out the door and called out a quote from Nicholas Nickleby over her shoulder. "The pain of parting is nothing to the joy of meeting again!"

When Vi arrived once more at Enid's room, she found her finishing a cup of tea with Juno and Ceres. The room was too small to comfortably fit more people, so after a brief admonishment to Vi for taking so long to get there, Juno excused herself. The actress's ire over Vi's impromptu appearance backstage evidently was not lessened by her ministrations to the star. Vi tried not to think how annoyed Juno would be once she found out the throwing knife act was out. Unless of course she was relieved, which was just as likely at this point.

Vi explained the salve to Enid and showed her how to wrap her bandages tightly enough for protection, but loosely enough not cause her any more discomfort than necessary. Ceres promised to help, and Vi was glad that not all members of the Belles were as petty and jealous as Diana. Of course, Diana had Vi fooled with all of her talk of respecting Juno and not feeling slighted by the addition of Enid to the cast. Prudence's distaste for actresses was starting to make a whole lot more sense.

"You will want to sleep without them at night, mind," Vi said. "The blisters need a chance to breathe and drain, and best to do it while you are sleeping rather than moving around. The skin will be raw for a few days, and you will probably have some scarring."

"It's a good thing we wear those tights on stage," Ceres said.

Enid nodded. "Oh yes. It is not as though I cannot walk. And if I can walk, I can walk onto that stage. I wouldn't dream of disappointing the girls."

"As they say, 'The show must go on'."

Vi wondered how much of that sentiment belonged to them and how much of it was Juno, but in the end, the result was the same. "I admire your commitment." Vi wagged her finger a few times. "Just make sure to get plenty of rest, as well. Otherwise your body will not have the energy to heal you." Once Enid agreed, Vi put the change of bandages and pot of poultice onto the bedside table. "Do you know where I might find Diana? I have a question for her."

"Juno sent her down to the dressing room," Ceres said. "She is supposed to improvise something else for Enid to wear now that her other dress went up in smoke."

"Poor thing." Enid shook her head. "She worked so hard on it. And I don't know that she slept a wink last night. She looked awful this morning, did you notice? Now, she'll have to work around the clock to get something new ready before tonight."

Vi was far less sympathetic. She knew better than most what effect a guilty conscience had on one's sleep. With one more reminder not to push herself too hard, Vi said goodbye to Enid and Ceres, and left for *The Piasa*.

The floating theater and her tow were rounding an immense island as Vi made her sojourn between ships. The water flowing through the narrowed channels pushed them along faster than usual, and Vi recognized the pull against the stores of energy she had gathered flowing along with it. New Orleans had to be over seven hundred miles away yet, and despite hurtling towards an unknown enemy, Vi was eager for her time on board to be over. Hopefully, now that she had the culprit within her grasp, she would not have need to push herself for the rest of the journey and her wound would have proper time to heal.

The Piasa's deck was quiet, which made sense given the events of the night before. A lone lookout at the prow tipped his hat to her as she slipped inside the theater. The interior was even quieter than the deck, the footlights on but only barely casting any light, what those in the theater world called the "ghost lights." Oftentimes, an empty theater gave Vi a thrill of anticipation, but knowing why this one now stood empty made the silence eerie and disconcerting. She wasted no time heading backstage.

Vi heard Diana singing to herself before she saw her. Her voice was not bad exactly, but she was pitchy and tentative, even while singing alone. Even if Diana didn't have Enid to compete with, she likely would never be a featured performer with the Belles or anywhere else no matter what Charles had promised her. It was a state Vi knew well; she carried a passable tune, but she was certainly not talented enough to ever be considered for a lead in that regard.

Still, a pang of nostalgic longing swept through her as she realized all over again that her brief return to the stage was over. Though Vi planned to threaten to tattle on Diana to the rest of the company in order to keep her from trying anything similar in the future, she knew in that moment she would probably never actually do it. If this got out, Diana would never work in the New York theater scene again. That was quite a price to pay for a few youthful indiscretions. Granted, most youthful indiscretions did not involve arson, but far be it from Vi to cast the first stone in a glass house.

Vi crept to the dressing room. The door was ajar, so she peeked inside and saw Diana kneeling in front of what remained of Enid's dress. She had a pin held in the corner of her mouth, bobbing along as she sang and making the words garbled. Though the lacey overlayer had been the main victim of the flames, the layers of fabric below were stained gray and brown. The hemline on the same side as the worst of Enid's burns had been eaten away by the fire, leaving a wide gap. Based on the bolt of fabric and sewing scissors at her side, Diana evidently intended to repair the damage rather than starting from scratch.

The door creaked on its hinges as Vi pulled it open wider and she cleared her throat to announce her presence. Diana turned to her with a delighted smile, but it faltered when she saw who it was at the door. She had dark circles below her eyes and she slumped under the weight of fatigue; both factors that shored up the premise that she had been burning the midnight oil in the course of her sabotage.

"Expecting someone?" Vi asked, arching a brow.

Diana sighed and pulled the pin out of her mouth. "I'm busy. Do you need something?"

"Strange about the dress, wasn't it?"

To Vi's surprise, Diana's face crumbled and she managed to look even more dejected. "It was all like some horrible nightmare."

"Not just for you, I imagine." Vi stepped farther into the room and slid a chair out from the makeup counter.

"Well, of course, poor Enid! It must have been terrifying. When I saw what was happening, I just froze," she replied, shifting her gaze back to her work.

"Ironic, is it not? To freeze in the face of fire."

Diana picked up her scissors. "She was lucky you were there and had your wits about you, at least."

Vi swallowed roughly. "Is that really how you feel?"

"What? Of course I do!"

"But you were jealous of her, weren't you?" Vi asked. "Her and Daphne?"

Diana shifted out of her kneel so she sat on the floor, gazing up at Vi with blue eyes wide and doll-like. "Is that what they're saying?" she whispered.

"Answer the question."

"Well, I suppose a little, but—"

"And you had access to their costumes."

Diana scoffed. "Of course I did! I have access to yours as well."

Vi eyed the pair of shears she still clutched in her hand. "Is that a threat?"

"No!"

"How did you manage the sandbag?" Vi asked, leaving her no space to think. "Did you ask Charles to do it for you? Jack?"

The other woman scrambled to stand, nearly toppling over in her haste. Vi shot to her feet as well, careful to keep the chair between her and the potential weapon. No eddies told her Diana intended to use it, not yet at least, but a pang of anxiety told Vi that it was better to be safe than sorry.

"You really think I am capable of such things?" Diana asked.

Vi's brows crept up her forehead. "So, you're not denying it?"

"Of course I am denying it! This is preposterous!" Her hands shook, the knuckles of the one holding the scissors pale with exertion. "I have put my whole life into this show, this company. Why would I throw it all away?"

The quiver in her voice and the strain on her face made Vi wonder if she was questioning the right person. She shifted tactics. "I know about you and Charles."

Diana gawked for a moment before regaining some semblance of composure. "I have no idea what you are talking about." This time, her rapid blinking and the way she reached to her ear with her free hand revealed her tells to Vi. She had not exhibited either behavior a moment before. Could she have been telling the truth?

"Do not fret," Vi said, gentling her tone. "I am not planning to tell anyone."

Whether because of the verbal onslaught or her exhaustion, Diana let her facade fully crack. She reached out to the dressmaker's dummy beside her to steady herself before sighing, "Thank you. Juno would fire him for sure."

Vi made herself sound as sympathetic as possible, inveigling some trust between them before continuing with her questions. "I think you are probably correct. Those two are like oil and water."

"They were getting along fine until he and I...."

Vi gave her a commiserative nod, then offered Diana the chair she held before her. The other woman gratefully took the seat and set the scissors down on the table.

"Tell me. Do you think he might have done it? Done it for you, I mean?"

Diana craned her neck to look at Vi's face. "What? Dropped the sandbag?" Vi nodded and the other woman looked back at the floor in front of her, anger rising in her tone. "That was an accident. But if you are so keen on accusing him of something, he will be here any moment. You can ask him yourself."

Vi moved to kneel in front of her. Now that Vi knew her newest suspect was on his way, she needed to make progress with his possible accomplice fast. "Diana, what would you say if I told you it was not an accident?"

"How do you know?"

"That does not matter right now." Vi dismissed her concern with a flick of her wrist. "And what if I told you what happened to Enid was no accident either?"

Diana blinked numbly for a few heartbeats before murmuring, "But why would anyone do such terrible things?"

"Perhaps because he was not able to marry the girl he loved?"

"No!" Diana cried, struggling to rise and failing. "I don't believe you!"

Vi returned to her feet. "No one ever wants to believe the worst of people. But look at the facts."

"Who do you think you are? You've known Charles and me for what? A week?" This time when Diana pushed herself out of her seat, she succeeded, but rocked unsteadily on her feet. "And you have the gall to make these kinds of accusations? To say...to say...."

The dancer's knees buckled, her eyes rolling up into her head. Vi barely had time to catch her as she crumpled to the floor.

CHAPTER 28

Vi laid Diana out on her back and called her name. Her eyes did not flutter, not even when Vi gently tapped her cheek. This appeared to be a good, old-fashioned swoon of the type Vi had occasionally pretended to succumb to as a distraction during a job, but had only experienced in real life en route to Chicago. If Diana had not looked so haggard nor wobbled on her feet like a newborn colt for the moments leading up to her fall, Vi may have suspected the dancer of the same kind of subterfuge. But as far as she could tell, Diana was not faking.

A voice rose up in the hallway, accompanied by the thud of footsteps. "Diana?" Charles called. "Are you all right?"

Vi put some distance between herself and the unconscious woman just as he burst through the door like a berserker.

"What happened?" he asked, his wild eyes flashing between Vi and his beloved. He crouched down beside Diana and gathered her into his arms. "I heard shouting."

Vi fought to keep her expression neutral, wary of what he might do if he knew about her suspicions. She put a small quaver of theatrical panic into her voice. "I don't know! She just collapsed."

Charles stroked Diana's cheek and whispered her name, his throat constricted with the force of his emotion. Her body remained limp, her head lolling. He scooped her up as if she weighed nothing and moved toward the door.

"Where are you taking her?" Vi asked as she followed him down the hall.

"I...I have no idea," he rasped. "Help. We need help."

"Has anything like this ever happened before?"

"No. Not that I know of anyway."

Vi trotted ahead and held the side door open for him. "Take her to her room. It is likely just exhaustion."

"Yes. Exhaustion," he repeated.

They crossed the knee, and Vi tugged at his sleeve, bringing him to a stop. "I am going to ask around if anyone has any salts. I will meet you there. Yes?"

He nodded, then rushed across the deck. Minerva and a handful of the rest of the troupe were scattered around, but at the sight of Diana's drooping form, they all dropped whatever conversation they'd been having. They had the good sense to leave Charles to his errand, but immediately accosted Vi with questions. She told them a version of the truth. Before she could ask if anyone had smelling salts, Minerva held up her hand for silence.

"What were you doing over there in the first place?" she asked, jutting out one hip and placing her hand on it.

"I was giving her an update on Enid," Vi lied. "She will be just fine, in case you were wondering."

Minerva tossed her hair and rolled her eyes. "Yes, I know. I have been to see her."

"Diana, on the other hand, could use some smelling salts. Does anyone carry them?"

Most of the people murmured and glanced around nervously, but Minerva huffed a sigh. "Yes, I have a vinaigrette, but not here. It is in my room."

"If you would be so kind as to fetch it for me and meet me at Diana's cabin?" Vi asked. "I want to find her brother and tell him what happened."

The juggler piped up. "Last I saw him, he was with Bulloch up in the pilothouse. I can bring him down if you want."

Vi bobbed her head in thanks and he took off at a run. She gave Minerva a by-your-leave gesture, and the pair departed for the boiler deck. Bonnie was descending from the hurricane deck just as Vi reached the level where the Belles were housed. She was clutching her head—no doubt to ward off the pounding of her alcoholic breakfast—but she dropped her hand when she caught sight of Vi.

"I heard a commotion," Bonnie mumbled, eyes bleary. "What is happening? Is it Enid?"

Vi's bruised pride made her stand up tall, her chin held high. "Nothing that concerns you."

"Have it your way." Bonnie turned on her heel, her hand once again gripping her head. "I'm going back to bed."

Minerva looked between the two with a probing glance, but instead of prying, she pointed to the door behind Vi. "That one is Diana's room." She pointed at another room a few doors down. "That one's me. I will be right back."

As she waited, Vi upbraided herself for her display of disdain toward Bonnie. It undoubtedly would not help her return to her friend's good graces, but the instinct to put even more distance between the two was stronger than her desire to reconcile, for the moment at least. Vi walked to Diana's door as she hardened her heart against the inevitable moment Bonnie finally left her just like everyone else.

Vi twisted the knob and stepped into Diana's quarters. The state rooms were larger and better appointed than the crew quarters, just as Sam had said, but he was also right about the quality of air. Vi dragged the still, humid air into her lungs, made all the heavier by Charles's rapid breathing. He had his fingers twined through his hair as he paced, and he rushed to Vi as she entered.

"Did you find any salts?" he asked.

Minerva entered at the same moment, a phial in her hand. Her eyes flicked between the still form of Diana on the bed and Charles's tortured expression before she passed over the metal bottle, no larger than Vi's thumb. Vi unscrewed the top and waved the vinaigrette under Diana's nose. When the first pass had no effect, she gave the bottle a sniff. The salts had been dissolved into a perfume, but the shock to her nostrils was unmistakable. She tried again, but there was still no hint of movement from Diana.

"Wh-what does that mean?" Charles asked. "Is she going to be all right?"

"It may be more than exhaustion," Vi admitted, screwing the cap back onto the smelling salts and bending closer to Diana. Vi gently pulled one eyelid open, then the other, but only the whites of her eyes showed.

"I'll tell you what it is." Minerva's voice dripped with bitterness. "It's the curse. We're jinxed, just like the papers said."

Vi twisted to look at her. "That's absurd."

"We cannot seem to catch a break!" Minerva huffed. "We lost our first Venus, and by some miracle we found Enid. But now she's hurt. Diana's, well, look at her! And Juno is...beside herself." The pause was incremental, but enough to make Vi wonder what Minerva's first choice of word had been. Embezzling? That would certainly jibe with Charles's complaints. Terrible to work for? That would fit, too. "I think we must be haunted or something," Minerva finished lamely.

"That is even more absurd." Vi allowed one side of her mouth the curl. If there had been a ghost at work, she definitely would have figured that out by now. The living were far more difficult to get a read on.

Minerva opened her mouth to reply, but as Jack stepped into the room she changed her mind and melted out of the way. Vi stood up to allow him to sit at his sister's side.

He took her hand and held it to his heart. "What happened?"

"Where have you been?" Charles asked.

Jack shot him a frustrated glare. "I had some words with the first mate, but I came as soon as I heard about it."

"I-I just found her this way." Charles's fingers snaked back into his hair, leaving furrows and spikes in their wake. "She won't wake up."

"She has not yet woken up," Vi corrected. "That does not mean that she will not."

Jack nodded absently and touched Diana's hair. "What can I do?"

"Give this a try again in an hour." She held out the phial of smelling salts. "Do not panic if it does not work the second time either. She may just need to sleep for a while. If three hours pass and it still does not rouse her, then perhaps, *perhaps*, we shall need to take stronger measures. But there really is not much else we can do until we make port next."

He took the bottle. "What was Minerva saying about being haunted?"

"Oh, nothing. Just something the papers put in her head."

A storm cloud settled on his brow. "I think she may be right."

"Piffle," Vi said. "There is nothing at all supernatural at work here. People faint. Accidents happen." Her confidence wavered as she spoke the last words. Except for her own problems on the stage, nothing else that had happened since they all boarded *The Piasa* had been an accident. A curse did not require magic to be real; just someone willing to see it through.

Vi had been assuming that all of the so-called accidents had been committed against a single individual, but it was looking more and more as if anyone could be a target.

CHAPTER 29

During the next several hours, *The Piasa* wended its way through bends rife with sand bars. Many members of the crew came over to help with steering. Vi would have liked to have offered assistance, even if just for a distraction, but between Bulloch's words and the fear of running into Bonnie again, Vi stayed in her room on *Apple Blossom* for most of the day.

She was far from lonely, however, with the pair of ghosts keeping her company. Even though she had done little that day, Vi found herself growing more weary with every passing moment. She tried to convince herself it was just the stress of the day, but she could not ignore the telltale pull of energy out of her body via the gash in her aura. Her head throbbed, and she had her face buried in the crook of her elbow to block out the light, which did nothing to block out the iridescent shapes of the ghosts nor their bickering.

Upon Peter's request, she'd retrieved a checkerboard Henry had found in a cupboard in the mess hall. Now the ghosts were engaged in what was proving to be an interminable tournament. They had been trading wins all afternoon and were now trying to decide the best of seven. Peter knelt beside her small desk, his eyes level with the board and face stony with concentration. He reached out a hand and furrowed his brow as he attempted to pick up the checker to take one of Henry's pieces. Vi sensed the energy coalescing in his fingertips where he gathered his strength as a brighter glow, but despite his effort, he only managed to nudge it.

"If you can't jump it, then you can't take the piece and you will have to forfeit," Henry said, his voice imbued with a tone of indelible truth.

"I've been doing it all day," Peter whined. "And that sounds like a rule you just made up because you know I'll win." He glared even harder at his red checker and made another attempt to pick it up. She could not see the checker itself, but based on how he moved, the game piece stirred but did not rise. He groaned out his frustration.

The other ghost lifted his hands defensively. "I don't make the rules."

"Yes you do," Peter replied, getting to his feet. "You did it just now."

"This is *dead man's* checkers. It's got its own rules."

"You made that up, too!"

Henry crossed his arms. "I assure you, I didn't. You reckon we're the first spirits to play checkers? I learned the rules from someone else." Peter made a rude noise by way of response, so Henry continued. "Reg'lar checkers is about strategy, but dead man's checkers's also a battle of wills. You have t' be stronger than your opponent in more ways'n one t' be the victor."

"And that is why you wanted to play me," Peter accused. "You knew that you were going to last longer."

"Maybe I just enjoy checkers."

"Cheater!"

"Children!" Vi snapped, throwing her arm to the cot beside her and turning on her side to face them. "If you are incapable of playing together like good little boys, I shall take the toy away." She rose from the bed and stomped over to the board. Before either of them protested, she picked up the piece she thought Peter had been attempting move and jumped it over one of Henry's black pieces. "There. Your move."

Henry mumbled something like "now who's cheating?", but his grousing was interrupted by a knock at the door. Vi swore to herself, worried that whoever it was on the other side had heard her outburst. She steeled herself and opened it enough to let her face fit through the crack.

Charles stood outside, twisting his cap in his hands. He looked as exhausted as Vi felt, but even more so for the sorrow on his face. "Sorry to bother you, Miss. But Di...Diana, she hasn't woken up. Hasn't moved at all."

"Her breathing is still steady?" Vi asked, widening the opening. She was careful to keep the checkerboard out of his line of sight, lest he think she was not only talking to herself, but playing the game alone.

Based on his glassy eyes and drawn face, he probably would not have noticed if Vi had an elephant in the room behind her. "Yes'm. She looks real peaceful, but even when Jack shook her just now, she didn't move a muscle."

Vi closed her eyes against the pounding in her head and pinched the bridge of her nose. "This is beyond my expertize, I am afraid. There are a few hours yet before we are going to tie up for the night. I think if her condition has not changed in that time, you had best fetch a more experienced doctor to look her over."

"Is there something else we can do right now? Anything at all?"

"Just make sure she's comfortable. That is really the only thing we can do from here. You could turn her on her side, I suppose, just in case she retches." He blanched at the mention of effluvium, so she added a hasty, "But I do not think that is likely."

He thanked her, donning his wrinkled cap as he left, the weight of defeat heavy on his shoulders.

"Our Snow White is still sleeping?" Henry asked as the door clicked shut.

Vi leaned her back against the door. "And I am starting to wonder if her sleep is every bit as unnatural. Tell me, if we were dealing with our own version of a poisoned apple, what would be your guess?"

He quirked an eyebrow at her. "I thought Diana was your prime suspect. You think now she's another victim?"

"I am not ruling out the possibility. So, what do you think?"

Henry rubbed his hands together, excited to use his skills once again. "She just collapsed out of the blue?"

"Well, no. Not completely. She was pretty shaky on her feet just before she fainted. Even this morning when I first saw her, I noticed she was looking a bit under the weather."

"That means we can rule out cyanide," Henry said. "It's nearly instantaneous. And with no foamin' at the mouth, I'd say strychnine is also off the table."

Peter interjected, "If it is poison, that would be a whole lot more direct, not to mention deadly, than anything else that has happened so far. Do you really think the perpetrator would change tactics so drastically? Perhaps this could be a coincidence, and she's just exhausted, as you originally thought?"

Vi smirked. "Do you remember what Pru said about coincidences?" She turned her attention back to Henry. "What else could it be?"

"Arsenic is fairly easy to get ahold of. It doesn't have a taste or smell, and though it doesn't dissolve in water, the powder is simple enough to mix into food or sprinkle on top. It can even be inhaled if a poisoner wants and then goes to work in a few hours."

"Easy to get from where?" Peter asked.

"Oh, a general store might carry it. It is good for pest control. Or you can definitely get it from—"

"An apothecary," Vi interrupted. "Like the one we saw Minerva leaving in Memphis."

Peter took a moment to consider. "But it sounds as though she would be the last person to do anything to hurt the show. She wants it to go on."

"That is what she *says*, but who knows what she really *feels*?" Vi asked. "I have hardly spoken with her at all, aside from trading barbs here and there. If the girls are under contract, for instance, and she wishes to break it once they return to New York, breaking up the act on the way home would be an easy out."

"She was on the stage when the sandbag fell, wasn't she?"

"We already theorized the culprit was not working alone," Vi pointed out. "There were at least a dozen people mulling around when that happened. It easily could have been someone else who dropped the bag. I thought before it was Charles, but you saw how wrecked he is by what happened to Diana. There is no chance he was the poisoner."

"If there even *was* a poisoner," Peter added.

Vi waved away his objection. "For the time being, I think we need to operate as if it were poison, at least until we can rule it out for sure. I need to get into Minerva's room and find out what she bought in Memphis. If I don't find anything, that will not mean too much because she may have thrown the evidence overboard. Or someone else did it. But if I do find something suspicious, at least I would be able to go to Juno with something more concrete than a bad feeling in my gut."

"I will come snoop with you," Peter declared. "I am tired of checkers, dead man or otherwise."

"So, does that mean you forfeit?" the other ghost asked archly.

Peter scowled, but before he could respond, Vi said, "Go ahead and finish your game. I need to figure out where she is first and whether or not I can even go in and take a look around right now." She smirked. "If you need a little extra juice to move the pieces, why not go snack on Bulloch? He must be skulking around somewhere."

"I thought you were against that kind of thing," Henry said.

"For that odious man, I think I could make an exception."

Peter pulled a sour face. "If that is my only option, I'll pass. I find him just as repellent as you do."

"I agree," said Henry. "There's somethin' awful strange about his aura."

Vi slipped on her shoes. "I will leave the two of you to puzzle that out. I have my own mystery to solve."

"Be careful," Peter said. "And I think you should start wearing your knife around again. Just to be safe."

She chuckled as she reached for the door handle. "It would not have much affect against arsenic. But if it will make you feel better, I will."

Joking aside, the thought had occurred to her as well. Her personal knife and harness were still in the dressing room with the rest of the trappings of the act. In all of the hullabaloo, Vi had not yet gotten around to telling Juno she would no longer be performing. Whether or not she would need them, collecting her personal affects was a good excuse to go roaming around the ship and see if Minerva was occupied.

If the cat was away, this mouse would try to catch herself a poisoner.

CHAPTER 30

This time when Vi entered the theater, it was like night and day. The musicians were at their places on the floor in front of the stage, and the Belles were gathered above. Everything was set for the opening of the second act. Enid was in the middle of singing her solo and moving around the stage, more than likely trying to acclimate herself to the pain of her burns. She still had no new costume, but instead wore a plain muslin dress. Her bandages were visible when she moved, but Vi could not see any indication that there was any bleeding despite her being up and about. Enid kept at least three feet between herself and the footlights even though they were cold and unlit at present.

Juno reclined on her chaise, but watched the singer attentively as she did her number. Vi was at the edge of the stage just as Enid finished and took a bow. The plucky girl spotted Vi and waved to her, then bowed again to imaginary applause. Soldiers were the ones who had the reputation for being tough. Knowing what kind of pain Enid had to be in right now, Vi couldn't help but think the honor should be shared with actresses as well.

"That will do," Juno said, rising. "As long as you feel up to it, I see no reason why you cannot perform. And our resident nurse agrees?"

Vi startled and replied, "Giving some more recovery time would help, of course. But yes, I think she will be up for it by the time we reach Vicksburg."

Juno put her hands on her hips. "We are going to do Helena, actually. It is somewhat of a backwater, but we need to make up for Memphis. And perhaps we shall stop in Greenville as well."

"But that would mean performing tonight! Aren't you a woman down?"

"Luckily for me," Juno said, jerking a thumb at the wings, "I had a willing replacement on hand."

Vi looked to where she pointed and found Bonnie standing alongside Minerva and Ceres. Unlike the rest of them, the little brunette was in costume, the one Diana had worn during the second act. Minerva was giving her some instructions about where she needed to stand, and what cue to listen for. Bonnie must have felt the weight of Vi's gaze, because she looked over at the same time before pointedly turning her attention back to Minerva.

Vi leaned on the edge of the stage and beckoned Juno closer. "Do you really think that is a good idea?" she whispered.

"She fits the costumes. And she will not need to remember more than a few lines." Juno regarded Bonnie with greed in her eyes. "I think she has some real potential."

"I have no doubt," Vi replied. "But what I mean is, well, given everything that has happened...?"

Juno let out a sound of disgust as she straightened. "Please do not tell me you believe in this curse business as well. I thought you at least had a more level head than that. I have had a difficult enough time as it is keeping things together in the face of that nonsense. We need this. And besides, I hear it is none of your business anymore."

"Ah, yes." Vi grimaced. "So, Bonnie told you?"

Juno regarded her for a moment, then nodded curtly. She spun on her heel and paced over to Enid, casting her words over her shoulder. "It is a shame you are not feeling up to it, your act was a crowd pleaser. Before everything happened with Enid, I was meaning to tell you so. But if you are not willing—"

"But I—"

"Or able," Juno said, her voice dripping with condescension as she flashed a glance at Bonnie and raised her brows. "Then I think you should collect your things and be on your way. We do not have much time before we reach Helena, and there is much work to be done."

Vi sighed and nodded. Whatever Bonnie had said to Juno by way of explanation, it appeared to leave little room for argument. Even though it had been Vi's intention to quit anyway, Juno's words stung, though not as much as the knowledge that Bonnie was now squarely in the crosshairs. Vi took the stairs leading up to the stage and went straight for where Bonnie and the pair of Belles were working together.

"Next, you will need to bring in the flower arrangement that Midas touches," Minerva said.

Ceres indicated a prop table on the opposite side of the stage. "It is the one that is normal on one side and gold on the other. Juno conceals it from the audience, and then she turns it around to achieve the effect."

"Excuse me, but may I have a word?" Vi asked, barely containing her ire at Minerva's proximity.

Bonnie and the other women exchanged a heavy glance before the little brunette nodded. "I will be with you in a minute," she said.

Once the Belles had moved a short distance away, Vi hissed, "This is a very bad idea."

"What does it matter to you?" Bonnie said. She tried to convey an air of imperiousness with the set of her shoulders and the rise of her chin, but she could not hide her pout.

"It matters quite a lot," Vi replied. "I do not want to see you get hurt."

Bonnie's nostrils flared, but she did not point out the irony. Instead, she whispered, "Look, you were right. I admit that. Something terrible was about to happen and your focus was split. You should have told me what was happening, but I do understand why it happened. However, if we are not doing our act together, you are not going to be here to keep anyone safe. So the least I can do is step in." She crossed her arms and raised her voice. "Besides, *they* need me."

Vi scoffed, "*I* need you." She lowered her tone back to a whisper. "And most importantly, I need you alive and unharmed."

"This is not your decision." Bonnie did a half-turn, but Vi could still see her trying to contain her quivering lip. The young widow may have wanted to toughen up, but she still had a long way to go.

"You do not know what you are saying." Vi flicked her eyes to Minerva and back, trying to put as much meaning into glance as possible, but Bonnie refused to look her in the face. Vi whispered, "There are things you do not know. Important things."

Bonnie mistook Vi's meaning and her frown deepened. "I am a fast learner. I will get the part right."

"No. I mean you could be in very real danger. *Everyone* could be. Not just Enid or Juno."

The other woman's expression softened. "What do you—"

Minerva's voice cut in. "Bonnie, dear, we really need to get back to work."

"Be right there!" she called. To Vi she said, "We can talk later, all right? And you can tell me everything. But right now, I have to go."

Before Vi could say anything else, Bonnie skipped off to heed Minerva's call. More talking was not going to solve anything at this moment anyway. What Vi needed to do was try to find some proof of wrongdoing. With something concrete in hand, she could hopefully talk some sense in to Juno about canceling the show. And at minimum, at least, Vi now knew that none of the Belles would be returning to their rooms any time soon.

She went into the dressing room and retrieved the knives, then beat a hasty retreat back to the state rooms. With almost everyone over on *The Piasa* either helping to steer or getting ready for the next performance, she did not meet anyone on her way back. So, there were no witnesses as she approached Minerva's door. Even so, her heart thudded as she used her knife to jimmy the lock.

For as neat and tidy as Minerva always appeared, her room was more akin to the scene after a tornado touched down. Frilly undergarments and other accoutrements were strewn about the room without rhyme or reason, and nearly every drawer was ajar. It was possible someone else had already come rifling around, or perhaps this was simply the natural state for the dancer's bedroom. At least it would mean that Minerva would probably not notice if anything was out of place when she returned. However, it would make Vi's job more difficult.

She started with the dresser drawers, then checked under the bed. When that did not turn up any packet of white powder, she moved to the writing desk. As in Sam's room, there was a bottom drawer that could be locked, but Minerva had not taken advantage of it. Vi worked her way from the bottom to the top. She reached the final drawer.

There was a small packet inside stamped with the apothecary's mark. She held it her palm, turning it this way and that until she found a loose corner. Gently, Vi slipped the parcel open and pinched the edges to make the opening wide enough to peer inside. Instead of the loose arsenic powder she was expecting, she found about a dozen pills.

A tingle crept across Vi's shoulders, and she looked around her in a panic as she realized someone was approaching. She hid the packet behind her back as they drew closer and tried to figure out a place to hide. Finding none, Vi took a deep breath and pushed her extra layer of awareness out to feel for the shape of the approaching presence. She touched on Diana first, the flicker of her outline barely visible. If Vi had not sensed Charles so strongly sitting next to her, she may not have believed it was a person lying on the bed at all.

To Vi's great relief, it was the glowing blue shape of Peter who made his way down the promenade rather than Minerva. Vi pulled her power back, and though it had made her head swim again to do it, she was relieved when she knew to anticipate the ghost passing through the door rather than a flesh and blood person.

"Did you find it?" he asked.

Vi held out the packet of pills for him to see. "I found something. But I am not really sure what it is."

Peter squinted at the contents. "Those are mercury tablets."

"Mercury? Are you sure?"

He snickered. "Spending hours in a cigar lounge with a group of rascals taught me more than how to blow smoke rings," Peter said. "You have heard the saying, 'One night with Venus and a lifetime with Mercury'?"

"You mean syphilis?" Vi asked, shaking the packet until one of the pills landed in her hand. "Surely not. She does not show any signs of it. Aside from a general nastiness, I suppose. But that is not a mood swing. She if *very* consistent in that regard."

"It could be for treating something else, I suppose," the ghost replied, holding his hands wide. "But those pills are a common treatment for the Spanish Pox."

Vi arched a brow as she examined the tablet. "Mercury can also be quite detrimental to one's health, can it not? People sometimes suffer as much or more from the treatment as the disease itself."

"You think this is what Diana took?" His brow furrowed. "It would be much harder to hide this than arsenic."

"Still, it is a possibility," Vi replied. "Enough of a possibility that I can at least talk to Juno about it."

"Is there anything you can do first to find out if it was mercury poisoning?"

Vi tipped her hand until the pill rejoined its brethren in the parcel, then she folded the edge back over and slipped the packet down the front of her dress. "Bonnie is a Belle now. Or at least, performing with them for the time being. I do not want her to spend a second more on that stage with Minerva than she has to."

"Now, Vi," Peter said. "Though she is not pleasant, if Minerva is afflicted rather than guilty, it could be terrible for her if people find out. What if you get her fired?" He crossed his arms and raised his brows. "Are you sure this is not about Sam?"

"Certainly not!" Vi said.

Peter's skepticism remained written all over his face and his tone turned acerbic. "I saw the way you were together. How you are drawn to him, the tension. You think I do not recognize the signs? If you were a stranger and I was playing another round of 'case the place,' I would definitely peg the two of you for a couple."

As the ghost's words pelted her, Vi's breath came fast and shallow. "I told you," she gritted, "we are just friends."

Peter's spirit flesh was eddying now, his whole body a series of miniscule whirlpools made of dark clouds. "Yeah, friends who make doe eyes at each other."

"You are being ridiculous."

"Am I?" he roared.

The force of his tone set Vi back on her heels. No, not just his voice, he had pushed against her with an outpouring of energy. She dropped her gaze to his legs, and found that fissures were seeping into the mist of his body, cerulean fire creeping around the edges.

Vi swallowed down her anger and lowered her voice. "Peter, I do not think you are well."

"You just do not want to admit it!" The ghost started to pace. "He makes you feel normal. Like you belong. And I, well I—"

"You have been on the water too long, and you are overextending yourself," she said, taking a step forward. "You are not yourself."

"You are just trying to distract me!" His voice dripped with malice as he came undone. The last voice that she'd heard sound that angry was in the memory of Jane. She did not believe Peter would ever hurt someone on purpose, but the monster standing before her may be capable of anything on instinct.

Vi inched closer and raised one hand. "Peter, please, let me help you."

As he readied himself for another verbal onslaught, the cracks in his body widened. Vi did not allow him the opportunity to protest this time and thrust her hand through his chest. She pushed out with her energy, sharing the last of the reserves she had been able to gather in Memphis. Her body grew cold, and she acutely felt the additional energy she was wasting flowing out of the gash in her aura, but he needed any power she had to give far more than she did right now.

When she was spent, she pulled her hand back. His legs were whole again, his body blazing for a moment before Vi's vision dimmed. She could tell from the clarity of his outline that he had been restored, though her own lack of power now made him more difficult to see than usual. Peter stood frozen, incapable of doing anything more than stare at her as the power coursed through him.

"You are welcome," she said, her mouth taking on a sardonic tilt. "And despite your hysterics, you are right. I should see if I can determine whether it was mercury that brought Diana down or not before I go to Juno."

CHAPTER 31

Vi left Peter to absorb what she had given him. Despite her head's best impression of a paddlewheel, she managed to keep from stumbling until she was out of Minerva's cabin. As she steadied herself against the wall, a shiver wracked her body. All Vi wanted to do was to go to sleep for three days. However, she had a patient to check and a show to stop, and they drew closer to their destination every moment. Her leaden feet did not wish to move at first, but after a brief argument, she convinced them to shuffle her along to Diana's room.

She slouched her way in, and Charles immediately shot to his feet when the door opened. With everything else going on, she had forgotten he would be there. "I need a few moments with Diana, if you please."

"Has there been news? Do you have a way to treat her?"

She did not want to crush the light of hope in his eyes, so Vi replied, "Perhaps. But I need to do an examination. Just us ladies. And I think you could use a break."

"Right," Charles said, brushing the wrinkles from his clothes. His stomach evidently detected the shift in subject matter and gurgled its seconding of Vi's suggestion. "I could do with a spot of something to eat, I suppose. It has to be, what? Noon already?"

Vi smirked. "Try sometime after four. I would say well past time for some lunch. You go on and get your strength up. No sense having you pass out from exhaustion as well."

She stepped into the room to let him pass, eager to take his vacated chair. But before she could sink into it, Charles turned back and said, "Thank you for looking after her."

Vi gave him a nod of acknowledgement and waited until the door had closed fully before she slumped into the wooden chair by Diana's cot. In reality, the only thing she really could do was smell the other woman's breath and check for the telltale metallic tang that mercury could leave behind. It had already been several hours since it would have been administered, though, so even that was a long shot. Still, she needed to be able to say she had tried everything within her power before she went to Juno.

Jack had taken her advice to move Diana onto her side, and she looked for all the world like she was simply sleeping. Vi hesitated for a moment before remembering that if anything she did were to wake the other woman, it would be cause for celebration. She reached out and gently pulled Diana's lower jaw open. Vi put her face in the path of her patient's nearly non-existent stream of breath. Though she did not detect the scent of metal, Vi did feel the trickle of her senses warning her of danger. She was far too depleted to reach out and determine who, so she settled for sitting back in her chair and awaiting whoever happened to enter the room.

The handle rattled and the door opened a few inches to reveal a tawny, close-cropped beard. "May I come in?" Sam asked.

Vi swallowed hard before replying in the affirmative, her mind shifting to their last conversation that had nearly sent both *The Piasa* and his hopes for the future sinking to the bottom of the river. "Well hello, Captain," she croaked.

"Oh, it's you. I mean...that is to say...hello."

Sam's ears flushed pink as he stuttered, and Vi could not help but smile. The invisible string between them tightened, and despite him being on the far side of the room, she swore she could smell him.

The moment stretched and he looked more and more uncomfortable, so Vi tossed him a lifeline. "Come to check on our patient?"

"Why, yes," he replied, gratitude making him sound far too chipper to be visiting a woman in a coma. He cleared his throat and continued with a far more sober tone. "Has there been any change?"

Vi shook her head. "I am sorry to say no, except that she may be getting even weaker rather than stronger from her time in bed."

"This is what my pride has wrought," he said miserably. "I wanted the Belles to perform even though they were just finishing a tour. But they were all exhausted. I never should have asked."

"You cannot blame yourself," Vi said.

"Sure I can!" he cried bitterly. "They were tired, all of them. And they made mistakes that got Enid hurt. And now Diana is so spent she will not even stir! This was a stupid, selfish enterprise, and I dragged them into it."

Sam looked so dejected, so heavy under the invisible weight of guilt and failure. In that moment, Vi wanted to take away some of the burden shining through his eyes. The sweet, laughing boy she had known had been replaced by this sorrowful man. Before she even realized she'd stood, her palm rested against the familiar curve of his cheek. Sam leaned into the unexpected touch, eyes closing and his hand rising to rest against hers and press her closer. For a few heartbeats, they breathed together into the moment. A warmth trickled from Vi's fingertips and up her arm until her own face flushed.

"None of this is your fault," Vi assured him.

His reply was barely a whisper. "You don't know that."

"Yes, I do." She stroked the ridge of his cheekbone with her thumb, longing for him to meet her gaze. "They were accidents." A white lie to ease his suffering, followed by the truth. "There was nothing you could do."

"I am the captain. I'm responsible for everything that happens on my ship," Sam insisted.

Vi's extra knowledge of events rattled against her desire to keep her abilities hidden from him. He was her last vestige of her life before the war, before she took the path that led her to the person she'd become. Even if he believed her about seeing the dead and her pronoia, he would never look at her the same way again. No one ever did.

Her struggle vanished as Sam rotated his face until his lips could brush against the delicate skin of her wrist. The heat spread down her neck and cascaded through her spine as he spoke. "Vi, there's something I have to tell you. I—"

"Please, don't." She could not bear to let him speak his feelings aloud again with her knowing there was no future. And though she would not be able to give him the solace of giving in, she could at least tell him the truth of what had happened over the past week and allay his guilt. Vi took a shuddering breath. "I need to tell you something first."

He brought his eyes up to meet hers for the first time since she'd reached for him. Some of the pain had drained away, replaced by a bemused affection.

"And what is that?" he asked, pulling her hand gently from his face but keeping her fingers cupped in his.

Vi cleared her throat and studied his collarbone. "It has been a long time, Sam. And things have changed. I have changed."

Sam's knuckle brushed against her chin, gently raising her eyeline. The love that had been glimmering in his gaze a moment before was washed away by fear. To her added surprise, he moved her chin sideways. As he gawked at her cheek, Vi's stomach dropped. She ripped her hand away from his and turned away in shame, the pleasant heat of their contact draining away instantly and replaced by the hollow cold.

But it was too late. He had seen her wound.

"Vi," Sam said to her back. "What was that thing? What's happening to you?"

Her body shook with frustration. Even though she had made the choice to tell him her secret, she had been robbed of the chance to determine how to go about it by the very same. The emotions that had sent her running from her old life now resurfaced, and she had no more power to change things now than she did with Peter. So she had run as far and as fast as she could. It had felt like the only choice left, the only way to protect both of them from her. And here she was again, right back where she started.

She knew she could not stay; but she'd be damned if she didn't get a proper goodbye this time.

"I will tell you everything. Every sordid detail of my life, Sam," Vi said. "But first, I need to do something because I do not think you will want me to afterwards."

Vi raised herself onto her toes and threw her arms around his neck. As their lips met, she was not certain if it was surprise or a shared desire that kept him from recoiling, but as his arms snaked around her back, she knew he would not break the embrace. If this were to be their final kiss, she would be sure to make the most of it.

The gentle rush of warmth morphed into sweeping fire, and she maneuvered an unresisting Sam until his back rested against the wall. She drank him in, his smell, his touch, his solidity. The loneliness of the past few years was like a wide, parched seabed that the kiss was filling. Vi'd had her share of kisses over the years, the most recent with Jeb only a few weeks before. But that had been a brief kiss to show her gratitude. What was happening now felt like her actual survival depended on it.

A low rumble came from Sam's throat, one hand rising to coil through Vi's hair and the other traveling lower. His fingers tightened, sending another rush of sensation all the way down to curl her toes, rippling and rebounding from the soles of her feet to reverberate through her entire body. She melted against him, taking in every drop of the comfort and ardor he had to offer. A sound almost like the tinkling of the tiniest of bells drifted into her ears.

The hand tangled in her hair spasmed, pulling her face away from his as he gasped her name. Her eyes had been closed so hard, shards of crimson light now sparkled along the edges of her vision like rubies dangled just out of sight when she looked at him. Vi felt an animal snarl distort her mouth at the interruption to her satiation, though his attempt to hold back and tease her only made her need stronger.

She moved in to kiss him again, but Sam held her in place. His grip was not so firm she could not have broken it, except that now with the precious inches between them, Vi could take in his glassy, faraway expression and the way his skin stood out stark and pale against the red of his beard. A puff of frigid air escaped as he murmured, "Vi...Stop."

Vi gave her head a shake to clear her vision, but the crystalline red refused to budge and the thousands of miniscule bells chimed even louder. Sam's head dropped forward and his body slumped. The wall behind him kept him from crumpling completely, and Vi managed to guide his leaden form to the floor. She knelt beside him, cupping his lolling face in her hands and calling his name, but his eyelids did not even flutter at her entreaties.

She propped him against the wall as best as she could and rose to her feet. Her wild, red-tinged gaze ricocheted around Diana's cabin in search of anything that might help revive him. The flow of energies Vi usually sensed as gentle breezes danced and roiled around the objects in the room, nearly overloading her senses. A pitcher of water sat on the side table, so Vi stumbled over to it, hoping if she splashed some onto Sam's face he would wake up. Her hands shook as she tipped it over a glass, the water sloshing over the edge and spreading across the table.

Vi took a deep, steadying breath and caught sight of her reflection in the mirror. Her own face looked strange, but it took her a few heartbeats to realize that it wasn't just the wash of red or the churning waves of energy around her that caught her eye. She reached up to where the seeping blue wound had been for the past weeks. Her cheek was now smooth and unblemished.

The jingling in her head grew even louder, and her sense of danger added its own screech of awareness to the sound. Vi spun around, trying to gather her thoughts enough to offer whoever had just entered the room some kind of explanation for Sam's prostrate state.

The doorway remained empty, the door swinging gently as the ship rocked along down the river. Then her gaze fell on the bed and the sleeping woman, and where she expected to see the pale, pearly aura of the living, a shimmer of orange surrounded Diana. The light refracted into ever-moving shards, but only extended a few inches from her body. What she saw blocking a section of the Titian glow stole her breath.

A creature was uncoiling itself from Diana's head and neck. Its body was made of something so dark that she almost mistook it for a shadow, except for the way the carapace glinted in the crimson of her heightened vision. On insectile, faceted legs, the foot-long entity drew itself away from its victim's spine, carefully removing a proboscis from the back of Diana's skull. Vi stood frozen in place as the obsidian thing regarded her with a set of ten crystalline spheres set into what must be its face, though the thing before her was so alien she could not know for sure if they were eyes or some other sensing structure.

It curled the front half of its body up, the upper legs shaking. The jingling sound growing even louder as it made its display. The thing rose into the air, its flat body undulating and whorls of aether eddying in its wake. It did not so much float as swim through the once invisible currents, flashing its iridescent underbelly at Vi before slipping through the wall.

She could still feel its presence for several seconds as it retreated, taking the peel of bells along with it. When she finally ripped her gaze away from where it had gone through the wall, her thoughts rushed to Diana, lying unconscious a few feet away. Vi scrambled to the bed and clutched the other woman's shoulder. She doubted calling her name would do any more good now than it had before, so Vi gently rolled her body to get a better look at where the thing had been clinging to her.

Though Diana's mussed, corn silk hair was in the way, Vi's ruby-lined vision showed her a round lesion, as if someone had pushed a finger through the base of her skull. When Vi touched it, a shining blue substance, both familiar and terrifying, came away on her fingers. The spirit energy seeped into her fingertips, blazing scarlet before fading into Vi's body as she absorbed it.

Vi recoiled in disgust at what lay before her, almost tripping over Sam's outstretched legs as she backed away from the bed. Her eyes fell on him as she steadied herself against the doorframe, and she noticed the halo of color emanating from his body for the first time. Except Sam was the purest, most beautiful shade of lavender she had ever seen. She stood in awe for a moment, catching her breath as her mind reeled. His condition appeared to be the same as Diana's, but Vi could not see any trace of a second presence or wound on his head to explain it.

Though the action would do nothing to remove the stolen energy from her hands, she rubbed them against her skirt until her palms were raw. Vi dared not approach either of the supine figures again—not that she had any idea what she could do to help either victim in the wake of the strange creature's attack.

And that's when she realized the horrible truth. Sam hadn't been the unwitting victim of a second shadow creature.

Vi was the monster. He was her prey.

CHAPTER 32

It was difficult to tell if a few seconds or a few hours passed while Vi stood in the doorway and willed it not to be true. The thing that finally snapped her out of her stupor was the all too familiar burning itch across her shoulders that told her someone or something was approaching. If the psychophage had returned for a second course, she was unsure what she could even do about it. She steeled herself all the same. With fists clenched, she focused on the approaching energy. As it resolved into the distinct shape of Peter, she let her hands relax.

Though he was still a full deck below her, she could clearly sense his movements as he climbed the stairs. It was one thing to feel an indistinct blur of spirit energy and its general vicinity, but this was almost like the ship itself was made of glass and she could feel every person distinctly. He rounded a corner and started up the next set of stairs, his face drawn with worry.

Somewhere down and to her right, Henry also blazed. He was surrounded by the shining masses of the living, but like the ghosts, they were far more distinct than ever before. Each person's aura was tinged with a different color, though far less distinct and clear than those in the room with her. Minerva had a golden glow, Enid was coral, and Ceres was a deep emerald. Juno had a pale indigo aura, though a kind of sickly dark also twined around her. Even with Vi's extra power, Bulloch remained an ugly, foggy gray.

On reflex, Vi reached out with her mind and touched Henry, and to her surprise, the faraway ghost reacted as if she'd actually tapped him on his shoulder. She could distinctly feel him turning his head this way and that, looking for the source of the sensation. As Mary and Peter had both proven in abundance, the dead were able to touch the living if they worked at it. Vi had never before actually made contact with a ghost like this, and definitely not at a distance.

Peter came barreling around the corner and skidded to a halt. His iridescent blue eyes grew wide as he gazed at her, jaw slack and haste forgotten. "You are...you are so...so beautiful," he whispered.

Despite the machinations of the past few minutes, Vi smirked. "No need to sound so shocked."

"No." His head moved slowly from side to side as he looked her over from head to toe. "You've never looked like this before. I was too far away to see you that night in Chicago, but I could feel you then, and I feel you now. Vi, you are blazing like the sun." When Peter finally tore his eyes from her, he glanced at the floor and took a few noiseless steps forward. "Dear lord! What happened here?"

"Wait!" A mix of panic and shame washed over Vi, and her arm automatically shot out, blocking his way.

Peter looked at it for a moment and sighed. "Let me see." He took a decisive step forward. Vi's gesture should have been futile, but rather than passing through her as they both expected, the ghost slammed into her arm and stumbled backwards. They stood together staring at the offending appendage for a few breaths before Vi sheepishly let him pass.

"There was...something in the room with us," Vi said, squeezing the bridge of her nose and clamping her eyes closed against the scene behind her. Even with her eyes closed, she still sensed the two comatose bodies and Peter moving through the room, examining the stricken people. "I think it may have been one of those psychophages Henry told us about. There was something dark feeding on Diana. Like a centipede from hell, as long as my arm."

The ghost leaned over the woman on the cot. "You saw it?"

"Yes," Vi croaked, rubbing her eyes. "It was wrapped around her neck, her head."

"Where is it now? It's not still in the room, is it?" His voice became shriller as his eyes darted to every corner of the cabin.

The sight of the creature's body flashed across her eyelids, and Vi opened her eyes to dispel it. Her voice grew more confident as she spoke. "Gone. I believe I frightened it. If such a thing is possible. And now Diana has a wound, just like the one I have." Her fingertips brushed across her cheekbone and she corrected. "Had."

The ghost shot to his feet and crossed back to her side. Vi turned her face so he could more easily see the gash had disappeared. He scratched his head, a bemused expression on his face. "I'll be damned. That thing, what, healed you somehow? And then attacked Sam? Or the other way around?"

"No. Sam collapsed, then I saw it." Vi ground her teeth together and studied the floorboards, wishing she could sink through them and out from under his gaze. "I think I did that."

Peter's brow knit together. "What are you talking about?"

Heat crept into her cheeks. "I kissed him." The ghost harrumphed, but she pressed on. "Just one kiss, I swear. A farewell of sorts before I told him about my abilities and that there was no chance for us. And then I nearly killed him."

His head swiveled between Vi and Sam a few times. The ghost took a tentative step toward the other man before crouching down beside him. With every moment of silence, Vi's dread squeezed her tighter. She wanted him to berate her, or cringe away in fear, to do something to reflect the disgust she was feeling about what she had done, but he just knelt there blinking dumbly as he looked the other man over.

Eventually, Peter asked, "He's not dead, is he?" His voice was even, as if he did not care about the answer. Perhaps he was still in shock.

Vi shook her head. She did not need to examine Sam closely to tell he was still breathing. His aura was diminished, but Peter should also be able to see that Sam still glowed like the living should.

The ghost shrugged. "Well, no real harm done, then."

"How can you say that?" Vi cried. She controlled her volume as she pointed to the collapsed form at her feet. "He looks rather harmed from here."

Peter returned to standing, brushing his hands together as if it could also brush away her guilt. "It sounds to me as though you did precisely what Henry advised—"

"Not on purpose!"

"—and people can recover from that—"

"Not always!"

"—Ergo, no harm done."

"Is that so?" Vi hissed. "Then why won't you look at me?"

"Because." The ghost turned his head over his shoulder far enough that she could see the corner of his mouth rising. Despite the small smile, sadness pulled at the corner of his eyes. "You kissed him."

"*That* is what you took from what I said?" she scoffed. "I just drained a man like some kind of vampire and left him lying unconscious at my feet, and you are concerned about a trifling moment?"

Peter finally turned to face her. "Is that all it was?"

"I am not going to do it again, if that is what you are asking."

"No, that is decidedly *not* what I asked." Agitation coiled through the fog of his spirit flesh, then calmed. "But as you say, I suppose it does not matter. This is our more immediate problem." He gestured at the two sleeping bodies.

"Indeed," Vi replied. "Diana is comfortable enough, and her immediate danger has passed. Hopefully, what she needs now is to rest and nothing more. But I do not want to just leave Sam there, and I cannot move him myself. I doubt even if I could convince Bonnie to help, she and I together could move him, especially not without being seen."

"So, what should we do?"

She pushed away from the doorframe. "All anyone else will know is that he collapsed just like Diana did. I should be able to get some of the men to help me get him to his quarters at least." The cogs of her brain clicked together faster as the ruby fog began to clear from her vision. "If they are suffering from a lack of spirit energy rather than some mundane cause, there may be something in the book that can help them. Pru's tea, perhaps."

"Glad to hear you are over your phobia of the book, even if the circumstances are less than ideal."

"Desperate times, as they say," Vi replied, shrugging. "I am reticent to use it for myself, but now there are two other people at stake."

"What about the thing you saw? Do you think it is gone for good?"

She threw her hands up helplessly. "I have no idea. It seemed frightened of me after I...took what I needed from Sam."

"I suppose without leaking energy, you were no longer a good target."

"It was more like it was afraid. As if I were the larger predator." Her eyes grew hot with disgusted, unshed tears. "The scarier monster."

"Lucky for Diana that you were!" Peter said with a grin. "Otherwise, that thing could have sucked her completely dry and we would never know the cause. You just saved her life."

Vi gestured at Sam. "And at what cost?"

"He will be fine." Peter wagged his hand dismissively. "Though he will probably wake up with a very sore neck if we do not get him into his own bed. That does not look comfortable."

CHAPTER 33

Vi clutched the bottle of whiskey as hard as the dread clutched her heart.

Once word spread around the ship that there had been a second mysterious collapse, of the captain no less, all hell had broken loose. Juno ordered her people to go to their rooms and stay there for fear of some kind of disease spreading around the ship. Bulloch stepped in to take Sam's place and ordered them to continue past Helena and on to Greenville where there was a proper hospital.

Vi knew it would do no good, but she was hardly going to protest. It would mean another overnight run on a stretch of river with little to no habitation, which also meant no help if anything went wrong. However, when Bulloch made the announcement, he seemed not only fully committed to the challenge, but confident in their success. Ironically, his habitually gruff demeanor now served to put others at ease. Though people worried about the threat of illness, they had remained calm as they retreated to their rooms. Vi had followed suit, and with her still heightened senses, was able to feel that everyone had indeed followed Juno's orders and were passing the evening alone. Except, of course, for Charles, who continued his vigil at Diana's bedside.

The ghosts, on the other hand, were anything but calm. When Peter told Henry about the psychophage sighting, it sent him into a panic. The two dead men decided to search the ship for any sign of the creature. Their motivation was more or less selfish, but it would have the added benefit of letting Vi know if it had found another living host that would need treatment. If she could figure out what treatment even meant.

Which now left Vi utterly alone with her guilt. Well, not *utterly* alone. She had her whiskey and the family tome laid out on the bed in front of her. The voices of the memories trapped inside spoke louder now than ever before. They may have been screaming offers of help or advice, or they may have been as horrified as Vi at what she'd done. Vi didn't have the stomach to face Alice yet and had been careful not to handle the book directly as she retrieved it from her things and placed it on the bed as she gathered her courage.

She yanked the cork out of the whiskey bottle with her teeth and spat it onto the bed before taking a swig. It was top shelf, imported; far better than she really deserved for all the trouble she had caused. The smoky smell of the peat-imbued liquor tickled into her nose as the tendrils of warmth reached into her belly and released some of the tension from her shoulders.

The red tint to her vision remained, but only barely, like seeing her own eyelashes if she squinted—a visual reminder of her latest sin in a long line of sins. There was deep remorse coursing through her, but the more Vi thought about her circumstances, the angrier she became. She had never asked for any of this, and she had definitely never intended to hurt anyone. She'd only ever wanted to *help*. (Turning a tidy profit came fairly high on the list, too.)

Instead, she spread chaos and destruction in her wake.

Vi sat back against her pillow and took another pull from the bottle. The events of the past week churned in her brain as she examined the different paths she could have taken. She was still no closer to figuring out who was sabotaging the Belles; Diana's collapse had been a red herring. Whatever reason Minerva had for buying the mercury, she had not used it to poison anyone. Vi wracked her brain but could not figure out who would benefit from the show being ruined, but she, herself, had inadvertently seen to it. Without the performances, Sam would continue to be under the thumb of whoever issued his loan when...if he ever recovered.

She glanced at the book and her eye twitched. Though it was true it would probably hold answers, Vi became overwhelmed with the fear that they would not be the answers she wanted. It was just as likely that she would discover she had done real and lasting damage and destroyed her friend along with the last vestige of the innocence in her past.

Vi shifted the bottle to her lap, taking a strange sort of comfort in its weight and solidity, its immediacy. As she ran her thumb over the lip of the bottle, she thought about the last whiskey she had been around. She chuckled at the memory of the happily drunk and perky Bonnie, then her face fell when it was replaced by the angry version of her friend. Now *there* was a situation where Vi could have done something differently.

Vi rose to her feet. She retrieved the cork and shoved it into the top of the bottle before tucking it under her arm. She regarded the book for a moment. "*You* can wait. I have something I need to take care of first."

As Vi left her room and moved to the next door down, part of her knew she was just avoiding the inevitable by delaying her next encounter with Alice. But another louder voice in her head insisted that making up with Bonnie was far more important at that moment and could not possibly be postponed. Besides, Vi needed someone to talk things out with her, and there was no one else she could trust.

When she got to her cabin, Vi felt Bonnie sitting at her writing desk inside her room.

Vi took a deep breath before she gently knocked. "Bonnie? Can we talk?"

The other woman hesitated a moment, but answered the door and beckoned her inside. It was Vi's first time being so close to Bonnie since she could see her color, and the serene, robin's egg blue barely visible at the edges suited her.

Once the door was closed, Bonnie asked, "Is it true? Is there some kind of sickness on board?"

"No," Vi replied with an emphatic shaking of her head. "At least, not anything that can spread."

Bonnie cocked her head. "But two different people have been afflicted. You must be so worried about Sam."

"Same affliction, two causes." Vi set the bottle down on the desk, her gaze wandering over to the letter the young widow had been writing.

"I am telling Mama Murphy about Tobias," Bonnie said. She took a shuddering breath as she moved to the desk and gathered the papers. "I may not have the courage to do it in person, but she should know what happened. And it should be in my handwriting, not something so cold as a telegram."

"You are wrong about me, you know," Vi said, sinking into the chair. "I am not brave. If there is a coward in this room, it is most definitely me. At least you are trying to do the right thing even though it is hard. Given the opportunity, I will run or hide. Every goddamn time."

Bonnie took a place opposite her on the bed. To Vi's surprise, she had a smile on her lips. "You are not hiding from what awaits in New Orleans. And you came over and warned me this morning."

"Yes, so about that—"

"—and you knocked on my door just now. That is something." She blushed and regarded Vi through her lashes. "I have not given you much reason to want to talk."

"Nor have I," Vi said, returning a sad smile of her own. "And I still cannot apologize enough."

Bonnie pointed at the desk. "Why not pour me a glass of your peace offering and give it a try?" Vi nodded gratefully. She stepped to the side table and picked up the glass resting beside the pitcher. The other woman continued, "But just one, mind you. I believe I have quite learned my limits. Most of that afternoon is a blur."

Vi poured a few fingers of whiskey into the glass, careful to keep her back turned as she asked, "What do you remember?"

"I was at the bar with the fellows. They really are a nice lot. Then you came and helped me back to the ship, correct?"

"Yes. But you were not exactly happy to see me." Vi steeled herself as she returned to her chair and passed the glass to Bonnie. She twisted to retrieve the bottle for herself and took a swig to fortify her.

Bonnie nodded her thanks, her face wrinkling as she tried to remember. After a few heartbeats, she broke out in a sheepish smile. "I bet you are glad now you did not give me those boxing lessons."

"It was a rather poor showing." Vi chuckled, then leaned forward, her tone earnest. "But I would still be willing to teach you. That is, unless you are planning to disembark?"

The little brunette took a sip of her drink. She coughed faintly from lack of experience. "Honestly, I have not made up my mind yet. And you did promise you would tell me more about what we might face before I had to decide. So, out with it."

Vi settled back into her chair. "Fair enough. So, as I've told you, I was in New York until I left for the front."

"Then you met Patrick and Peter. And then Peter and you started running confidence games. I know all this."

"There is a part in the middle there that I have not told you yet," Vi said. "And it is vital to the story, because it is the reason I do not trust easily. Not even with people who deserve it."

Bonnie scooted herself until her back rested against the wall. She crossed her ankles and smoothed out her skirt, then motioned at Vi to continue.

"The boys were not regular soldiers. In fact, they were not soldiers at all. They worked for people in the military, which is why 'Trick ended up in my care. But they were not enlisted men. Have you heard of the Pinkertons?"

"I think so. Are they the ones who stop train robbers and the like?"

"Among other things, yes. During the war, they took on missions to aid the Union army."

Bonnie tipped forward, resting her chin on her hand. "Really?"

"Yes. Some of the missions were publicized, but many of them were never acknowledged formally. And in many instances, the agents were sworn to secrecy."

"How exciting!" Bonnie gushed.

"It had its moments."

"Wait, are you saying you were one of them, too?"

"'Trick enlisted me. There were some things only a female agent would be able to accomplish, and he thought I was a good candidate. I had experience on the stage, and I could also act as a field medic in a pinch. And I can be pretty clever, if I do say so myself. So I joined up. I learned some boxing from my father, but 'Trick was the one who really taught me how to fight. And more importantly, how to win a fight. I had good reflexes, something I know now was tied to my rather specialized skillset. At the time we just thought I was an apt pupil."

"This is too much!" Bonnie cried, giddy. "You really are a hero from one of my books."

"I do not think that I would go that far, but things were good, for a time. Peter, 'Trick, and I made quite a team. We were making a difference." Vi huffed a sigh and set her bottle down on the floor beside her. "The only problem is that we were not the only team, and even though the whole Agency was supposed to be working together, we crossed a two-man operation, the Carmichael brothers, who had been taking money from both sides. We could not let it go on, but we also did not know far up the conspiracy went. So, we planned it all out, set ourselves a trap, and—" Her voice hitched.

Bonnie mistook the pause for Vi trying to build suspense. She motioned emphatically for Vi to continue. "And then what?"

"The plan went wrong." Vi swallowed around the lump in her throat. "And Patrick did not make it out. Took one of the Carmichaels with him on his way."

The other woman gasped, and she nearly spilled her drink as her hand became slack. She noticed just before the first drops hit her sheets and cried, "Oh, Vi!"

Vi pushed out the next words, afraid that they would choke her if she did not release them. "There was a third agent, one who was working with the other two. One that I trusted. And that trust cost me my husband." Tears threatened to blur Vi's vision, but she blinked them away. "That's when Peter and I ran. The only people we knew were on our side were each other. We could not take anything with us and we needed money, so that is how the confidence games began. We managed to get some information about the rebel army contacts who had turned our agents along the way, but honestly? Peter and I were both so angry at the world, we did quite a lot of things just out of spite or for amusement. To feel like we had some power back. I am not proud of it."

Bonnie nibbled on her lip. She did not have to say anything for Vi to know the young widow understood the kind of impotent rage Vi described. One moment, the person you loved was a certainty, and then they were simply gone, a puff of smoke in the breeze.

Vi continued, "The war ended before we found out exactly who had been paying off the agents and the trail went cold. Or so we thought. Sometime after my first encounter with a ghost, I met a dead woman who had a confession she needed to make before she could be at peace. It was about her husband, Colonel Edward Sinclair."

"*Your* Colonel Sinclair?"

Vi grimaced. "I prefer not to think of him as 'mine', but yes, the same. He was not just connected to the plot, but central to it."

"So you *married* him?" Bonnie scoffed.

"You must understand. Grant had pardoned the entire Southern army. The Colonel had not, in fact, broken any laws. He and his cronies were simply underhanded. So there was no authority to go to and seek punishment. If we were going to make him suffer, it had to be at our own hands. His wife inadvertently gave me everything I needed to ingratiate myself to him before she passed on." Vi's mouth had gone dry, so she retrieved the bottle of whiskey at her feet and took a swig. "And the rest, as they say, is history."

Bonnie was quiet for a minute, sipping her drink and thinking over what Vi had confessed. Eventually, she said, "Thank you for telling me. Our circumstances were different of course, but I understand. I am angry, too. Tobias...he would still be alive if I had spoken up. If I had put my foot down about his foolhardy idea to go West. I should have been braver. But I just let him convince me everything was going to be all right."

"Is *that* what this bravery talk has been about lately?" Vi asked.

Bonnie nodded. "And also...also I am so scared to be on my own. I knew Tobias since we were children. I have not really known this world without him. I am so lost."

Vi hesitated a moment before closing the other woman's fingers in hers. "And you think learning to fight will make you feel different?"

"I think it could," Bonnie admitted. "If I knew that if it came down to it, I could keep myself safe, then maybe I would not be so afraid."

Vi found herself nodding along to the other woman's words. They echoed her father's sentiment when he knew he would be leaving her alone much of the time and had first taught her about boxing. It was a position Patrick also held years later when he'd taught her everything else she knew.

"I promised I would teach you, and I will," Vi said, slipping her hand out of Bonnie's grasp and settling back into her chair. Her eyes fell to the bottle in her lap. "But there are many ways to be brave, and many ways to be cowardly. I, for one, cannot even bring myself to open Pru's book again."

"Why?"

"It feels as though every time I decide to take a step toward 'embracing my heritage', as Pru would say, only trouble follows."

"But it helped you to know there was something fishy going on with the Belles and the 'accidents.' And that is where you got that trap to contain Mary."

"Exactly my point!" Vi threw her hands up. "I used something in that book to protect myself, and a whole city suffered. Who can say what havoc I would wreak if I learned how to do everything within those damnable pages?"

"It is not as if you meant to burn it down!" Undoubtably Bonnie had intended her words to be reassuring, but they only made Vi cringe. She continued, "You did not make the wind blow. You did not make it the hottest autumn on record. You—"

"Lit the match," Vi sighed. "I lit the match."

Bonnie grabbed her by the shoulders and pulled her to standing. Vi never ceased to be amazed by how such a tiny woman could be so very strong. "If you want to blame anyone, blame that Mary character, or her boss. If she had not come after you, you never would have needed to light the match!" Vi opened her mouth to protest, but her friend silenced her with a stomp of her foot. "No. Not a word. That is the God's honest truth and I refuse to hear the contrary. You are standing here because you lit that match, Viola Thorne, and I refuse to be sorry about it. And neither should you. And furthermore," Bonnie said, releasing her grip so she could wag her finger. "We are going to New Orleans and we are going to find out what happened to Peter and what it has to do with ghosts. There is something happening down there, a person or people that are using the dead to do their dirty work, and there is no one else who can figure out who or why, Vi. No one."

Vi stood stunned for a few heartbeats. "See?" she murmured, "I told you."

"Told me what?" Bonnie asked, chest heaving slightly from her monolog.

A grin split the medium's face. "That I need you."

Without hesitation, Bonnie crushed Vi into one of her steel-girder embraces.

"Thank you," Vi continued, patting her friend's back. "That was exactly what I needed to hear. You are completely right, there are far bigger problems to face once we reach our destination. And I need to stop being such a coward."

Bonnie held out her hand. "Partners?"

"Before we shake on it," Vi said, her elation at their reunion sullied by the final secret she needed to share. "There is one more thing I need to tell you."

CHAPTER 34

Bonnie had finished her glass of whiskey and asked for another splash by the time Vi had finally finished telling her friend everything she had missed over the past two days—the paraffin leading to Vi's accusation of Diana and her subsequent collapse, searching Minerva's room and finding the mercury, and finally the revelation about the creature, and Vi inadvertently healing herself. Bonnie's reaction to what Vi had done to Sam was much along the same lines as Peter. Considering she had just absolved the medium for burning down a city, Vi should not have been wholly surprised, but she was grateful just the same.

Now, the pair of them were standing on the main deck of *Apple Blossom* where the light of the setting sun was still the brightest. Storm clouds were rolling in on the horizon, a menacing gray on top but candy floss pink on the bottom. Soon, some crewmen would show up to man the oars for the overnight run to Greenville and the storm threatened to break within the hour, but for now, it was an excellent place for Bonnie's first lesson. They were less than a week out from New Orleans, and there was plenty of work to do, so in spite of (or perhaps because of) the whiskey they had been sharing, they decided now was as good a time as any to begin.

Vi had equipped Bonnie with the men's clothes she had borrowed from Sam. As she was several inches smaller than Vi in every dimension, they sagged off her petite frame, but they were still better than trying to learn in stays and a skirt. Bonnie had her fists up before her, and one foot in front of the other for balance.

"Bring that one higher," Vi said. "Make your forward hand close to throat level. You will need your forearm to block anything coming at your face."

"I have been to a match before, but they were wearing gloves," Bonnie said, lifting her hand up a few inches. "I don't suppose you have any squirreled away among our possessions, do you?"

Vi pulled the other woman's left hand forward, then shifted her right fist back and lower to protect her midsection. "Yes, in a tournament or some such thing they would likely be using the Marquess's rules. But we are not training you for a fair fight now, are we?"

Bonnie threw a playful jab with her left fist, but Vi saw it coming and knocked it away. The little brunette laughed and bobbed her eyebrows. "No, I suppose we are not," she said, a slight slur to her words.

Vi smirked at the cheekiness, easily knocking away the next weak jab, too. "You will want to strike with the other hand, not the forward one."

"So, now that you know it was not poison," Bonnie said, taking a swing with her right that Vi sidestepped. "Do you think Diana did it?"

"No." Vi chuckled and reached out to flick Bonnie's ear. "You should have seen her when I was questioning her."

Bonnie pursed her lips and threw another punch, harder but not nearly hard enough. Even if Vi could not read the aether, the other woman broadcast her intentions in her stance. Something else to work on.

"Charles?" Bonnie asked.

"Perhaps." Vi gave the other woman a playful flick right between the eyes before dancing out of reach again. "If the motivation is indeed jealousy, it could still have been Minerva even if she did not poison anyone. Or someone else we have not considered yet for reasons I cannot fathom."

Bonnie tried doing two strikes in rapid succession. Vi countered them each with a slap of her open palm. The trainee let out a sound that was one-half frustration and one-half laughter. "I will get you someday. I am sure of it."

"That a fact?"

"Well," Bonnie said, dropping her fists. "I will get someone someday."

"Not punching like that you won't," Vi replied.

The two worked for a few minutes, Vi demonstrating how to add power to a punch by stepping or twisting along with the motion of the arm. Despite her earlier tipple, Bonnie was proving to be fairly coordinated and attentive to the instruction she received.

"Sometimes, you probably will want to strike with an open palm instead, like I was doing. Without gloves to protect your hands, you could easily break something if you hit a face in the wrong place." She remembered the posters plastered onto the Belle's various crates and beckoned Bonnie to follow her over to one. Vi pointed to the smiling woman at the center. "The eye may seem like a great target, and it will make your opponent flinch if they think you are going to hit them there. However, heads are easier to move than bodies, and as you are more than likely shorter than anyone you would face, the chances are good that you would make contact with a jaw instead of something softer. You could easily break your hand rather than your opponent's face."

Vi took Bonnie by the hips, squared her in front of the poster and had her do a few slow punches into the air to illustrate her point. A tickle on the back of Vi's neck told her that Peter was approaching. Hopefully, he had good news about the creature.

She brought her attention back to her pupil. "Doing a feint at the face can be effective though," she continued. "Especially if it looks like you are going to scratch rather than punch. It is only natural to jerk away to protect one's eyes, and that can leave the body more accessible. You will want to concentrate on organs like the kidneys and liver." Vi pointed at the two-dimensional woman's torso, indicating the most vulnerable places before leaving Bonnie to practice on her own.

When Peter finally arrived, she was waiting for him. "Did you find any sign of the psychophage?"

He shook his head, face drawn with worry. "No, I did not. But I also cannot find Henry. We were supposed to meet back together at your room half an hour ago, but he did not show up. As you were likewise absent but far easier to find, I followed you here. You are still shining quite brightly." He glanced over at Bonnie and raised his brows. "I did not expect to find you together. And definitely not doing this."

"We had a long talk, and all is well," Vi said. "She has been asking me to teach her, so I thought why not start now? The ship will not be stopping again until the morning, and who knows what tomorrow holds?"

"What did the diary say? Will the tea help them?"

Vi sniffed. "I no doubt cannot get the ingredients until tomorrow either. Even if there was a proper kitchen on board, these will not be your garden variety herbs." She feigned nudging him in the ribs at her bad joke, but with the effects of her excess energy wearing off, Vi made no contact.

He rolled his eyes, his posture indicating she was about to receive a lecture. Bonnie let out a cry of surprise that sent them both wheeling around. A ragged piece of the poster was fluttering to the ground, the printed woman's once-smiling face now obliterated by a diagonal slash. Vi paced back to the little brunette's side, and Bonnie said, "Sorry, I did not mean to startle you. I was doing what you said, scratching at the face. I caught the corner there and it came away. It must not have been properly glued."

Vi was about to make a joke about 'losing one's head' in a fight, but something about the exposed wood caught her attention. Beneath the poster, there was something stamped or painted onto the crate, something familiar. She reached up to the intact corner and pulled, working at the pieces until they were nothing but shreds at her feet. The symbol on the crate was about a foot across. It took her a moment to fully recognize what she was looking at; the last time she had seen that symbol, it had been embossed in a red wax seal rather than stamped in black ink.

She stepped back to give Peter a chance to look at it as well.

"I'll be damned," he said.

Vi nodded her agreement at the sentiment, but it was Bonnie who spoke next. "What is it?" she asked.

"That symbol was on the letter I got from the lawyer," Vi replied, her pointing finger tracing the circular outline.

"The one in Sacramento?" Bonnie's face screwed up in thought. "I do not understand. What does that mean?"

Vi placed her palm in the center of the design, murmuring, "There are no coincidences."

CHAPTER 35

Vi looked at the rapidly darkening sky. "Quick, we need a bar or something to pry it open. I have to see what is inside."

Bonnie followed her deeper into the storage area. No one had come by to light the lantern yet, slowing their search. "What do you think a lawyer would need to transport in a huge box like that?" Bonnie asked as she opened a cupboard.

"The letter was on stationery from the law firm, but this symbol was in the wax seal. It may not have even come from the attorney himself; it could have been added later by the true sender. Peter said they had been sending several copies of the same missive out. Either way, that is a very heavy crate; it did not even budge when we hit the sand bar the other night. And why would someone want to pretend it was part of the Belle's set? Aha!" Vi cried, triumphantly brandishing a crowbar.

When they returned to the suspicious crate, Peter still stood in the same place, stroking his chin thoughtfully. Vi made a shooing gesture at the ghost. "I want to come at it from this side so we have the light." As the carton was taller than either of them, Vi crouched down with her back to Bonnie and tapped her shoulders. "Hop on. I will hand you the crowbar."

"What if someone comes?" Peter asked.

"That is what our trusty lookout is for," she replied. "Go on over to the stairs and give a shout if any of the crew are coming."

Once Bonnie was situated, Vi stood up and steadied herself against the rough wood. She passed the crowbar up and the other woman set to work. From her position, Vi could not see what Bonnie was doing, but from the way the nails squealed and the wood protested, she had to be having some success. A moment later, there was an even louder whine as she lifted the corner.

"It is dark," Bonnie said. "What is inside, I mean. Almost black." Her weight shifted as she leaned over the edge for a better look. "Heavy...and mostly smooth. Metal? No, wood. No! Both!"

Vi's mouth went dry. "Guns."

Peter called. "They're coming!"

She cursed, then passed on the information to Bonnie, who brought the lid back down and used the crowbar to help pound the nails back where they belonged. She had to balance stealth and haste, and only just barely gave Vi a sign to bring her down again as the medium sensed the crewmen's auras approaching. The women slunk between the crates, careful not to alert the men to their presence. The pair were safely back by the cupboard where Peter awaited them before they spoke again.

"Well?" Peter asked.

Vi replaced the tool. "It was full of guns, or so we think."

Bonnie grabbed Vi by the wrist to allow her to hear Peter just as he scratched his head and said, "I thought carrying guns to the rebel states was illegal after the war."

"It is."

He crossed his arms, haughtiness pulling at his features. "So your beau *was* hiding something."

Vi thought back to the way Sam's face had lost color when he saw her throwing knives into the same crate, but that did not mean he was guilty of anything besides being a responsible captain. She shook her head. "He is *not* my beau. And do not jump to conclusions. Sam may not have a clue that is what is in there," Vi hissed. "It could be someone traveling with the Belles who is smuggling them without his knowledge. And it is not as though I can ask him about it at present."

"Could there be records somewhere?" Bonnie asked. "Up in the pilothouse, perhaps?"

"Let us hope not. That is probably where Bulloch is right now. And I cannot imagine he would be happy about me walking in and digging through drawers." Vi snapped her fingers. "But there is a drawer I could try in Sam's room. I found it while I was looking for his knife set. It was locked, and if he is the one hiding anything, it is more than likely in there. And I doubt he would object much at present if I were to go and take a look around."

Though discovering the weapons was decidedly a bad thing, her spirits were buoyed by having a new piece to the puzzle. When they reached the texas deck, the ship had passed fully under the cloud cover, which had now swallowed the sunset and plunged them into a murky darkness. Some of the gaslight sconces had been lit, but once the thunderhead broke, no one would be venturing outside but the unfortunate crew. The wisdom of the overnight run seemed to lessen with each passing moment, but it was Bulloch's call. She doubted he would listen to the objections of a woman, especially if that woman was Vi.

When they reached the captain's quarters, Vi barged straight in. She had been so focused on her task, she had not bothered to reach out and sense if anyone was in the room, and was surprised to find Minerva at Sam's bedside.

"What the blazes do you think you are doing, barging in here like that?" Minerva squawked.

Vi narrowed her eyes. "I am his nurse. I can come and go as I please. What are you doing here?"

Minerva met her glower for glower. "I thought he could use some company. Even if he is sleeping." She stood up and put herself between Vi and Sam, pointing out the door. "I think you should go."

"I need to check on something."

"You've already done enough, haven't you?"

"Me? What have I done?"

"Nothing," Minerva spat. "Or perhaps everything. I could not help but notice that both Diana and Samuel fell unconscious in your company. *Alone* in your company, I might add."

"You think I did this?" Vi cried. Though in Sam's case it was true, she still did not appreciate how painfully close Minerva was to being right.

The blonde woman clenched her fists. "All I know is that everything was going just fine, and then you came along. Are you really so petty?"

Peter pushed through the wall and stepped over to the bedside. "Do you think the lady doth protest too much?" he asked, quirking an eyebrow.

Bonnie slipped around Vi and over to Minerva's side. She patted the dancer on the shoulder. "Minerva, you are upset. You don't know what you are saying."

"Don't I?" she said, slapping away Bonnie's hand. "Everything was great with Sam and me, and he was giving the Belles this opportunity to earn some extra scratch. And then *she* got on board and strange things started happening." Minerva stepped right up to Vi, and she was surprised to see tears springing to actress's eyes. "I would understand if you came after me, on account of Sam, but why did you hurt Enid like that? Why would you hurt Diana? They didn't do anything to you!"

Peter passed through Minerva, who absentmindedly rubbed away the goose pimples he raised. He stepped over to the desk and pointed at the bottom drawer with a quizzical glance. Vi cleared her throat by way of answering, and the ghost got down on his hands and knees to look at the lock.

Though the other woman was not really a threat physically, Vi's extra senses were sounding their alarm. She may not be able to take Vi in a fight, but she could tell Minerva wanted to. Vi took a step back, her hands up in a placating gesture and voice soft. "I didn't hurt the girls," Vi said. "I assure you, I have no grudge against them at all."

"So it is just against me?" Minerva asked, closing the distance again. "Why else would you go through my things? It had to be you, I'm sure of it. Though I admit I have no idea why."

Vi kept her face blank, but her mind reeled back to the mercury tablets. So much had happened, she had forgotten to put them back. "I apologize, I should have asked first," Vi said, hustling skills kicking in as she continued, "You had the smelling salts on hand, so I thought perhaps you had something else that would be of use in treating the fallen. We have a rather limited stock of medicine aboard. I meant no offense. I can go and fetch your pills right now for you. Living with the disease cannot be easy."

"They aren't *mine*," Minerva scoffed. "And the salts, neither. I got them for Juno."

"What?" Bonnie asked. "Why?"

"Because that wretch of a husband of hers got her sick. She had no idea he was off sowing his oats elsewhere until it was too late. That is why we took the show on tour. She could not stand to be in New York with him. She wants to set us up to continue after she's gone, and she's agreed to make me the new manager. So, I help her out any way I can."

Peter frowned up at Vi. "Uh-oh. There goes her motive."

"I had no idea, poor thing," Bonnie said, hand over her heart.

Something in her tone made Minerva relax her stance slightly. "No one does," she said. "Juno has some sores, but not where anyone can see, at least so far. She is getting more erratic, and I do not I always agree with her decisions lately. We all needed to rest, especially her. We never should have agreed to perform here. Everyone has been chalking up the changes to the stress of being on tour so far. But it's only a matter of time before someone finds out." Minerva's tone turned pleading. "You cannot tell anyone. Juno is proud, too proud, and she would be mortified if anyone knew. Having syphilis is terrible, but how she got sick? Her reputation would never recover. She plans to retire after the Christmas show so no one is the wiser. So please, I do not want anyone to know. For her sake."

"Oh, of course," Bonnie said. "We will not tell a soul, will we Vi?"

"Cross my heart," Vi said, making the gesture as she said the words. "And I also promise you, I had nothing whatsoever to do with all of the strange happenings."

"It is true," Bonnie assured the dancer. "In fact, we have been trying to find out who is behind it before anyone else gets hurt. It is why we joined the show in the first place."

Peter interjected from his place on the floor. "Speaking of which...are we going to open this drawer sometime before dawn? It should be an easy enough lock to pick."

"And right this moment," Vi said, crossing to the desk and opening the top drawer. The ring of keys rattled as she did, and she held them up for everyone to see. "We need to check on something in Sam's records. I am hoping it could shed some light on what is happening."

"So, you aren't here to check on him," Minerva said, pursing her lips.

Vi sorted through the keys and located a small one the same color as the lock. "This could help him, even if it will not help him wake up."

"Why don't we go get a nice cup of tea?" Bonnie suggested. "And we can get Juno's pills for her at the same time?"

Vi had her back turned to the dancer, but she could feel her eyes boring into her back. "So you expect me to leave her alone with him?"

"I trust her," Bonnie said gently. "And you should, too. She just wants to help."

The words made emotions swell in Vi, and she gave her friend a nod of appreciation as she pushed the key into the lock. The tumblers clicked into place.

"I will go with you to get Juno's medicine, but then I am coming right back," Minerva said, far louder than was necessary.

Vi slid the drawer open and sighed. "As you wish."

The other women passed through the open door as Vi peered into the drawer. A neat stack of ledgers lay inside, and she pulled out the one with the most recent date. When she had it open on the desk, Peter stood behind her and looked over the neat rows and columns of script. Instead of a shipping manifest or other cargo record they had hoped to find, the ledger held the record of the loan and construction of *The Piasa*. Vi was about to put it back in the drawer and pull out another when her gaze snagged on the last line, which had no explanation but did put a positive amount of one hundred dollars against the rest of the out-flowing cash.

"Could that be it?" Peter asked. "A hundred dollars would be enough to tempt any man, and especially a man in debt."

As hard as it was to believe, the ghost had a point. Except for a few childhood pranks, Sam had always been so well behaved, so unwilling to step out of line. Of course, Vi had been the same way once upon a time, and she had stepped over plenty of lines plenty of times since becoming an adult. Her pleasant reminder of the simplicity of the past was proving to be far more complicated than she would have liked.

The air was heavy with the threat of the storm, and Vi could just barely make out a distant rumble of thunder. She pivoted to regard the sleeping man on the cot, so familiar and so alien at the same time.

"Oh, Sam," she sighed, taking a seat on the edge of the bed. Vi ruffled his hair the way she did when they were kids. "What has happened to us?"

His forehead was cool, his breathing steady but shallow. Some of the color had returned to his face, but there was still no telling when he would wake. Even once Vi had Pru's concoction in hand, and that was assuming she could get the ingredients she needed in Greenville, she would not be able to administer more than a few drops at a time to ensure he did not choke. And meanwhile they would be hurtling closer and closer to New Orleans and out of each other's lives all over again.

Vi could no longer make out the color of his aura, but something about him still drew her in. She could not say if it was their long friendship or some quality in his aura that drew her in. Though it was not as palpable as when she had been so sorely in need of energy herself, the connection between them was undeniable. And she realized, perhaps it was a connection that could go both ways. She shifted so she could place a hand on each side of Sam's face.

"What are you doing?" Peter asked. "If you are kissing him when Minerva comes back, she is going to scratch your eyes out."

Vi ran her thumbs over his cheekbones before closing her eyes. "Will you drop it already? I am doing nothing of the sort," she replied. "I am going to try to give back some of what I stole."

"You can do that?"

"I can try."

CHAPTER 36

The ghost paced behind her, gesticulating wildly. "This is not like what you did in Chicago, Vi. That was an explosion; it went in every direction. Even if some of it passes into him, and I am not saying it will, it would only be a fraction of what you would put out. Then you could wind up right back where you started and draw from someone else when you least expect it. Plus, if that thing did go away," Peter said with a shiver, "this might be exactly the type of thing that brings it back."

"I suppose I will need to do my best to explode in only one direction, then, won't I?" The ghost scowled and as he appeared on the verge of another diatribe, Vi added, "I did it for you. And I remember what it felt like to take. I think I can do the same, just in reverse."

She took a deep breath and focused on where her skin met Sam's. There was a slight vibration, a whispered conversation between his energy and hers. As she let out the breath, she concentrated on her fingertips and pictured sending the breath through her hands and into Sam. His skin began to warm under her touch as his body responded, and she pushed a little harder. An invisible gap widened, letting in the flow of power and allowing him to absorb it. There was some resistance, but it was more akin to surprise than any actual protestation from his spirit. Once the flow began in earnest, she did not need to push, she simply needed to allow it to happen. A cold sweat beaded at her hairline.

"I think that is enough. You are going pale," Peter said, a slight quaver in his voice. "You do not want to overdo it."

She opened her eyes, but Sam still lay before her unmoving. "Not until he wakes up," she insisted.

"You can't be sure that will happen. And what if he needs more than you have to give?"

The door to the cabin slammed open, aided by the wind kicking up from the storm. The shock of the sound and motion ripped Vi's hands away, stemming the flow. Minerva and Bonnie stood in the doorway for a heartbeat, as surprised by the noise as Vi. When she recovered, the Belle rushed to Sam's side and pushed Vi out of the way with her hip.

"Get off him!" the dancer shouted.

"Really, Minerva," Bonnie sighed, stepping into the room behind her. "Calm down."

To Vi, the blonde snapped, "Whatever you are doing, just stop."

"I was not hurting him," Vi gritted, reluctantly giving way to the bony hip dug into her and moving aside.

"I will be the judge of that." Minerva leaned down and examined Sam's face. Vi could perceive the gleam of infused energy receding into his flesh that the other woman could not see. She would just have to hope whatever she had been able to give him was enough.

Lightning flashed through the window, drawing everyone's attention for a moment. When Vi looked down at Sam again, his eyelids were just beginning to stir.

"See?" Vi said, motioning at him. "I did not harm him in the least."

"Samuel? Can you hear me?" Minerva asked, taking one of his hands in hers and gently patting it.

Ever so slowly, his lids lifted and revealed the gray of his irises. His stare was glassy at first, but recognition blossomed the longer he was conscious. Sam swallowed with visible difficulty, then rasped, "What happened?"

"You had a fall, dear," Minerva replied hurriedly. "But I have been here to watch over you." Vi did not fight the urge to snort, but Minerva was so focused on Sam she did not bother to glare. "How do you feel?"

"Groggy," Sam said. He pushed himself higher up on his pillow and caught sight of Vi over Minerva's shoulder and smiled weakly. "How long was I out?"

"Several hours," Vi replied.

Bile churned inside of Vi as Minerva asked, "Do you remember what happened?"

He rubbed his temples. "Diana. She fainted. I was in her room to check up on her...." Vi's heart pounded as the seconds stretched on, but finally he just shrugged. "And I woke up here."

"Can Vi get you anything, dear?" Minerva asked. The words were intended for Sam, but she took the opportunity to twist around like the snake she was to look at Vi and grin. "I am sure she would be happy to fetch you something to eat." She untwisted, her mask of sincere, maternal concern back in place when she was in his eyeline again.

"I believe my place is here with my patient," Vi said. She crossed to the desk and held up the ledger for Sam to see. He blanched slightly. "I have some questions I still need to ask. For his health."

Vi had the ledger hidden behind her back before Minerva turned once more to look at her. She scowled for a moment, then regarded Bonnie instead. "Perhaps you could go? I am sure he is hungry as a bear after missing supper. But he needs me."

Sam cleared his throat. "Actually, Minerva, I could use a cup of coffee. And you know just how I like it. Do you mind?"

She pouted for half a second before plastering on a sweet smile. "Of course. Anything."

When she opened the door, another gust of wind blew in, disturbing some stray papers on the desk. The first drops of rain were yet to fall, and the atmosphere buzzed with electricity. Bonnie struggled against the wind, but got the door closed as she followed Minerva.

Sam pushed himself the rest of the way into a sitting position. "I can explain."

"Can you?" Vi asked archly. "This should be good."

"In fact, I was going to explain. You were there, weren't you? In Diana's room?"

Vi's throat constricted. He remembered more than he had said. "Yes," she replied, her tone wary.

"I thought so. I think I was going to tell you then, but I must have blacked out before I could." Sam studied his hands in his lap, fists clenching and unclenching. "The whole thing is rather embarrassing. I cannot believe I just fell over like that...in front of you. Not really a trait a woman wants in her man."

Vi swallowed. "But...it is fine to lean on a friend when you need it. And we will always be friends."

He glanced at her through his lashes, his expression resigned. "I admit, I had convinced myself the terror on your face the other night was due to hitting the sand bar, but I'd held onto some hope it hadn't been my suggestion that we pick up where we left off." Vi could not draw enough breath to speak, but he continued quickly. "I am glad we can at least be friends and I did not scare you off completely."

She cleared her throat, then punched his arm the way she used to when they were kids. "You are just lucky I caught you. If you had hit your head any harder, who knows what else you may have forgotten." She took her seat on the side of his bed again. "And you *did* forget, right?"

He thought about it for a moment longer, but shook his head. "I hope I didn't embarrass myself."

Vi let out a relieved breath. "It was a rather short conversation, actually. Nothing earth-shattering transpired."

"Go on, ask him," Peter said. He had taken up a position by the writing desk and thrust his hand at the ledger. He did not pass the full force of the blow to the book the way a living hand would, but it was enough to send it toppling to the floor.

Vi shifted to retrieve the fallen ledger, pausing long enough to hold the ghost in her gaze and jerk her chin toward the door. Peter shoved his hands into his pockets before passing through the wall and out of sight.

"So," Vi said, holding up the ledger. "Tell me about this."

"Well, you know about the loan already."

"Indeed," Vi said, leafing through the pages until she reached the last one. She flipped the ledger around so he could see where she tapped her finger against the mysterious entry. "The one with unfavorable terms?"

"Yes. Hauling freight for them is one of the conditions. In exchange, they take away some of what I owe them."

She was afraid to ask, but posed the question. "And do you know what you're carrying?"

"No, it was an 'ask no questions' kind of arrangement," he replied, his shoulders slumping. "But I am not so naïve as to think it is anything I would want an inspector to find."

While Vi was glad to find out that he was ignorant to the extent of his crime, that same ignorance also made her angry. He might not consider himself naïve, but she did. With effort, she contained her pique. Instead, she asked, "And the other conditions?"

"They are charging a high interest rate, which will mean I while be hauling for them for quite some time. And I know it's wrong, Vi. That is why I wanted to start making money with the stage show as quickly as possible. You understand, right?" Sam reached out for her, but Vi moved away.

"Any other terms?"

He sighed. "And taking on Bulloch as my first mate."

"What?"

"We had never even met before. I was about to set off on the maiden voyage with *The Piasa*, and he was waiting for me at the dock. That is when I found out we would be picking up my first delivery in St. Louis, and he was coming aboard to oversee the transport. He assured me we would be together for quite some time. And though he is a capable enough sailor, I do not trust him."

"And I do not I blame you. I do not care for him much myself." Thunder growled outside as Vi tapped her chin in thought. That explained the presence of the surly first mate, but not the symbol on the cargo. "Who did you say gave you the loan again?"

"I did not," Sam said, fingers once again massaging his temples. "Because frankly, I cannot."

"Then how did you get mixed up with them in the first place?"

"They approached me. Said they knew about my gambit and my lack of finances and wanted to see me succeed. I had already dried up my own contacts, and no bank back East was willing to give me a loan. They said it was too risky, or that the floating theater days were past us. So you can imagine when this well-heeled gent appeared with a cartload of promises and the cash to back them up, it felt like a dream come true."

Vi's frown deepened. "Someone just walked up to you on the street and offered you money?"

"No, not precisely. I was at a tavern, drinking away my sorrows and trying to work out a new plan when this man offers to buy the next round. We get to talking, and I tell him about my scheme with *The Piasa*. He tells me I'm brilliant, and I tell him that may be so, but it's too late. Then he says he just came into some money by way of inheritance and is looking for an investment. It was perfect."

"When something seems too good to be true, it usually is," Vi replied with a sigh.

"So I have learned."

She moved closer again and patted his hand. If she were to design a perfect patsy, it would look just like Sam—desperate for not just money, but to prove his mettle; a creative type able to imagine possibilities without a crooked bone in his body. He was exactly the type of person she had preyed on in her day without giving it a second thought. Now, a pang of guilt churned her stomach. On an intellectual level, Vi had understood why Agnes had wanted to smash in her face for taking her little brother in with a line. Now, she actually felt the visceral need to do the same to the people who were manipulating Sam.

His voice brought her thoughts away from vengeance and back to him. "Has he done anything since I have been out?"

"What? Who?"

In the flash of lightning that followed, Sam's face was wide-eyed and desperate. "*Bulloch.*"

"Nothing really. That is to say, nothing bad. He rallied the troops to make haste to the hospital in Greenville after you fell ill, so now we are doing an overnight run."

Sam shook his head, sinking back against his pillows. Whatever energy Vi had been able to give him, it was fading fast. Or it could be the weight of his own mistakes dragging him down. "He is not doing it for my benefit, believe me. He simply wants to get the cargo down south as quickly as possible."

Vi's head jerked up. "That is his sole priority?"

"Yes."

"So anything that might cause a delay, such as extra stops between here and New Orleans, for instance...?" she trailed off suggestively.

Sam gave a derisive snort. "No, he was not pleased with me for bringing the Belles on board. We had a proper row about it, but that wasn't the first time we'd had words. The only way I could convince him it would be a boon rather than a hindrance in the first place was to point out that his crate would blend in better with the Belles' things than if it was alone."

"So, you added a promotional poster to make it look like it was part of the Belles' set pieces."

"I didn't do it. Bulloch must have. It fooled even me. I had managed to more or less forget all about it until I saw you throwing knives into a crate the night of the snag. Then, I realized it was his."

The door lurched open. Bonnie operated the handle while Minerva held onto a modest tray. The heady scent of coffee made Vi's stomach rumble, and she dared to hope Minerva had brought enough for everyone. Alas, Vi only spied a single cup and saucer when the dancer brought it to rest on the side table. Vi did not wait to be shoved aside this time and got well out of Minerva's way before she took up her perch on Sam's bed.

"Well, I will leave you in Minerva's capable hands," Vi said. "You are still weak though, so do not try to get up just yet. You may have been sleeping for most of a day, but try not to stay up too late."

Minerva caught Vi by the sleeve as she passed. "I am sorry about before," she said. "Bonnie told me everything, about how you two go all the way back to childhood." She pulled slightly on Vi's arm and she obliged by leaning closer. Minerva whispered, "Of course you would not hurt him. I was just so worried. I lost my head. I did not know what I was saying."

Vi regarded the other woman warily, but unlike the majority of the times Minerva had spoken to her, she did not seem to be concealing any barbs or slights within her words. Considering Vi had harbored her own wrong-minded suspicions about Minerva and how petty their feuding felt in the shadow of the larger threat she faced, she could not conjure the energy to hold a grudge.

"Apology accepted," Vi assured her, straightening up. "Take good care of him for me."

She beckoned to Bonnie, and the pair slipped out the door. Peter was waiting outside, hands clasped behind his back as he paced. "What now?" he asked.

"Now, I believe it is time to have a little talk with the first mate."

CHAPTER 37

October 22, 1871
The Witching Hour

Bulloch's voice echoed around the empty theater. "All right. You wanted me here. So, here I am."

He removed his hat and whacked it against his palm to free it of rain. He was in the middle of the stage, the ghost lights the only illumination besides the occasional flash of lightning from the storm raging outside. The footlights flickered and hissed as the water hit them, but recovered their eerie, golden glow.

From Vi's vantage point in the upper balcony, he looked small, but she knew better than to have this confrontation too close to those meaty fists. She ran her thumb over her flint as she watched him pull something from his pocket.

He waved around the note Vi had sent him, then squinted at it in the dreary near-darkness. Bulloch leaned into each of the words she had included to get her point across. "Your *aim* is clear," he read. "You have the Belles in your *crosshairs,* and I know why you are *gunning* for them." He folded the note and put it into his breast pocket. "You're clever, whoever you are."

"I thought so," Peter said, lounging in a seat a few rows behind Vi.

"What are you doing up here?" she hissed. "I need you down *there.*"

"Forgetting something, aren't we?" The ghost stood and walked through the intervening rows until he was standing next to the limelight canister. He puffed up his chest and held his arms wide. "You were going to give me a little something so I could pick up something heavy?"

Vi sighed and nodded. Waking Sam must have taken more out of her than she had thought if she could forget her own carefully laid out strategy. After she had filled in the blanks for Bonnie and Peter, the piece that she had not been able to bring to aid her was Henry. He was probably off ogling an unsuspecting Belle somewhere, and Vi did not want to take the time to look for him. Besides, the storm would probably keep everyone away from the cargo; only a suicidal person would be out on the slippery deck in the blasting wind without a good reason. Henry's presence as watchman for Bonnie would probably only serve to quiet the little voice telling Vi not to leave the other woman alone more than it would provide any tangible help. And Bonnie had made it quite clear she did not want protection.

Vi reached out to put her hand into Peter's chest as she had the day before, but he flinched away before she could.

"Are you up to this?" he asked.

Bulloch's voice rose up again. "You said you wanted to discuss the terms of your silence? Because I am willing to talk, but I can't wait here the entire night to do it. I've got a ship to run."

"Yes," Vi whispered. "I may be a little off, but I can keep him busy while Bonnie takes care of the cargo and you take care of him. Afterwards, I plan to sleep until we reach New Orleans."

The ghost eyed her warily, but stepped back into reach all the same. Vi's fingertips passed through the mist of his sternum, and she pushed outward. The energy trickled more than flowed, but the action of passing it between bodies—living or dead—was becoming second nature. The realization made her squirm, but that was a problem for another day. Today, she had an evil troll to vanquish and a handsome, bearded damsel to rescue. The sooner she could do away with the troll, the sooner Sam could turn this tub around and hopefully get out of range of whatever was cooking in New Orleans.

Peter shone bright and solid. With a grin and a wiggle of his fingers, he slipped through the floor of the balcony. He made no sound when he landed on the main floor, but Vi could see him emerge from beneath the overhang a moment later and jog toward the stage.

"It's now or never!" Bulloch called. "You are robbing me of my generous mood."

The limelight blazed to life the moment Vi struck her flint. The beam of white light landed squarely on the first mate, who winced at the shock and put a hand in front of his face to shield it.

"It will be now," Vi said.

Even at a distance, she could see how the force of his scowl made his caterpillar eyebrows touch. "Oh, good," he grunted. "It's you. I should have known."

Vi was not sure if it was sarcasm or something else coloring his voice. "Who else were you expecting?" she asked cautiously.

Bulloch took a few steps to his right, trying to leave the pool of light. Vi pushed the canister to follow him and keep him blinded. He would not be able to see Peter no matter what, but he would notice something floating through the air at him if she gave him a chance to find his balance.

Bulloch shot her a yellow-toothed grin. "That how it's gonna be, eh?"

"Yep," Vi replied. "As I see it, I am the one holding the best hand of cards here, so we are going to do this on my terms." She crept back from the light, careful to remain in the thickest of the shadows.

The burly man gave up trying to see her against the burn of the stage lighting and looked out over the empty theater to blink the spots from his eyes. "Sam woke up and told you, is that it?"

"Would it matter if he did?"

"My employer would be interested to learn he's a stoolie." Bulloch snickered.

"And who might that be?" Vi shouted.

"Would it matter?" he asked, doing an aggravating imitation of a female voice. He shaded his eyes again and tried to steal a glance at her. "How about you come on down here so we can talk like civilized people?"

"How about you answer my question?"

"All you need to know is the League would be more than happy to have me take over operations here if anything were to happen to the good captain. And I don't think you want that, do you?"

Vi's blood boiled at the not-so-veiled threat, but she had a name. Or at least, part of a name. "The League" did not mean anything to her immediately; however, it was a direction to take, and that was more than she'd had before.

When she stole a glance at the stage once more, she found Peter with a board in his hands. He crept up slowly, keeping himself directly behind Bulloch's back to keep from giving himself away.

"No such luck, friend. Sam's no stool pigeon," she yelled back, craning to get a better view of the impending strike. "I found out all on my lonesome. He's none the wiser. Has no idea about this little meet of ours, either."

"What about that other little bird of yours?" Bulloch asked, shoving a hand into his pocket. His face twisted as he paused to pull out a handkerchief and mop the rain from his face. "The pretty one. What's her name again? Bonnie?"

"You saw that scene," Vi said, putting an annoyed snarl into her tone to sell the lie. "You think I would cut her in on something this good after she was shoving me around like that? Nah, this is our little secret."

Bulloch replaced his rag. He stroked his beard with one hand and fondled the ever-present pocket watch with the other. "Here all alone, huh?"

Vi wrinkled her brow. She was the one who needed to stretch out this conversation, but he seemed more than willing to help her do it. "You going deaf?" she asked, attempting to sound casually annoyed but coming off as cagey. "That's what I said, didn't I?"

"You're braver than I gave your credit for."

She chuckled. "Funny. I was just telling someone the opposite was true. So, we going to talk business?"

"Smarter, too," Bulloch said, though somehow it did not feel like a compliment.

He could snark at her all he wanted if he would stand still just a few seconds more. Peter was almost in reach, he just needed to take one more step to be close enough to swing. He lifted his foot, but it only hung in the air before him. The ghost pushed out with his foot, and it grew brighter as he put more power behind the action. He gritted his teeth and tucked the board beneath his arm before leaning with his full body, but something would not allow him to make more progress. His face shot up to Vi, confused and plaintive.

"Not smarter than me, though," Bulloch said. He turned on his heel so he faced Peter full on. For a horrifying moment, Vi thought he must also be a sensitive. When he took a step forward and it made Peter stumble back in his wake, however, she knew he was something else entirely. She crept out of the shadows to get a better though uncomprehending look.

The board clattered to the floor and Bulloch stooped to retrieve it. He turned back to the limelight before breaking the wood across his knee.

Peter gathered the strength he could for an assault. The ghost smacked into the same invisible wall and ended up sprawled on the stage floor. He did not have any breath to be knocked from him, but he sounded for all the world as if he'd been socked in the gut. "Run, Vi," Peter gasped.

"Your dead friend can't hurt me," he roared, using one end of the board to point at her. He thumped it lightly against his chest, snarling, "I've got myself protection."

Vi realized her jaw was hanging slack and snapped her dry mouth shut. "I-I don't know what you are talking about," she stammered, leaning against a seat as her head whirled with confusion. "Where do you suppose that came from?"

The big man sniggered. "Not feeling like you've got the best hand now, are you, Vi?" Bulloch asked, shaking his head and tutting. "Or should I say, Annabelle?"

Before Vi could react, a piece of board came hurtling through the air. It crashed into the limelight, throwing a shower of sparks in every direction. Then, the world went black.

CHAPTER 38

Vi was not much of a screamer on a normal day. Today, however, was turning out to be anything but normal, so she shrieked in surprise as she dived out of the way of the cascading sparks. Red and gray spots floated in and out of her vision against the background of darkness. She knuckled her eyes to clear her vision, but became aware of a stinging sensation on her legs. A few sparks had landed on her skirt and were eating their way through the fabric. Vi scrambled to a seated position before frantically patting them out.

The shock of Annabelle's name, her most dangerous name, on Bulloch's lips addled her as much as the white wash of sparks. It was only the sound of Peter's voice that brought her back to herself.

"Vi! Get moving!" the ghost yelled, his voice impossibly far away even though he was only as far as the stage. "He's on his way up!"

Vi gave herself a mental slap before pulling herself to standing. It wouldn't take someone like Bulloch long to climb the stairs to the balcony, and she had already lost some distance to her stupor. She picked up her skirts with one hand as she bolted up the aisle and held the other out before her to ram open the door.

Being at the back of the audience put her at the front of The Piasa, and she sailed through the foredeck door just as Bulloch's muttered curses reached her from the aft staircase. Vi skidded across the slick decking, dropping her skirt in order to catch the rail. The hem was immediately soaked with rainwater and clawing at her legs as she made her way up the narrow, metal staircase to the roof.

The lights of the pilothouse blazed, a beacon atop the windswept vessel. The shore on either side showed no sign of life, just the blurry black of a landscape that would afford her no assistance or rescue. She was vaguely aware of the sound of men's voices rising up in song from the lowest deck; the crewmen in charge of the oars were making the best of a miserable night. Vi considered calling down to them, but she had no idea who Bulloch had bribed or threatened to help him with his endeavor.

The tarred surface of the roof gave her more purchase than the polished wood of the deck, but it offered no shelter from the storm. Wind ripped at her hair, sending tendrils free only to get bogged down with water and stuck to her face. Stinging drops of rain pelted her as she gathered her skirts once more and took off for the far end of the roof.

There was a loud flapping sound, and as a bolt of lightning crackled across the dense clouds, she saw the line of flags tossing in the wind between the two craft. She reached the flagpole that held them on this end and squinted into the darkness at where the line was affixed to the smokestack. Making her way hand over hand to the towboat would be difficult even without the storm, and now that she stared down at the churning water and the distant deck, it felt impossible. The gleam from the single lantern below was faint and only highlighted how far away it was. There were hints of movement, and she considered shouting down to Bonnie. With only a single boxing lesson under her belt and a far more important job to do, Vi decided against it. She clung to the pole as a fit of dizziness seized her.

"You're at a dead end!" Bulloch roared. "Best to come quiet-like."

Vi put her back against the pole and held up one placating hand. "We can talk about this."

"Doubtful. There's a bounty on you, girly, and I intend to collect it."

Part of her itched to ask him how high of a bounty, if only as a point of pride, but she kept the thought to herself. Instead, she asked, "How did you know it was me?"

He took a slow step forward, and Vi's muscles coiled. With the rain and his general bulkiness, she might just be able to slip past him and back down the stairs.

Bulloch followed the line of her eyes and adjusted his angle. "You don't work for the League without picking up a few tricks," he said, patting his watch pocket. "Or trinkets. This lil' beauty lets me know when there's a dead man close by and keeps them from getting too close."

"Sounds like you're quite well informed about the operation, but you do not trust your boss. Or is it bosses?" she asked.

Whether the wind kept her words from reaching his ears or he was simply ignoring her, he did not answer. Instead, Bulloch's face split into a wicked grin and thunder rumbled to underscore his menace as he took another pair of steps. "When you walked into that hotel bar in St. Louis, my watch got hot as all get-out, so I had my suspicions. We knew to be on the lookout for this Annabelle wench, and you fit the description, right down to having a ghost in tow. Well, I thought it was Christmas."

Vi took in his wide stance, the slant of his shoulders. The rain was cold, so cold that might slow him down half a step, but she was shivering, too. Her dress was completely soaked, trapping her legs. It was looking less and less like she would be able to lose him that way. She was sure that once he got his arms around her, he'd be able to squeeze the air from her lungs with little effort. Slowly, Vi bent her right knee and lifted her foot up behind her, hoping to bring her knife into reach before he realized what she was doing.

"And you couldn't wait, could you?" Vi asked. "You wanted Christmas to come as soon as possible. But Sam had other plans."

Bulloch licked the rainwater from his lips and shrugged like a man with no choice in the matter. "I couldn't very well risk you getting wise, or worse, getting off, before we got to New Orleans."

"So, you set Enid on *fire*?" She laced her voice with outrage and rebuke to draw his attention to her face as she reached back with her right hand. With the tangle of sodden fabric in the way, she could not feel her way to her holster. Vi risked a quick look over her shoulder, whipped the heavy, wet muslin away, then pulled the blade free. "Not another step!" she cried, holding the knife out before her. "We both know what I can do with this."

He hesitated, but took another step forward. "Yeh, I don't believe you will though."

"Watch me," Vi said. She grabbed onto the line of flags, plunged the knife into the coil of rope, and twisted. Several strands broke, and when she pulled it down as hard as she could, only a few strands were left to hold it together. Bulloch bellowed and charged at the same time she put the blade in her teeth and launched herself at the rope.

Her hands met the twine a few feet away from where she'd cut the line, and it gave way under her weight. Vi twisted the rope around her arm for a better grip as she hurtled toward *Apple Blossom*'s glistening deck.

CHAPTER 39

The rope hit the railing of the upper deck of the tow, throwing Vi into an aisle between the shipping containers. Her feet hit the deck, but the rain took them out from under her and she slid along the planking on one side. Vi had never been so happy to be wearing bloomers in her life.

She had been so focused on her landing, Vi hadn't looked for Bonnie on her way down, but trusted she was somewhere among the wooden crates. The lantern swayed on its hook, buffeted by the storm. It cast eerie, ever-moving shadows around the deck. Vi put her knife back in its sheath, then scrambled to her feet. In her depleted state, the world slanted on her way up. A cold much deeper than the rainwater spread through her body. She had banked on Peter needing her power more than she did, and now she was only strong enough to stumble.

"Bonnie! I hope you have those guns overboard, because we've only got maybe two minutes before he comes down from the roof."

Vi rushed out of the cargo area and headed for where the knees held the two ships together. If she could detach *The Piasa* before Bulloch made it across, she would buy them both time and distance to figure out their next move. The v-shaped lengths of wood were lashed down, so Vi attacked the rope with her knife. Even if she could get them free, pushing them out of alignment would take more than one person.

"Come over here and bring whatever tools you were using. We need to get these moved now!" she called.

A few heartbeats passed before Vi realized Bonnie was not answering her. Vi whipped around and found the gun crate cracked open and weapons spilled across the deck. Bonnie must have used an axe to break right through the side rather than trying to get the cover off on her own. In the next burst of lightning, Vi discovered both where Bonnie was and why she could not speak.

A lanky man stood behind her, the handle of the axe Bonnie had been using pressed into her throat. She also had her hands on the wooden handle, face creased with the strain of pushing it away from her windpipe, but she was no match for her captor.

Vi sprang toward them as a weedy voice ordered, "Not another step!"

"Jack?" Vi asked, wiping the hair plastered to her face out of the way to make sure she could believe the truth of her ears. Even in the dimness, his thin, black mustache was unmistakable. "What the devil are you doing?"

"Stopping her from destroying the cargo," he said, the nonchalance in his voice at odds with the struggling woman before him.

"You can see why though, can't you?" Vi gestured at the assortment of firearms scattered at their feet. "It's contraband."

"No," Jack sneered. "It's my ticket out of this life. Mine and Diana's."

That day on the St. Louis waterfront flashed through her mind, and pieces clicked together. Vi murmured, "Of course. He wasn't working alone. You were the one who loaded the cargo for Bulloch."

"And there is a pretty penny in it for me," Jack said. "Not to mention the look on Juno's face later when I finally give her a piece of my mind. But we couldn't quit until we had some security. Bulloch is providing that."

Vi scoffed. "Pretty enough of a penny that you'd let him commit murder?"

The man before her lost a few years, revealing the boy inside as his face fell. "I didn't know he was going to do that to Enid. I agreed to bring on the shipment and scare the girls a little. I didn't want any of them to get hurt."

The whimper in his voice gave her an idea. "Like your sister?" Vi asked, voice gentle and hands out before her as if she approached a skittish colt and not an axe-wielding enemy.

"She fainted from exhaustion. You said so," he replied. "Because Juno is relentless."

"Are you sure about that?"

Jack shook his head. "No! He didn't do that. I asked him."

"And you think he told you the truth?" Vi took a tentative step forward.

The young man's eyes grew wide, and he relieved some of the pressure from Bonnie's throat as he considered her words. It was not enough to allow his captive to get free, but enough that she could breathe easier. He recovered some of his aplomb, but his voice still held a hint of quaver when he replied, "I don't believe you."

"Think about it. The fire wasn't enough to keep the show from happening, so he stooped to poison. The captain, too. They were both in his way." Vi was only a few arm lengths away now. Jack's face was screwed up in confusion, and she pushed on. "I examined them, remember? I have medical training. They were poisoned, I swear it," she lied.

"But I...he...."

"I was afraid of what he would do, so I didn't tell anyone." Vi reached out her hand and rested it on Jack's forearm. Despite the rivulets of rain, there was an unexpected heat to the contact as their energies interacted. She imbued her next words with as much understanding and sincerity as she could muster. "You were afraid, too, weren't you? After what he did to Enid?"

Jack scowled at her and tightened his grip, twisting aside to get out from under her hand. Bonnie was now balancing on her toes, her eyes bulging as the pressure returned. Jack snarled, "We'll just wait and see what he has to say for himself. Stay back, hear? Or she goes into the river." He dragged Bonnie closer to the railing, and she sputtered and choked in his grip.

Accusing him of fear had been a misstep, so Vi dropped her motherly tone and threw his rage back at him instead. She followed him step for step, her voice slicing through the howling wind. "Do you really think Bulloch gives a damn about you or your sister? About anything other than being paid?"

"He cares about revenge!" Jack said. "About getting some justice for the fallen."

This stopped Vi short, and she regarded him in confusion. What revenge? What fallen? Then she remembered Bulloch's tattoo, the one from the Rebel navy.

"You're a secessionist?" Vi guessed.

"Damn straight."

"But you are too young—"

"No one was too young," Jack hissed. "Diana and me lost a brother and a father to that fight, but I made it out. And for what? So she can parade around in her knickers and I have to beg for scraps from that harpy?"

Another wave of dizziness hit her, and Vi pinched between her eyes to help her focus. Jack was using Bonnie as a shield; getting a clear shot at any vital organ would be impossible even if she did want to take out her knife. He could easily throw her friend overboard before Vi could stop him. Bulloch would be there any second, and she didn't think she would be able to get away from him again in her current state.

It was time to kill two birds with a single stone.

Vi painted on a pleading expression and put a quiver into her voice to sell the ruse. "Please," she begged. "Please don't throw her over. Bonnie can't swim. You'd kill her!"

Vi had no idea if that was true, but neither did Jack. His Adam's apple bobbed and he gave a curt nod. In the moment of calm, Vi's arms shot out and she gripped the bare knuckles of Jack's closest hand.

"Thank you," she said, pouring all of the gratitude she could into her eyes. She pulled.

Warmth spread into her hand as she opened the gateway between them. He had a different essence, a different flavor than Sam, but the surge of energy had the same primal, seductive effect. She smiled as the power flowed into her, widening the invisible gap and urging it to surge forward and give itself to her. When Vi opened her eyes, the crystalline red tint had returned to her vision, and Jack's grip was going slack. Bonnie pushed the axe handle away and ducked out from under it. Jack's face was set in a rictus of surprise as he slowly sank to his knees, the axe clattering to the deck. It balanced for a moment on the edge before tipping and disappearing into the dark water.

As it had before, the entire ship lit up with the auras of the living. Bonnie burned with her sky blue light, strong and true as ever. Minerva and Charles continued their vigils at the bedsides of their dearest ones. Diana's aura was deeper and stronger than before, though still weaker than those around her. Juno sat alone in her room, her body wracked with a fit of pain that made her color churn. The rest of the troupe slept, oblivious to the drama unfolding below, while the crew on the front of *The Piasa* passed a bottle around and started another round of singing to stay warm. Peter was sprinting his way along the promenade, only a dozen paces or so from where the two ships met. The muddy, gray aura a few paces behind had to be Bulloch, the effects of his special watch making him difficult to detect even in her heightened state of awareness.

Vi touched on something that was Henry, but not Henry, at the same time. It was so faint, she was not sure she would have been able to feel it on a normal day. Now, with so much energy pulsing through her, she felt something akin to the hint of a spirit. As she touched him, he took notice and the dissipated fog of him made his way toward her at breakneck speed.

But it was not just Henry on its way; something dark and menacing followed close behind.

Something hungry.

CHAPTER 40

"Vi! Vi, let go!" Bonnie shouted, gripping her shoulder.

She snapped back to attention and released her grip on Jack. He slumped to the deck. His eyes were rolled up in their sockets, and even in the meager light, she could see his skin had taken on a bluish pall. The best and the worst part of it all was that she didn't care about the state she had left him. It just felt so good to have done it. The stolen energy rolled through her in waves, vibrating from her bones out to her skin and back again.

"What happened with Bulloch?" Bonnie asked, her voice hoarse. "I assume your dramatic entrance means things did not go as planned?"

The question was so small, so inconsequential compared to the power coursing through her, Vi did not answer at first. When Bonnie touched her again, Vi startled. "He knows." She shook her head to try to clear the throb from her brain. "And not just that we are on to him. He knows about me, about ghosts," Vi replied. "And Peter cannot even get close."

"What do you mean? Why?"

"This organization, the 'League' he called it. They are far bigger and more organized than we thought. And they are all looking for me." Vi took a steadying breath. "You have seen that watch he always carries? Well, it had something done to it. Something that affects ghosts and my ability to sense him. He must have gotten it through the League somehow? To protect himself from ghosts?"

"Or to protect himself from them," Bonnie said.

A wave of ill-intent reached Vi through the aether as Bulloch closed the distance between them from one side. Henry and the psychophage barreled down on them from the other. Being the meat in a malice sandwich should have made her shake in her boots. Instead, Vi smiled.

She took Bonnie by the shoulders and looked her square in the face. "I will explain the details I gleaned later. But right now, he is coming. So I need you to do something."

"What?"

"Hide."

Bonnie shook her head. "No. Absolutely not. You are not sending me away again."

"He doesn't know you are here. I want to keep it that way." The other woman opened her mouth the protest, but Vi didn't give her the chance. "But only until the right moment. I am going to need a distraction. And you are my secret weapon," she said with a wink.

Bonnie's aura grew a little brighter, buoyed by Vi's confidence in her. She nodded her understanding, then ran to the nearest gap between the crates. Vi strode back out into the open and took up a place in the middle of the scatter of firearms. She stooped and retrieved a pistol. She pointed it at where she knew Bulloch would cross to *Apple Blossom*.

Peter and Bulloch crossed the knee a few seconds later. The ghost barreled across with no hesitation, but the man's pace slowed when he saw her. Satisfaction twisted his features as he took in the scene. "Decided to stop running, eh?"

"There is not anywhere to go," Vi said.

He eyed the gun in her hands. "You know how that thing works?"

"Yes." She pulled back the hammer.

"Then you know it won't fire," Bulloch said, crossing his arms. "Even if we were moving them loaded, which would be risky, the powder'd be wet."

"True," Vi said, bringing the pistol close to her chest with the barrel pointing skyward.

Peter stepped up to her side. "So much for your brilliant plan. Though speaking of brilliant, you are shining quite bright. What happened?"

She used her eyes and minute tilting of her head to indicate the slumped body of Jack by way of answer before grinning at Bulloch. "This damn thing is useless to me." She flipped the gun to hold it by the barrel, then sent it flying end over end into the river. Vi stooped down and picked up another firearm, ready for a repeat performance.

Bulloch growled, "I am gonna need you to stop doing that."

"What? This?" She sent the second gun flying.

The splash was swallowed by a rumble of thunder. The rain had let up during her encounter with Jack, but the slick decking shone with the reflected light of the lantern. She could sense the mist of what remained of Henry's spirit flesh coiling through the cargo hold and the psychophage in tow. Vi wanted to warn Peter of what was about to happen, but there was no time nor any way to do so without letting on to Bulloch that something was amiss. She glanced around her feet and bent to pick up another gun.

"Do you really think taunting him is the best course of action here?" Peter asked.

The big man stomped over and kicked it out of her reach. He tried to grab her around the waist, but Vi anticipated the action and sidestepped. Bulloch turned to face her, now standing with his back to the darkened hold.

"You know, girly, the League may want you alive, but they didn't say anything about unharmed."

Vi didn't need her eyes to sense that Bonnie was on the move, coming down the aisle in a crouch. When she reached the League's crate, she slowed and cautiously reached for a rifle, her face never leaving Bulloch. Peter saw her at the same moment and his eyes grew wide. "What is she doing?"

"Being brave," Vi whispered.

"Talking to the dead man?" Bulloch sneered, his hand in his watch pocket. "I know here's here, but he can't help you. Now, you can make this easy, or you can make it fun. It's up to you."

As Bonnie slid the rifle free, the pile shifted and another gun's barrel scraped against the floor. Bulloch began to twist at the waist, but Vi stepped right up to him before he finished the action and saw Bonnie skulking behind him.

Vi held her hands out before her, wrists together as if waiting for handcuffs. "You are right. It was silly of me to try to resist."

Henry slithered between Bonnie's feet as she stood, rifle held by the barrel and the butt high above her head like a club. The ghost's straight path was interrupted when he encountered Bulloch's aura, and the mist pooled for a moment before passing by him at a safe distance.

Peter saw his threadbare counterpart and gasped, then his face swiveled around as he did a wild search for the psychophage. The creature undulated through the aether, but stopped a few meters away when it became aware of

Vi. The ghost backed away from the threat, terror written on his face. "V-Vi, it's here."

Bulloch narrowed his eyes at Vi's outstretched arms and stroked his beard thoughtfully. "Just like that?"

"Just like that," she said.

Her fingers snaked toward Bulloch's pocket, and she was surprised to feel a definite, energetic resistance, as if she was pushing against taut fabric. The effect of his charmed watch was not as strong on her as it was on the ghosts, but the energies involved were similar enough that it was fighting her. What was left of Henry's spirit flesh twined between Vi's feet like an affectionate cat, and she felt a weak, plaintive tug. She didn't mind using the stolen power to help restore him, but she had other plans for it first.

"Well," Bulloch said, his voice dripping with arrogance. "Nice of you to come to your senses. It don't mean I'm not going to teach you some manners." He cracked his knuckles before one heavy paw shot out and grabbed Vi by the back of the neck. Bulloch twined some of his fingers through her hair and jerked her head back in order to sneer down at her face. Though unpleasant, allowing him to do so also got her closer to his pocket. Bulloch either could not feel the frisson of their auras meeting, or he ignored the crackling of his protective layer in resisting her proximity.

"Please, don't hurt me," Vi whimpered, urging her borrowed power into the hand closest to the watch. As the energy flowed, she became aware of tiny gaps she could widen, like pushing a needle in between threads. Sam had already been weakened, so an influx of power from her gave him strength. With Bulloch intact, the surge of energy was too much to take in. Vi willed the power outward, feeding it into his invisible wall and overloading it with energy. Shafts of a sickly, chartreuse light flared through the muddy gray of his protective layer as it broke down. In the next breath, she had her fingertips on the watch fob.

Bulloch's thumb slithered from her jawline to her jugular and his mouth twisted into a satisfied smile. "Not so brave now, are you?"

His head jerked as the rifle butt cracked against his skull. Bonnie's blow was not hard enough to knock him out, but it did get his attention. Bulloch cursed and swung around to face his attacker, releasing his grip on Vi to take on the new threat two-handed.

As he turned, she pulled the watch out of his pocket. There was a tearing sensation as it came away. At first, she thought it was simply the fabric of his waistcoat tearing as the watch chain ripped free, but when she looked down at her hands, she found a shimmering blue residue. The psychophage must have sensed the hole she had just punched in Bulloch's aura, because there was a distinctly happy tinkling of bells.

"What do we have here?" Bulloch snarled. He rubbed the back of his head as he stalked toward Bonnie. He grabbed the rifle out of her hands, and Bonnie fumbled backwards, tripping over the pile of weapons and falling against the crate.

The red facets at the edges of Vi's vision were mirrored in the smooth sheen of the creature hovering near the scene. It bobbed and circled in midair. Based on the way the volume of its call increased, it seemed to find Bulloch appetizing, but it did not approach. It flashed its belly at Vi as it had on their first encounter, and to her horror, it turned to go. It was deferring to her once again. However this time, she needed it to feed. If she walked away, perhaps it would return, but Bonnie would be left to the mercy of the angry man and his powerful fists.

As Bulloch loomed over her, the widow let out a squeak. Vi tucked the watch and chain into her bodice, then scrambled onto her front, throwing herself between him and her friend. The wound she'd left at his belly oozed phosphorescence.

"Don't," she said, raising a hand. "No one needs to get hurt. We'll both come quietly."

He sniggered. "As I see it, you both need to come down a peg or two first." Bulloch pulled back his arm, intent on landing a backhanded slap across Vi's face.

Vi's forearm shot up on instinct, stopping the blow before she grasped his arm with her other hand. His energy now welcomed her touch, even as his physical body became rigid from the unexpected resistance. She willed another surge of power into him, but with the wound to his aura, much of it came pouring out of the hole she had created. The gap widened, and it and the small fissures throughout his aura started leaking the glowing blue residue of excess power. As it flowed away from her, the red receded from Vi's vision, but not before she heard the chiming chatter of the psychophage's return. Now that she no longer represented a threat, it was free to satiate its hunger.

Bulloch ripped his arm out of her grasp and glared at the offending appendage. "What the hell was that?" he growled.

"Call it a gift," Vi said. She pulled out the watch and held it up for him to see. "Or rather, an exchange."

Though Vi could no longer see the phage, from the way Bulloch stiffened, then tottered, she knew it had to be latched on and drawing the power out. He took a confused, weaving stumble backwards, his hands clutching his head to fight the dizziness Vi knew all too well.

"What's the matter?" Vi asked sweetly. She got to her feet and gave Bonnie a hand up. With the contact, the other woman could see the cerulean cracks all over his body and the vapor leaking out of his belly. Bonnie's free hand came up to cover her mouth and stifle her gasp.

"She hit me...harder than...than I thought," he slurred, pointing at Bonnie. "But I'll...I'll...."

His knees buckled and hit the deck. Bulloch caught himself with his hands as he tipped forward, his breathing labored. The puddle of Henry's spirit flesh coiled around his arms, drawing even more power away. The pool of fog expanded as he used the energies to gather more aether to him. By the time Henry was more or less man-shaped again, Bulloch's elbows bent beneath his weight, and he had nothing but his face to break his fall.

CHAPTER 41

October 22, 1871
Approaching Greenville, MS

After the long night of pouring rain, the whole world awoke to the smell of green and the cool, fresh breeze.

Humidity clung to the windows of the pilothouse, leaving the interior a foggy imitation of itself. Vi did not need her eyes to see it was Sam alone inside. She shifted the pair of steaming mugs to one hand and knocked on the door.

"Come on in," Sam said cheerfully. He did not turn when she entered, just continued scanning the pale, golden horizon.

Vi took in the view for a moment, the weight off his shoulders and his vision fixed on what was to come. Now that the wound in her aura no longer begged for sustenance, the pull between them had diminished. He was still undeniably handsome and she had warm feelings for her friend, but leaving him no longer felt like such a burden.

Vi stepped up to his side. "I thought I might find you here." She carefully set down the mugs of coffee with a smile. "And that you might need this."

He picked up one of the mugs and held it to his nose before sighing happily. "Right on both counts. I was up most of the night."

A smirk pulled at Vi's mouth, and she hid it with a sip of her own coffee. "Did Minerva talk your ear off?"

"Yes, she stayed up with me, for most of the time, at least. She's sleeping now."

"I am sorry to have left you alone with her like that," Vi said, nudging him playfully. "I can only imagine how much she enjoyed her captive audience."

"Actually, I enjoyed it, too. We seem to have more in common than I had realized. And she's smart. I would call her shrewd, even."

"How so?"

"Did you know she's going to take over the Belles?"

Vi leaned against the wall. "Yes, she told me right before you woke up."

"Well, when we got to talking, she made me an offer."

She nearly choked on her next sip. "What kind of offer?"

"She's taken a shine to *The Piasa* and its facilities." He gestured at the expanse of dark water outside. "Not as fond of this part of the Mississippi, though. If I am willing to head back north, she's proposed a more permanent arrangement between us going forward."

Vi chuckled. "Business or pleasure?"

"It makes a lot of sense from a business perspective. She takes the money that she would need to spend renting a theater and pays back my loan, and I've got a permanent show to bring in the gamblers." The telltale flush crept up his neck as he gave her a sheepish grin. "But you know something, Vi? I am really starting to like her."

"I am glad to hear it. You deserve to be happy."

"You do, too." Sam put a sympathetic hand on her shoulder. "If even it isn't with me."

Vi was not sure she agreed, but rather than argue the point, she said, "So, she is paying back your loan. You will get to be pickier about your cargo again."

"Yeah, about that," Sam said, setting down his mug and leaning back, arms crossed. "It was a good thing I was awake early, because I got to hear direct from the night crew that they came upon my first mate in a rather strange state. There he was, just lying in the middle of the deck next to an *empty* crate."

"That so?" Vi asked, keeping her voice steady.

"Uh-huh. Someone appears to have cut the crate open with an axe." He matched her nonchalance. "Funny thing is, the axe and the pieces they cut away can't be found. There are no identifying marks of any kind."

She painted on a look of mock-concern. "Surely you have records you could consult about the sender or the nature of the cargo?"

"Well, see, I was going to do just that." Sam crossed his arms and leaned against the opposite wall. "Unfortunately, I accidentally knocked my candle over, and wouldn't you know? The last page of the log burned right up."

"Those open flames can be tricky. Perhaps you should switch over to a lantern," she replied, pumping her eyebrows a few times. "Well, between that and your new business arrangement, does this mean you are not going all the way to New Orleans anymore?"

He took a gulp of his coffee. "It would probably be for the best that I do not. I hear one can actually use a telegraph to arrange for money transfers now, so I can repay the loan from anywhere once Minerva and I have the arrangements all set. She's going to talk to Juno about canceling their last appearance, considering everything that has been going on. They can regroup and have a fresh start on the Great Lakes or somewhere else this boat can go. But where would that leave you and Bonnie?"

"Much closer to our destination than when we started," she said with a grin. It faltered when she thought about the League watching the docks. Vi cleared her throat. "As it happens, I was already feeling rather tired of traveling by water. Perhaps we shall enlist a coach to take us the rest of the way."

"Are you sure? It can be a rather bumpy ride, rattles the bones."

"And things aboard *The Piasa* have been so smooth?"

"Fair point," he said with one of his deep rumbles of laughter. "Well, I wish you a pleasant journey, however you decide to travel. We will be in Greenville in the next hour or two. I plan to leave Bulloch there; he can be the hospital's problem. But I do not know what to do about Diana."

"Oh, you did not hear?" Vi asked casually. "She's awake. I just came from her room and she will make a full recovery, just like you." Despite the coffee, Vi had to stifle a yawn. Diana would have to finish recovering on her own, but the medium had at least been able to seal up the wound the psychophage had left behind.

Sam twisted the tip his beard. "I am relieved to hear it. Let us hope Bulloch is not quite as lucky. I would like to put some distance between us before he comes to."

"I would not worry about that. I expect him to be asleep for quite some time."

"Do I want to know how you know that?"

"Probably not." She had gotten through this mess without having to reveal herself to Sam, so she saw no reason to tell him Henry and Peter were keeping an eye on the phage to make sure it stayed where they'd left it until Bulloch was unloaded. Vi reached into her pocket and pulled out a package the size of her palm. "I almost forgot. I have a few parting gifts for you."

Sam unwrapped Bulloch's battered pocket watch, but showed no signs of recognizing it. "When did you have time to get this?"

"Just something I picked up along the way," Vi said airily. "I thought you could use one, especially after your last one fell into the drink. Something told me this was exactly the right one for you. There is no chain, I am afraid, so you will have to make sure to keep it close and be careful not to lose it." She took Bulloch's charmed watch out of his hand and tucked it into his waistcoat pocket. The chain had been spirited away among her things. It carried the same aura-muddying power as the watch, which would no doubt come in handy once they got closer to the League.

"I think I can manage that." He nodded and patted the bulge. "Did you say parting gifts?"

Vi pointed to the paper he still held in his hand. "That is an old Thorne family recipe. Something you should drink that will aid you in your recovery. Diana has a copy as well."

"And here I thought the only thing I would get from your family is doors slammed in my face," he joked as he looked over the scrawled instructions. She knew he was referring to Prudence, but as Vi had also rejected his advances, the remark stung a little. "I may have to ask around some to find it all, but I should be able to manage this as well." When his eyes left the paper, he beamed at her.

"Good." Vi retrieved her mug, then drained the last of her coffee to help relieve the lump gathering in her throat. "Now that is settled, I should go pack my things."

CHAPTER 42

October 26, 1871
Approaching New Orleans

The carriage ride down to New Orleans was every bit as uncomfortable as Sam had predicted. At least, that was true for the living passengers. The ghosts, on the other hand, had a marvelous time watching the countryside roll by from their perch on top of the coach.

For her part, Vi more or less ignored the scenery. It was difficult to see anything with her face buried in the family tome. Alice and the other memories trapped inside had not disappeared, but rather receded into the pages, as if confident she would call on them when she needed them.

Her reading was only interrupted by stopping at an inn for the night and the occasional projectile. Now that they knew the breadth of Vi's pronoia, Bonnie enjoyed testing it. Over the past three days, Vi had caught a walnut, a nickel, a dinner roll, and an assortment of small stones the other woman tossed at her. The stirring of the aether told Vi she was about to receive another volley. She used her index finger to mark her place and closed the book before glancing up.

Bonnie feigned innocence, using the hand that had been poised to throw something a moment before to prod her hair instead. She tried to keep a straight face, but it cracked when Vi cleared her throat and held out her hand. "Oh, fine," Bonnie said. She presented Vi with the chestnut pod she had been poised to toss at her head.

Vi received the spiky, chartreuse ball and held it up near her face. "That would have hurt."

"I knew you were going to catch it."

"Because I knew you were going to throw it. You've held onto that since the last time we stopped to water the horses."

"You knew that whole time?" Bonnie sighed and sank into her seat. "I thought I was being sneaky."

Vi tossed the chestnut out the window. "I did not see you pick it up, that part was expertly done. But the breeze coming off your fist has been present since we got back into the coach. I was relatively certain you were not going to punch me, so I put two and two together."

"Not without some more lessons, but maybe with enough practice, I shall be able to surprise you some day," Bonnie said, grinning. She rose and deposited herself next to Vi on the opposite bench. Even with her diminutive stature, the coach ceiling made her slouch her way over. Bonnie ran her thumb over the edge of the remaining pages of the book. "More than halfway done already. It must be an exciting read."

"Well, there are no highwaymen or vampires, but it certainly holds one's interest." Vi lifted her finger to allow Bonnie a glimpse at the contents of the page. There was another illustration, though this time in a walnut ink rather than the full spectrum of watercolor paints. It showed a woman standing with her hand outstretched. There were layers of ink around her in roughly the shape of her outline, each one lighter and less distinct than the last as they radiated out from her. Vi assumed it was meant to signify the aura and the energy put off by a medium. Around the hand, however, the different shades were close together at the wrist, with a ball of energy surrounding the hand and extending beyond it.

Bonnie read the title of the drawing out loud. "On moving objects at a distance." Her eyes grew wide as she tore them from the page and shifted them up to Vi's face. "You can do that?"

"Not to my knowledge. It would be a nice way to get a bottle off the top shelf at the saloon." Vi chuckled, Pru's words about reaching her full potential drifting into her mind. "But at least one of my ancestors could. So, I suppose that means it is conceivable."

There was a thump on the ceiling, followed a moment later by Peter's upside-down face peering down at them.

"Won't be long now," he said, his spirit flesh swirling with excitement. "We need to decide exactly where we are going."

"Whether or not they have been preparing it for her arrival, 'Annabelle' will certainly *not* be making an appearance at the St. Charles house." Not yet anyway.

"My place was paid up a few months in advance. We could go there."

Vi shook her head. "It has likely been compromised. The League found you once. It seems they would be able to find you again. And if they are expecting us, they will be watching it."

"They took me from the club, not from my home. But point taken. Though I would like you to retrieve a few things at some point."

Henry's disembodied head appeared beside Peter's. "I know a place. An old 'haunt' if you will."

"Will you two please come down here so we can have a proper conversation? Bad puns aside, I find I cannot take anything you have to say seriously looking like that."

Bonnie touched Vi's wrist in order to see what the ghosts were up to. Her fingers first came to rest on the watch chain Vi had started to wear the previous day to conceal her true nature. She wanted to see whether it changed anything about how her senses functioned. Thankfully, it did not hamper her ability to communicate with the ghosts. The other woman shifted her hand, and the ghosts must have come into view because she giggled. The dead men obliged, pulling themselves through the ceiling and coming to rest on the opposite bench.

"So, where is this place of yours?" Vi asked. "Not a bathhouse or anywhere else full of scantily clad women, I trust."

"A friend," Henry replied.

She furrowed her brow. "You are not exactly in a position to make introductions. How do you suppose we should explain ourselves?"

"No need." He beamed. "She's a sensitive, too. That is how we met."

Given his past, this statement should not have surprised Vi, and yet the coach felt like all of the air had been sucked out it. Aside from Prudence and August, she hadn't met many people like her, and it was not as if she had long in Chicago to discuss their shared experiences.

The hair on the back of Vi's neck rose in the wake of a gentle, aetheric breeze. There was no hint of malice, but something was definitely headed their way. Though Henry's mouth was moving, she could not hear the sound as the sensation crept over her body. Neither he nor Peter showed any sign of detecting what she felt.

Vi glanced down at the book in her lap. The feeling could have been one of the memories trapped in the book trying to get free, but none of her skin was making contact. This was something different.

"Vi," Bonnie whispered. "I feel...strange." Unlike the family diary, Vi was making direct contact with the young widow. Her eyes were trained on the invisible horizon. "Do you feel it, too?"

A wall of energy crackled through the carriage. It hit the ghosts a moment before it reached the two women. The normal, gentle blue shine of the dead men flashed so bright it was blinding. The light breeze became a storm front, slamming she and Bonnie against their seats and stealing her breath. The tide receded as quickly as it had come, trickling in rivulets around her body as it drew itself back into the distance.

The swell of power was weaker than when Vi had reached into Jack, but it fed her in the same way. She turned her head to Bonnie, who was gasping for breath beside her. Dully, Vi was aware that the other woman's fingernails were digging into her wrist. She twisted her arm free for fear of what effects the energy could be having on her friend.

"Are you all right?" Vi asked.

Bonnie's mouth opened and closed a few times before she found her words. "Was that...was that someone passing over?"

"I do not believe so. Or if it was, it was the most powerful passing I have ever felt."

A movement across from Vi caught her attention. Henry had his hand up before his eyes, a grin splitting his face. The mist of his body was nearly solid, the eddies frozen in place while he glowed twice as bright as usual. "This must be what the rumors were about," he murmured.

An equally solid Peter found his voice. "That was...amazing."

Bonnie let out a squeak, followed by, "I can see you! A bit at least."

"Well, of course you can," Henry said. "You're touching—" Bonnie held her empty hands up in the air. "Oh."

"It is not like when Vi shows me what she sees, but I do see...something."

"I do not understand," Vi said. "What was that? How is this possible?"

"Is it permanent?" Peter asked.

Henry shook his head, his face awash with wonder. "I hope so."

The carriage had trundled into the edge of town, the cobblestone streets of New Orleans adding their staccato to the ever-present bouncing of the wheels. With the energy pulsing through her, Vi felt the presence of both the living and the dead outside their walls clearly. She edged over to the window, and the rest of the party followed suit.

At least a dozen dead men and women were strolling along the street. To Vi, they all shimmered unnaturally bright and clear. The living people went on with their lives, seemingly oblivious to what had just occurred.

"Do you see them, too?" Vi asked Bonnie.

"I see...shapes, I guess you could say? But almost as if I am seeing them through the corner of my eye." Bonnie pulled away from the window. "If I did not know what I was supposed to be seeing, I am not certain I would notice them at all. The lights are already fading."

Vi turned back to Peter to confirm, and he was indeed no longer gleaming quite as bright. "So, it is not permanent."

"Have you read anything that might shed some light?" Peter asked.

"No, nothing at all." Vi ran her hand over the book. "But I have not finished yet. There could be something."

Henry's excitement bubbled out of him. "This is extraordinary!"

"Extraordinary," Vi said, "and worrying."

Peter pulled back from the window. "Do you think it could be tied to the League?"

"We should not jump to any conclusions. Perhaps it is some kind of natural phenomenon. Something to do with the magnetic field?" Henry clapped his hands together like a child about to ride a pony for the first time. "I cannot wait to investigate."

Vi stroked the family tome and returned her gaze to the city unfolding around them. "Neither can I."

EPILOGUE

Though the tapping of Mary's foot made no sound, her master shot her a look curdled with annoyance. "Are we boring you?" he asked, adjusting his spectacles. "Perhaps you would prefer to return to the docks?"

The ghost stilled her foot and mumbled. "My apologies, sir. Madame Corneau."

The stately woman by the fireplace removed her hood and peered at Mary down the length of her nose. She turned to Mary's master. "I do not understand why she is here in the first place. Her presence is far from required for this meeting."

"A demonstration may be in order," he replied, vaguely gesturing in Mary's direction.

Madame Corneau's chin raised incrementally, but it was her only outward sign of disapproval. "We do not wish for the League's supernatural ties to become public knowledge. Do you believe he can be trusted?"

"He'll keep any secrets we pay him to keep." He pushed away from the desk. Once he stepped out from behind it, he pulled out a second chair for the woman. "And don't forget, Colonel Sinclair trusted him."

She eyed the seat and remained standing. "Even so, we shall approach this as an ordinary business transaction for the time being."

"As you wish."

Mary wanted more than anything to ask them who they were talking about, but if she called attention to herself again, she might be told to leave. The last thing she wanted was to remain on the outside of whatever this was.

Especially if it meant taking Abernathy out for another meaningless day of watching ships come and go.

"Speaking of our more mundane business," he continued, retrieving a missive from his desk. "The fourth shipment of firearms has arrived."

"I am far more concerned with the ship that did *not* arrive," she snapped. "If Bulloch was correct in his suspicions about that passenger, Annabelle should have already been here and serving her purpose." Madame Corneau gave up her place at the mantel and finally took the proffered seat.

"Which is why are we are bringing in someone else to investigate."

A sharp tapping on the door interrupted the conversation. She bade the knocker enter, and a modestly dressed man came into the room. The most remarkable thing about him was how aggressively unremarkable he was. He removed his mud brown bowler hat to reveal a balding pate, and he squinted at Madame Corneau through a pair of brass-rimmed spectacles like a mole who had been dragged into the light.

A sneer curled Mary's lip. It was bad enough to have them question her ability to ferret out the wayward medium, but to be replaced by the rodent before her was a slap in the face – especially as this particular rodent had no clue there was a ghost standing in the room with him.

Once the niceties were completed, the little man took the second chair opposite Mary's master. "Let us get straight to the matter at hand. There is someone we would like you to find."

The mole man removed his glasses and polished them with his handkerchief. "Man or a woman?"

"A woman. A rather peculiar one."

"Will that be a problem for you?" Madame Corneau asked.

"Not in the least," he said, replacing his spectacles. "A job is a job."

Mary's boss leaned back in his chair with a satisfied sigh. "I am glad to hear it. I was not sure if the Agency had any sort of policy in that regard."

"They do not, but I am also no longer with the Agency." He folded his hand over the hat in his lap. "Let us say we had a difference of opinion when it came to our methods."

"Excellent," Madame Corneau said. "We cannot be sure if she has arrived yet in the city, or if she is still on her way. We have prepared a dossier for you." She snapped her fingers and a slim sheaf of papers was slid across the desk. "I am afraid there is no photograph, and she has quite a few aliases."

"Which are?" he asked, taking up the file.

"We are seeking her as Annabelle Sinclair, heir to the Sinclair fortune. We no longer believe she was using her real name during her time here. However, one of our associates encountered her under another name."

Madame Corneau glanced in Mary's direction for the first time. The ghost swallowed down her surprise and murmured, "Viola Thorne."

When the woman said the name for the living's benefit, the little man became perfectly still. "Could you repeat that, please?" he asked silkily, eyes never leaving the papers in his hands.

"Viola Thorne."

"And she is on her way here. You are sure of this?"

"She was in Memphis a few days ago and heading south. We have, unfortunately, lost track of her for the moment, but we have every reason to believe she is on her way. However, I doubt she will make a spectacle of herself once she arrives. That is why we need you to find her."

His face remained placid, but his fingers tightened around the crown of his Bowler. "And for what purpose?"

"That is *our* business."

"Nothing pleasant, I hope."

Mary pictured the medium strapped into the machine a few stories below, and she couldn't help but snicker. Neither of her living colleagues answered, which was an extremely telling answer in itself.

Delight creased the rodent's face. "I will take the job." He was on his feet and reaching out to shake the master's hand in the next heartbeat.

Madame Corneau rose as well. "Are you certain, Mr. Carmichael?"

He took her hand in his and laid a gentle kiss on her knuckle. "Oh yes, I am certain."

"But we have not worked out the details, Mr. Carmichael. Your payment," the master said.

The little man's eyes glinted wickedly. Mary had not imagined he was capable of looking menacing, but in that moment, she was glad she would not be his prey.

"As you say, those are the details. We shall apply my standard rate, though truthfully, I would take this case for free," he replied, donning his hat. "Ms. Thorne and I have a score to settle."

ABOUT THE AUTHOR

Phoebe Darqueling is the pen name of a globe trotting vagabond who currently hangs her hat in Freiburg, Germany. She writes curriculum for a creativity competition for kids in MN and works with both fiction and nonfiction authors as an editor. She loves all things Steampunk and Gaslamp Fantasy, and released an informative reference book entitled *The Steampunk Handbook* in 2020. Her first novels, *Riftmaker* and *No Rest for the Wicked: Mistress of None Book 1*, were released in 2019. You can find her short stories in the *Chasing Magic*, *The Queen of Clocks* and *Other Steampunk Tales*, *Harvey Duckman Presents Volumes 2&3*, and *Cogs, Crowns, and Carriages* anthologies.

NOTE FROM THE AUTHOR

Word-of-mouth is crucial for any author to succeed. If you enjoyed *Nothing Ventured, Nothing Gained*, please leave a review online—anywhere you are able. Even if it's just a sentence or two. It would make all the difference and would be very much appreciated.

Thanks!
Phoebe

Thank you so much for reading one of **Phoebe Darqueling's** novels. If you enjoyed the experience, please check out the beginning of the *Mistress of None* series!

No Rest for the Wicked by Phoebe Darqueling

"...an action-packed, spectacular good time."
–Leanna Renee Hieber, award-winning author of the *Strangely Beautiful* and *Eterna Files* series'

www.ingramcontent.com/pod-product-compliance
Lightning Source LLC
Chambersburg PA
CBHW011132100726
47898CB00009B/2944

* 9 7 8 1 6 8 4 3 3 5 5 8 9 *